THE WIFE'S BOYFRIEND

a humorous tale of marriage and murder

ROBERT McCRACKEN

Published by The Book Folks

London, 2022

© Robert McCracken

ISBN 978-1-80462-026-7

www.thebookfolks.com

For Suzie, Sarah & David.

Chapter one

When Barbara turfed him out, he didn't even put up a fight. He could have said:

'But I love you, Barbara.'

'I'll change.'

'I'll settle down.'

'No more drinking.'

'I'll work hard.'

'I'll help around the house...'

What actually came out was, 'Right then, I'll see you sometime.'

The front door slammed behind him.

A new life beckoned, free and single once again, and he couldn't get up the road fast enough. An hour and a half later, his tummy rumbled. He had to decide what to eat, never mind how to cook it and whether a tin of tuna actually needed cooking. Already, the bachelor-reborn idea had shed a little of its charm. A day later – his supply of Heineken drained and his last clean shirt covered in spaghetti sauce – he wondered about Barbara. She'd suffered enough. Pending her apology, he was willing to forgive and forget. He called round expecting to kiss and make up. Instead, he found a terse message pinned to the front door.

Charlie,

I've packed all your stuff into boxes. They're in the garage. Hope you're enjoying your new life of freedom. I'll listen out for your name on the news.
Barbara.

That sort of confirmed it. She needed more time to come round. Feeling a bit miffed, he decided to keep a mental note of the passing days. When he'd achieved all his goals, earned a fortune and made his mark on life he would know how long it had taken since leaving Barbara.

One year, three weeks and five days flew by. For no reason other than one year, three weeks and five days having passed, he attempted a second homecoming. He was convinced a welcome, nine-point-eight on the open-arms scale, awaited him. True, they had learned a valuable lesson. But they were made for each other; they were meant to be together. Charlie needed Barbara, and he was certain she needed him.

He still had his key. A whirl of excitement rose in his stomach at the thought of seeing her. He pictured the evening as he slid the key into the lock. Apologies exchanged, a kiss and a cuddle, a nice cup of tea in front of the telly, or maybe a DVD. He was more than happy to watch one of her weepies, or that rom-com where the New York fashion editor girl gets lost in Ireland looking for her fiancé and ends up falling for a turf-digger from Connemara. He didn't mind. It was her company he craved.

He pushed open the door and stepped inside. All was quiet, lounge to the right and dining room to the left deserted. He could see down the hall to the kitchen; no one there either. Floorboards creaked above him. He climbed the stairs, reaching the top step.

'Who the hell are you?' Charlie asked.

He was over six feet, naked and standing in the bedroom.

'Who are you?' the man said with not the slightest inclination to cover up.

'I asked first,' said Charlie.

He was Tarzan, golden-brown from head to foot and most points in between.

'My name is Malcolm Palmer.'

He sounded like bloody Michael Caine.

First impressions weren't good. Handsome, he had to admit. Cheerful, too, with an undercurrent of, 'Trust me, I know what I'm doing.' Charlie knew exactly what Tarzan was doing all right, or what he was about to do.

'Where's Barbara?'

Her timing exquisite, she emerged from the bathroom.

'Charlie! What are you doing here?'

Charlie glanced at her naked parts then back to the stranger. His eyes made the connection, but his brain was having trouble with the final piece of the puzzle. She darted to the bathroom and returned with a towel held across her front.

'What's *he* doing here is more the question, don't you think?'

'If you'll excuse us, we're kind of busy,' said Malcolm Palmer, his voice mannerly yet commanding.

'Not anymore,' Charlie said. 'Time you were on your bike.'

'Hold on a minute,' said Barbara. 'I'll decide who comes and who goes. It's my house.'

Charlie couldn't prevent his eyes from taking in the nakedness to his left and right. Admittedly, she was looking better since his departure. Her auburn hair had ventured below her shoulders, and her visits to the gym were proving a success. Not that she needed to lose much weight, but her figure, he thought, was now blooming in all the right places. He didn't think much of where Tarzan was blooming.

'You're a little pervert, aren't you?' said Tarzan.

'You're the one who's bollock-naked.'

'Will the both of you stop it,' Barbara shouted. 'Charlie, I want you to leave now please.'

'What about him? I'm your husband?'

'My estranged husband. You walked out over a year ago, remember?'

'You threw me out.'

'No, Charlie. I suggested you left to experience the fantastic life you claimed to be missing on account of me.'

Her face reddened. She fired him a dismissive stare. Tarzan, hands on hips, smiled priggishly through his little victory.

'Fair enough,' said Charlie.

Stomach churning, he descended the stairs disappointed that Tarzan didn't have a Jane instead of his Barbara. Wrapping the towel around her, she followed him downstairs into the hall.

'What do you want, Charlie?'

'I was thinking that I should come home now. That we can make a fresh start. Put the past behind us.'

'I don't think so.'

'I realise that I made mistakes in the past. But we were good together; we love each other. Come on, what do you say? Marriage is all about give and take, you know.'

'You're dead right. You gave me too much grief, and I could take no more.'

He didn't have much of an argument for that. He'd been a prat back then and an even bigger one now, thinking he could stroll back into her life as if holding on to his key was all it took. He needed a better plan.

'Worth a try, I suppose. Anyway, sleep on it. Let me know what you decide.'

'You're not listening, Charlie. You're not coming home. You wanted a new life, you got one.' She opened the front door.

'I'll go then.'

'Now you're getting it.'

Dutifully, he stepped outside. The door slammed.

In the pain of his disappointment, and picturing naked bum cheeks wearing Michael Caine glasses, a new plan was forming in Charlie's head. It was clear Barbara needed more convincing that she was wrong to have thrown him out. He knew what he must do.

Step one: get his life together.

Step two: do something to really impress Barbara.

Step three: convince her that she didn't need a man like Malcolm Palmer, Michael Caine or Tarzan.

That decided, he went to the pub.

Chapter two

Ballymenace is a confusing sort of place, south of North Down or north of South Down, depending on how you look at it. People don't care that much, but for the precious few to whom it matters Ballymenace is definitely in mid-County Down.

If New York is the city that never sleeps, Ballymenace never got its wake-up call. It is a small town, nestling below well-tended hills and strategically placed ten miles south-east of Belfast. Critics have suggested it is a giant barricade on the road to somewhere else. Somewhere more important, somewhere more appealing. In a land renowned for blockades, barriers and ghettos, they probably have a point. Not surprising that when plans were proposed for the construction of a bypass no one, inside or outside the town, lifted a finger in protest. Now, unless they live or work there, people don't worry about the place at all. The centre comprises a dozen streets, a town hall, courthouse and market square. On the periphery are several housing estates, a leisure centre and a shopping mall where, five years after opening, half the units remain vacant.

At some point in its four-hundred-year history a dedicated soul thought the town worthy of a newspaper. The biggest headline *The Ballymenace Explorer* ever had to print was to announce, in the 4 March 2008 issue, that the long-awaited Daniel O'Donnell concert in the leisure centre was cancelled.

It was after ten o'clock when Charlie reached *The Explorer* office, a cream-painted, three-storey tenement just off the market square. The ground floor housed a small reception, with a printing shop to the rear. In the news office, on the first floor, Carol, secretary-cum-receptionist-cum-junior reporter, was tapping at her PC. She always looked great, cheerful and efficient – the last person he wished to meet when suffering from a size-ten hangover, a swollen nose and a psychedelic shirt. He knew where he'd got the hangover, but he wasn't too clear about the nose and the shirt.

At nineteen, Carol was a little plump from too many chocolate biscuits between tea breaks. She didn't actually eat at break times, because her mouth was far too busy describing her latest crash diet.

She didn't even have to look at him.

'Rough night?'

'Don't even ask,' he replied, heading for the kitchen. He filled a glass with water from the tap and returned to the office.

'What are you doing here anyway?' she asked, her eyes still fixed on her screen. He could usually detect her sarcasm at twenty paces.

'I still work here, you know.'

'Not this morning, you don't. You're supposed to be in court.'

He only went to court on a Wednesday.

'No I'm not,' he said. 'What day is it?'

'It's Wednesday. But since you're here you may as well speak to Trevor. He's been waiting to see you.'

'What have I done now?'

'There's no danger of it being work.'

Ignoring yet another jibe, he set the empty glass on her desk and made a beeline for the door.

'Tell him I'm in court. I'll catch up with him later.'

'Can't do that.'

'Why not?'

'He just watched you parking that rust-bucket of a car.'

'I suppose I should see what the big boss wants then?'

'Good idea. I'll hold your hand if you like?'

'No thanks. You don't know where I've been. Not too sure myself.'

He climbed the rickety flight of stairs to the editor's office and knocked on the door. Usually he didn't bother, but this morning he reckoned if he were in trouble a little respect for his superior would not go amiss. When he opened the door he saw Trevor behind an untidy desk, sipping coffee from his beloved Arsenal mug and reading *The Sun*.

'Morning, Charlie. Rough night?'

'Wild night, rough morning,' said Charlie, his head spinning. He had visions of a girl in a black leather miniskirt and fishnet stockings. He didn't know her, couldn't picture her face, only the skirt and the legs. Fabulous legs.

Trevor gave a faint nod and resumed his reading. He didn't do wild nights. Couldn't even picture one. He was thirty-eight with a waistline pushing forty. What was left of his dark hair was cut in a short back and sides. His gold-rimmed glasses were poorly chosen and sat awkwardly on a shiny nose. Neither Charlie nor Trevor would pass muster as a Chippendale, a fact unimportant to Charlie and unimagined by Trevor.

He sat opposite, leaning over the desk, reading upside down what his boss found so interesting. Trevor liked the problem page. Today the headline was, 'MY WIFE WILL ONLY HAVE SEX IN THE CONSERVATORY'.

Trevor continued to read, while Charlie wondered why his boss had asked to see him. Right now, he would feel much better at home in his bed. Impatience kicked in.

'Carol said you wanted to see me?'

'I do,' Trevor replied, sipping from his mug. He leaned back in his leather swivel chair and rested his feet on the edge of the desk. 'Joan and I have booked a wee holiday in Tenerife. We're going next Wednesday.'

'Very nice. Can I come?'

'Funny you should say that because I want you to look after things while we're away.'

'Why me?'

'You're the senior reporter. I mean, you're the deputy editor.'

'Oh right,' said Charlie. That was news to him.

'Besides, Billy only writes about the gee-gees, and Jill would have you colouring in to make the paper look pretty before it hits the streets. Please, Charlie, don't mess up on this one. I need a break, but I don't want to come back to find you've gone mad on one of your tabloid-style reports.'

'No harm in sniffing out a good story.'

'This is Ballymenace, Charlie. It's the boring bit between Belfast and Dublin. I know you'd love to work for *The Sun*, going undercover, hacking phones, digging the dirt, but nothing ever happens here. Report the news from court, the council meetings, the hatches, matches and dispatches around the town. Don't make it sound like the Bronx.'

'You can trust me, boss.'

'Charlie, we both know that's not true. So promise me, while I'm away, there'll be no scoops.'

Charlie laughed, unwise for an aching head.

'Just promise me, Charlie?'

'OK, I promise. Besides, I have nothing at the moment except for that wife-swapping story on Yonhill Estate.'

'There you go again. I'm not even out the bloody door, and you're planning four pages of poppycock. There *is* no wife-swapping in Yonhill. Have you seen the women up there? You need safety glasses just to look at them. You couldn't donate them to white slavery with cashback never mind convincing some poor sod that your grass is greener than his. Just mind the shop for a couple of weeks, stay off the booze and keep out of trouble.'

Trevor had moved to the window and was gazing into the street.

'Do you think you can manage that?' he said.

'I suppose so.'

He was sure Trevor's attention was fixed on the dainty blonde from the jeans store across the road, returning from the bakery with a couple of doughnuts. He watched out for her every morning. Bit of a sad case really but not his fault. Any poor soul married to Joan would have little joy in life other than to watch pretty girls walking by.

'I know things have been difficult for you, Charlie, but it's time you made a fresh start. Strike out on your own. Maybe this is the chance you need.'

Charlie browsed the text messages on his mobile as Trevor poured out his advice. There was a reminder from Barbara:

> *Don't forget lunch with M. At one. Please don't mess it up. B.*

Twice he'd been told not to mess up, and it wasn't even ten-thirty. Talk about a lack of trust?

'You and Barbara have been separated for two years now...'

'One year, nine months, two weeks and four days,' said Charlie.

'Time to start thinking of your future. You can't turn back the clock, you know?'

Through an adjacent window, Charlie noticed the blonde in conversation with an equally hot brunette. An extra-special treat this morning. Trevor took it all in.

'Joan and I were devastated when you two split up. We're still your friends, you know? We don't want to take sides, but we're concerned about you. Barbara is worried too.'

'She's told you that, has she?'

'She told Joan about your drinking and that you're not looking after yourself.'

'You mean she's been whinging to Joan about me?'

'C'mon, you know what women are like when they get together? They rehearse exactly the right words to use against us so we don't stand a chance in the heat of battle. Having said that, I reckon she is genuinely concerned for you.'

'Pity she wasn't so concerned when she threw me out.'

The blonde laughed as if she'd just heard about Charlie's pathetic life and withdrew to her shop. Trevor's gaze lingered a moment longer until the brunette moved out of sight.

'Maybe it's time for a clean break,' said Trevor.

Charlie jumped to his feet. Perhaps Trevor was right. Taking charge of the paper for two weeks might be the very thing to impress Barbara. A couple of exciting stories on the front page, penned by her clever husband, and Malcolm Palmer could be on his way.

'I've work to do,' he said with a newly found enthusiasm.

'For goodness sake, Charlie, can't you even manage a clean shirt? Looks like you slept in that one.'

He didn't remember going to bed never mind what he'd been wearing.

His blue shirt had a purple stain on the chest. Snakebite & black. Several pints of Snakebite & black.

Now he remembered showing the girl in the leather miniskirt how he could drink through his left nipple. Judging by the orange stain across his stomach, he'd had an altercation with a portion of sweet 'n' sour chicken outside the Lotus Flower Takeaway. A throbbing nose and the blood on his sleeve reminded him that the altercation had also involved a lamp post.

'And, for goodness sake, wash your face,' said Trevor. 'You'd make a fortune selling *The Big Issue*.'

'Certainly more than I do here.'

* * *

In recent times, a glimmer of light sparkled on sleepy towns such as Ballymenace. 'Location, location, location,' was the PR phrase of the day, and as cities spewed further into the countryside men with an eye for property and a fast deal were quick to deliver. Malcolm Palmer was such a man. His eye roved further than most, and soon little-arsehole-of-nowhere by-passable towns, with diminishing prospects of ever staging a Daniel O'Donnell concert, were suddenly heralded as desirable 'locations'.

Both friends and rivals had said Malcolm Palmer was not one to miss a quick lay. Foundations, to bricks, to floorboards in just eight weeks, he didn't hang around. How he treated his women was another matter and entirely his affair. Charlie was a recent graduate to the 'I hate Palmer brigade'. Quite simply, Palmer was the bane of his ever-decreasing aura of happiness. All this played on his mind as he tried to think of a good excuse not to have lunch with the guy. He realised, of course, if he cried off he would suffer death by sharp-tongue from Barbara.

At one o'clock he told Carol he was going for lunch and might not return in the afternoon. He felt another hangover coming on, anticipating the drink he would consume when he was finished with Mr Palmer.

A magnificent, metallic-blue Aston Martin V8 Vantage was double-parked in Main Street when Charlie stepped outside. Malcolm reached across to open the passenger door.

'Hello, Charlie,' he said, exuding a cheery confidence. 'Glad you could make it.'

The sudden acceleration pushed him into the leather upholstery as he struggled with the seat belt. Miraculously speeding through the lunchtime traffic, Charlie looked dead ahead refusing to be impressed by this four-wheeled beauty. Some say that a sports car is compensation for a natural deficiency. He smirked at the thought.

'Fir Tree Lodge sound all right? I have a three o'clock nearby. Thought it might be handy.'

'Fine,' Charlie replied.

Malcolm was a charmer. Charlie had decided that much from their first meeting, nine months ago. At least this time he was wearing something. His clothes were expensive but not flash. He looked like a man who took care of himself: fine features, unblemished skin, veneered teeth and the perfect weight for his age and height. Charlie hated to admit it, but he could see why Barbara was taken with him. At forty-four, he was ten years older than Charlie but looked five years younger. He was fitter, richer, and definitely happier. If Barbara was into comparisons then her estranged husband didn't stand a chance. He couldn't begin to imagine how to compete with this guy. The theory of sports cars and penis extensions returned, but he fought it off bravely. The very thought of his Barbara copulating with Palmer and he endowed with any penis, regardless of size, made him feel queasy.

He thought he heard *Ride of the Valkyries*. Palmer switched on his hands-free phone.

'Palmer, here,' he said loudly. 'Yes, Margaret. That's fine. I'll be finished at' – he checked his Tag Heuer watch – 'three-thirty. I'll call on my way to Bangor. Can you move my four-thirty to eleven, tomorrow morning? Thanks, pet, I'll catch you later.'

There were two more calls on the short drive over the hill to the Fir Tree Lodge. Charlie didn't mind; it saved him the trouble of being offhand with the man who was taking his wife.

Palmer led the way into the pub-restaurant, a pseudo-American log cabin, set within a copse of fir and spruce, a popular watering hole for locals and the odd tourist who'd got lost on their way from Belfast to Dublin. An attractive waitress, in black skirt and smart white blouse, greeted Palmer like he owned the place and led them to a table by a quarter-paned window. While they browsed the menu, Palmer ordered a pint of Guinness for Charlie and a sparkling water for himself.

'Well, Charlie, I suppose you realise why I wanted to see you?' *Ride of the Valkyries* again. He pulled a mobile from the breast pocket of his grey suit. 'Hello, Mason old chap. How the hell are you?'

Charlie wondered why such airheads were so big in the world of high finance and why so many were called Mason, Ralph or Liam.

'Sorry about that,' Palmer said when he'd finished touching base with Mason. 'Now where were we?'

The phone rang again; Palmer rolled his eyes, sighed, and launched into another conversation. Charlie could take no more. As he headed for the toilets he heard Palmer, judging by his tone, rhyming off a list of orders to one of his lackeys.

At the urinal, an impish thought suddenly occurred to him. In the pocket of his seldom-worn sports jacket he retrieved his seldom-used mobile phone. He wasn't averse to mobiles; in fact, he'd lost count of the times he was stranded outside a pub after closing time without one. Lately, the odd curt text was his only line of communication with Barbara. The problem with mobiles was they needed charging every few days, and his memory didn't work like that. Usually, what he carted around was a flat battery. Today, fortuitously, a trickle of charge showed on the display. He called up the number of *The Explorer.* Bad idea, he should have finished peeing first.

'Hello, Carol? It's Charlie. I'm at the Fir Tree Lodge. Call me on my mobile in about ten minutes?'

'OK,' she said.

He replaced the phone in his pocket and, with some toilet roll, tried his best to soak up the stain on his beige trousers. Never seemed to be wearing black when this sort of thing happened. He removed his jacket, held it over the wet patch and returned to the table.

'I took the liberty of ordering for you,' said Palmer, staring at the motley collection of stains on Charlie's shirt. 'A medium rib-eye sound all right?'

'Fine,' said Charlie. 'As long as it's expensive. Not much point in coming otherwise.'

Palmer smiled, seemingly unoffended by the quip.

'Well, Charlie,' he began once more as if conducting a job interview. 'You and Barbara have been separated for two years now.'

'One year, nine months, two weeks and four days.'

'Pardon?'

'We've been separated for one year, nine months, two weeks and four days.'

'Right,' said Palmer, a little put off. 'I was about to say that Barbara has reached the point in her life when she believes it is time to move on. Close one door, open another, so to speak. I must say, I totally agree with her.'

Charlie's eyes locked on target, cold, unflinching and definitely hostile.

'Barbara and I were wondering how you feel about a divorce?'

Chapter three

He fought hard to keep his cool and took a few seconds to compose a reply. He thought it prudent to borrow his rival's pompous style.

'Awfully nice of you to raise the subject, Malcolm, but really there's no need. Barbara and I are merely on a trial separation. Only temporary. No reason for you to get involved.'

The waitress brought their food and, since his stomach hadn't finished with the sweet 'n' sour chicken from the night before, he merely toyed with the generous portion of steak. Having cooled down a little, he listened as Palmer presented his wife-stealing case.

'Barbara wants stability for herself, but she also cares about your future. We think it's a good idea to sell the house.'

All said with the polished delivery of a salesman, an estate agent to boot. Not exactly the best platform to earn a man's trust. Charlie was tempted to riddle his face with a mouthful of *petits pois*.

'I have already chosen a site in Cultra,' said Palmer.

'Moving up in the world?'

'The least Barbara deserves. We think it's fair if you have the money from the sale of number forty-seven. It might help get you settled.'

'That's mighty decent of you,' Charlie said, fuming at this imperious, puffed-up housebuilder, selling his home, the home of the Geddis family for three generations. 'I assume Barbara and you are moving in together?'

'That's the idea,' Palmer replied, taking a mouthful of steak.

Charlie tried to stay calm by eating some food and washing it down with beer. His three-step plan was now in tatters. Not that he'd made much progress. His life was a mess of dull days, and lonely drunken nights with little hope of improvement. Nine months on from his first encounter with the naked Tarzan, he hadn't yet achieved step one. Then suddenly he asked, what must have sounded to Palmer, a businesslike question.

'How much can be made on the house?'

'Well, my company can handle the sale, and I'll waive the agent's fee. Bearing in mind the cottage could do with modernisation, rewiring *et cetera*, I think 260 K is a realistic figure. And if you wish, to hurry things along, I will advance you that sum pending the sale.'

'You're very generous, Malcolm.'

'The least I can do, Charlie. Barbara means a lot to me.'

'There's just one tiny little thing.'

'What's that?'

At first Charlie wasn't conscious of waving his steak knife in the air, but then he noticed the unnerving effect it had on Palmer. He lifted his Guinness and sat back in his chair, still brandishing the knife.

'If you ever so much as put a 'For Sale' board on my property you'll live to regret it, understand?' His three-step plan was back on track. 'As for your advance, you can stick–'

'Excuse me, gentlemen,' said the waitress. 'There is a telephone call for Mr Geddis at the bar.' Charlie left the table and followed her.

'Hi, Charlie, it's Carol. You asked me to call you back?'

'Yes, Carol, but I asked you to call my mobile.'

'I tried, but you must have switched it off. What's the problem?'

'It doesn't matter.'

He replaced the receiver and examined his mobile; the remaining charge had disappeared. Even the simplest scheme to put one over on his rival had failed. Smothered by his rotten fortune, he returned to the table.

'You should get a mobile,' said Palmer. 'Saves the hassle.' He was off again, this time oozing sincerity. 'I realise this may have come as a shock. You might have other plans. Barbara and I want to help. She has your best interests at heart, and all she's asking in return is to settle into her new life with me.' He glanced at his watch. 'Must dash,' he said, rising from the table. 'I've already paid the bill. Can I drop you somewhere?'

'No thanks. I'll have a few more beers.'

This was the defining moment in his hapless existence. This was the day, the hour, the minute when he could no longer stand by and watch as this man took the woman he loved. With the help of God, and five or six policemen, he would fight to get her back.

Palmer summoned a cool-guy smile and moved through the crowded dining room.

'Malcolm,' Charlie called. Palmer spun round. 'Keep taking those pills. Use lots of ointment when it gets sore. And for goodness sake, be careful the next time you visit Bangkok.'

Looking disgusted, Palmer quickened his step as heads turned. Two old dears at the next table looked bewildered.

'It's OK,' said Charlie, 'I'm his GP.'

After three pints of Guinness, he moved to the bar and set about the row of optics. First the vodkas, which were easy, then a rough period as he tackled the gins. He hated gin, found it depressing. On one occasion, after half a bottle of White Satin, he had been reduced to floods of tears watching Manchester United lose to Chelsea in the Cup Final. A generous selection of whiskies slowed him down, and by late afternoon he struggled to order a Slouthren Cromfort.

Except for an elderly couple having afternoon tea in a corner booth, the Fir Tree Lodge was now deserted. Charlie had never liked the place and liked it less now because Palmer had chosen it for their meeting. He didn't think much of the snooty bar staff either; they had no friendly chat. Talking to someone made drinking more enjoyable and stopped him feeling sorry for himself. What could he do now to get back with Barbara? Just when he'd begun to sort himself out, she asks for a divorce. Didn't even have the nerve to ask him face to face. She got her rich boyfriend to do it. And she was prepared to use his money to buy off her husband. If it were only down to money, Charlie wished he had the funds to buy her back. But it seemed that Barbara wanted a successful man – a decent man, a rich man, an everything-under-the-bloody-sun man. For the moment that was not him. Maybe tomorrow.

By the time the room filled with evening punters, calling in for a drink or taking advantage of the Early Bird Menu on their way home from work, he was far beyond conversation. Several business types chatted at the bar ignoring the drunk at the far end, who was tearing beermats into little pieces and playing with them like a jigsaw. These people reminded him of Palmer: eloquent, confident and successful. He needed some air before he threw up.

* * *

He walked a perfect straight line on a winding road. Weren't drivers supposed to give way to drunks? He slowed down as a car roared by. He tried a hand gesture and nearly fell over. Sober eejits. Shouldn't be allowed. Drunks needed protecting from people like that. He staggered faultlessly to the entrance of Ballymenace Glen. Now he was safe, no cars in there. The path ran along the riverbank, but he couldn't catch it. Too quiet, how about a song?

At the sight of the approaching drunk, a middle-aged dog walking her woman changed direction and hurried off through the trees.

'Sell my house, would he? Pompous git. Charlie Geddis, *News at Ten,* in a big forest.'

Light under the trees was fading, and in the hue he stumbled onto an old wooden bridge. He knew the place, used to play here as a kid. The stream below opened to a large pond, home to several ducks and a few fish, and in summer it remained deep enough for swimming. Draining from this pond, the Ballymenace River ran from the hills into farmland recently sliced in two by the new bypass. Leaning on the railing of the bridge, he tried to focus on the dark shapes beneath the surface. He'd never seen a revolving pond before.

He didn't feel too good.

Clinging to the railing for dear life, he was startled by voices nearby. At least he hoped they were nearby and not in his head. He'd enough problems talking to himself without someone else butting in. The talking became shouting. He eased his head from the railing to look around. Maybe someone could help him, put him in a taxi and send him home. He glimpsed figures under the trees on the far shore of the pond. There was something disturbing about their voices. They didn't sound like pleasant bodies; certainly not the sort to help a pitiful drunk. His hearing, like his vision, was going in and out of focus. There were four figures, dressed in black from head to foot. Make that three. If only they would stand still for him to count. Three dressed in black and one other, with frizzy, red hair and a barf-coloured shirt. Not a redhead in the natural sense, more like a clown. He tried to make out what they were saying.

'I don't know...'

'Shut...'

Arms swung; a foot was raised. A loud yelp was followed by several groans.

'...knees.' Or maybe, '...trees.'

'No...'

'...angry...break...off.'

'...told you...Palmer...'

Another yelp, a dull thud, although it may have been his head on the railing.

'Please!'

Thuds, grunts and a cry of fear.

His eyes rolled; his legs buckled. A crack like a pistol shot. The red-haired man splashed into the revolving pond. Wood splintered and then darkness. Gasping for breath, the cold unbearable, Charlie was taking in water. Despite arms flailing and legs kicking, he sank deeper. The cold on the back of his neck paralysed him, sucking him further into sleep. I'm drowning, he thought. This is it. My demise. He spiralled into darkness, growing colder, stuttering to a halt like a car on a frosty morning. Suddenly a brilliant light shone beneath him. He was passing to the other side. Barbara, a black leather miniskirt, sweet 'n' sour sauce and an Aston Martin seeped into his head. *Ride of the Valkyries* pounded in his ears. He went limp, and there was no more pain. The light grew brighter. He was no longer aware of time passing. Suddenly the cold returned, and he crashed to the surface gasping and flapping. There was something around his neck, choking him, dragging him, kicking and splashing across the pond. Clumsy, like an elephant seal, he hit the beach and rolled onto his back caressing his aching throat. Looking up, he met the stern face of a man looking down.

'Are you all right there, young fella?'

Scrambling from the mud and stones Charlie struggled to his feet, shivering. He was too cold to answer as he tried to focus on his rescuer. He was old, no more than five and a half feet, with a crook in his hand a foot taller. He wore a flat cap and a dark grey suit with a pinstripe. His face had more grooves than the bark of a tree, but his green eyes were friendly and drew Charlie to trust him.

'What happened?'

'You fell in the river, from the bridge.' He pointed with his crook at the broken railing. 'Lucky I was passing, ye boy ye. Could've met your end.' He looked Charlie up and down and sighed with a high-pitched wheeze. 'Ye may come up the house with me before you catch your death. Soon get you warmed, young fella.'

Without waiting for a reply, the old man strode off through the trees. Charlie began to follow but suddenly remembered the events before his drenching in the pond. The far shore was deserted. There was no sign of a body floating in the water, and the dark figures had disappeared.

'Wait. There's a man over there.'

The old boy stopped and slowly turned around.

'What's that ye say?'

'There's a man. He was shot, and he fell in the pond. We have to get him out, tell someone. The police. We have to call the police.'

'He's dead, is he?'

'I think so.'

The old man didn't look convinced. Understandable, considering he'd just rescued a pathetic creature that swayed as he walked, and every word he'd spoken so far began with *ssh*. He tipped his cap back, rubbed his nose between thumb and forefinger, and set off again.

'You'll be needin' out of those clothes, young fella,' he said over his shoulder.

'But what about the man?'

'If he's dead like you say he'll not be in much of a hurry.'

Chapter four

Once beyond the trees they came to a gate that opened into a pasture, busy with a herd of Friesians. The man climbed aboard a rusty tractor and gestured for Charlie to sit on the flat-back trailer. The engine burst into life and, surprisingly, the chassis didn't fall to bits with the strain. They trundled up a narrow lane, rising above the glen, and jerked to a halt in a farmyard beside a whitewashed cottage with tiny windows, slate roof, and a shiny red door.

Not only did Charlie now believe he'd died and had passed to the other side, but heaven was back a century or two. Apart from the tractor, this place hadn't made it to the twentieth century, never mind the twenty-first. Charlie followed the man into the house ducking his head to avoid the lintel of the door, not bad reactions for a drunk who was soaking wet, hallucinating and possibly dead. The room had a polished wooden floor and a black-leaded fireplace, with kettle and griddle hanging from a sturdy mantelpiece. Against the opposite wall stood a large oak dresser adorned with delicate crockery in blue and white. Close to the window was a heavy table with a huge oil lamp in the centre. There were several vases of fresh flowers about the room, and a pair of rocking chairs sat by the fireplace. The smell of bread baking fired his appetite and, instantly, he became a hungry drunk. A brown and white collie lay on the floor, looking up at its master and the waterlogged stranger. This was a rustic heaven.

'Woman!' the man bellowed, a fierce voice erupting from such a wizened body.

A woman of about sixty appeared by a door beside the dresser. Much taller and wider than her spouse, she wore a green print dress in a leafy pattern, and a white apron. Her glassy eyes looked welcoming, but her chubby face lacked a smile. She said nothing, merely waited for the man to speak.

'Some blankets for the boy and bring the barley,' he said. 'Go on in there, young fella, and take them wet clothes off ye.'

He showed Charlie to a room lined with shelves crammed with pots of jam, preserved fruits and honey.

He was wringing out his boxers into a sink, when he heard a gentle tap. When he peered round the door, the woman handed him two blankets. Without a word spoken, he realised that he should surrender his wet clothes.

When he emerged wearing the blankets, one around his waist the other on his shoulders, the man was rocking by the fire and drinking from a tankard.

'Have some barley, young fella,' he said, nodding to a second tankard and a clay jar on the table. 'Sit down. Take the weight off your feet.'

Charlie sat at the table and took a gulp from the tankard. He gasped for a breath, and his eyes bulged. The man looked bemused as Charlie's blanket slid to the floor.

'What is this stuff?'

'Just a wee brew from last year's barley.'

'Phew! I thought it was a fruit drink, not paint-stripper from Homebase.'

'It'll warm the cockles of your heart.'

'Pickle it more like.'

The woman returned before he had the chance to wrap up. She looked unimpressed by the manifestation of banality before her, while he scrambled for the blanket, forgetting the corrosive reaction in his gullet. She set a tray on the table, with mugs of tea and scones smothered in clotted cream and jam. The hot tea soothed his puffy head and settled the turbulence in his stomach. He was happy to avoid another mouthful of gut-rot from the jar. The old boy joined him at the table but didn't speak as they ate and drank. In the silence he couldn't help thinking how nice it would be to live here with Barbara. It felt like such a homely place.

An hour later, he was very relaxed indeed with little inclination to share his life with anyone, including Barbara, ever again. Sitting in the rocking chairs, the dog between them, he asked the man if his wife was coming to join them. The man told him that she went to bed early in order to rise in time for the milking. Bliss. Such a contented life.

It wasn't long though before his thoughts drifted back to events earlier in the evening, events he was certain had taken place. The old man seemed convinced nothing had occurred beyond a drunk crashing through the handrail of a rickety bridge.

'Should we call the police about the body?' said Charlie.

The man filled a pipe with tobacco from a leather pouch. His eyes sparkled like someone who already knew the answer to a question that no one else did.

'Do you have a name, young fella?'

'It's Charlie Geddis.'

'And what do you do, Charlie?'

'I'm a reporter for The Ballymenace Explorer.'

'Ah! A newspaper man?'

'If you could call it that.'

'Well, come on, tell me what you saw?'

Charlie told him about the voices, the dark figures, and the red-haired man splashing into the pond. He explained about the loud crack, a gunshot maybe. There was no sign of shock or even disbelief on the man's face.

Having lit his pipe, he rocked on his chair puffing clouds of smoke towards the chimney.

'I can't believe you didn't hear it,' said Charlie, his impatience growing at the lack of concern. 'We should go down there and have a look.'

'Maybe later,' he said. 'So tell me about yourself, young Charlie.'

He couldn't see the point of the question, but he told the man his pitiful life story, omitting the recent encounter with a girl in a black leather miniskirt, the portion of sweet 'n' sour chicken and the lamp post. When he'd said enough to put the most conscientious therapist to sleep, he sat back in the rocker awaiting the old boy's comments. It felt good talking to someone who seemed happy to listen. Having a good natter with someone who wasn't being judgemental was a rarity for him these days. The man's pipe rested on his mouth, the flames from the fire reflected in his lively eyes.

'So the Gods have not blessed ye with good favour?' Rising from his chair he poured some barley into the tankards, handing one to Charlie.

'One way of looking at it, I suppose. Don't you think we should do something about the body in the pond?'

'Have a drink of barley, and we'll talk some more.'

Cautiously this time, he took a sip and was surprised that now it resembled a ten-year-old single malt instead of paint-stripper. A crack from a log on the fire broke an eerie silence. Charlie jumped, a shiver running down his spine. Unease seemed to wash over him from the surrounding darkness, his gaze fixed on the red glow of the burning logs. Was this the point where the man explained that he was actually the killer? That as a witness Charlie might not expect to see out the night? That the woman had drugged the scones and soon he would be tatty bread? Maybe he'd passed to the other side already and a glorious heaven was not to be his destination.

'The man you saw falling into the pond, did you know him?'

'I don't think so. And he didn't fall; he was pushed, and that was after he'd been shot.'

Judging by the weak smile, Charlie got the feeling the old man was trying to humour him. Toying with him.

'Who do you think might have done the shooting?'

'I don't know. Drug barons, paramilitaries, friends of paramilitaries, a splinter group of the Women's Institute, haven't a clue. It's not like they introduced themselves; they didn't even see me.'

'You're sure about that?'

Another shiver raced up his spine, a wave of fear through his jumbled head. What if they had seen him? Worse still, recognised him? He was a witness to murder, and they would come after him. He pictured a gang of masked men rushing up the stairs at *The Explorer*, shoving Carol out of the way and Jill screaming to high heaven. Poor Trevor, in the wrong place at the wrong time. Shots thump into his chest, his body jolts in the air, in slow motion, crashes through the window and smacks on the pavement below. The key witness flees the country, and helps the Amish build a barn in Pennsylvania.

'These boyos, did they say anything?' The man refilled Charlie's empty tankard.

'I couldn't make out all they said; they were too far off.' He didn't mention that his head was swirling at the time, and anything spoken made little sense.

The man poked the fire, restoring life to the dying embers. In the silence Charlie started thinking how easy his death had been. Was this his final resting place, or would he pass on to the room where they handed out the wings? So far death was quite painless and very relaxing. Certainly the barley helped. In a short time, he'd come to know it as his friend. As for his other friend he'd learned very little.

'I'm sorry,' he said, 'I didn't catch your name?' He was half expecting to hear something like Gabriel, Old Father Time or Saint Peter, when the old boy got to his feet.

'Herbie Smyth,' he said.

Such an ordinary name for the keeper of the Pearly Gates, Charlie thought. At least, drunkenly he thought.

'Well, Herbie thanks for getting me out of that bloody pond. It's time I went home.'

'Boyo, you'll not get far in your condition. There's a bed made for ye upstairs. I'll bid you goodnight. Sleep well, young fella, pleasant dreams.'

He hadn't finished with the body in the pond, but Herbie was already stomping up the stairs. Charlie looked at the dog lying at his feet.

'I don't suppose you fancy a walk?' The dog raised his head, seemed to ponder the question then went back to sleep.

Chapter five

He awoke from the most pleasant sleep he could ever remember. His bed was soft and deep, sheets and pillows a crisp white and smelling of fresh air. Morning sunlight blared through a gap in the curtains and, to his surprise, he could bear to look. Drunk for most of yesterday and yet this morning he felt good, more than good, as if all his lurid fantasies had come true at once: Cameron Diaz, Beyoncé and Carol Vorderman. He'd always loved Carol. Every man had his older-woman fantasy, and she was his. Carol Vorderman and Kylie. OK, Carol Vorderman, Kylie and Princess Caroline of Monaco. Always had a thing about her pink palace. Spoiling this moment was the man in the pond and the question of his own demise. How dead was he? Would he be all right for work? Would Barbara recognise him, or would it take a medium to get the conversation going. One thing was for sure, it was a hell of a drinking session, although that barley stuff seemed to have prevented a hangover.

Rising from the bed, he found all his clothes washed, dried, neatly ironed and draped over a chair. There was a jug of warm water, a basin, soap and a towel ready for him on a small dressing table. He washed and dressed then inspected himself in a mirror hanging on the wall by the door. Could do with a haircut, and he needed a shave, but he was taken with the new cool Charlie staring back. He was oblivious, however, to the blood-shot eyes, pinched cheeks and still swollen nose.

'God, but you look stunning, young Charlie,' he said to himself. 'Have a nice day.'

Opening the curtains, he met brilliant green fields sloping down to the glen, the trees vibrant with the colours of spring. It felt great to be alive or, quite possibly, dead.

A hearty Ulster Fry of bacon, sausages, egg, tomato, black pudding, potato farls and soda bread was set before him on the table by the woman of the house. The last Ulster Fry he remembered eating was three years ago in Torremolinos.

'Good morning, Mr Geddis. I trust you slept well?'

'I did, thank you, Mrs Smyth,' he replied, startled by her friendly manner, a definite improvement on last night.

She filled a blue delft mug with strong tea, set it on the table and left without another word. He wanted to ask her views on the body in the pond. Plainly, she was not a killer, nor were her scones. Had Herbie mentioned anything? Did they both think he was bonkers? He wanted to apologise for turning up wet. But the woman didn't seem interested in any of his woes. Perhaps heavenly bodies didn't judge new arrivals; they simply got on with their job. He laid into the food, his first heavenly breakfast.

* * *

Later that morning, idling by his desk, he felt cheated that he wasn't actually dead. He was sure he was alive now, because everyone in the office was treating him as normal, scolding, slagging him off or simply ignoring him.

His eyes studied *Daily Star* beauty, Maxine: dark hair, tanned, wet, and naked. With his right eye closed, and squinting through his left, he thought Maxine looked quite like Barbara. Not so much the naked parts, more the cool, serious face. Again he wondered if Trevor leaving him in charge for two weeks would be just the thing to impress her. How did it fit within his three-step plan? His life was back on track. He was in charge of the newspaper. He had survived a night of terror, had made new friends and probably would not go near strong drink ever again. Barbara would be proud of him.

'Steps one and two achieved in one fell swoop,' he said.

'What are you babbling about?' said Billy Norton, lurking by the kitchen door, waiting for the kettle to boil.

'Nothing. I'm just pissed off.'

'Aren't we all, sunshine? And what major problem does our local paparazzo have today?'

Lost in his thoughts, Charlie didn't answer.

Unfazed, Billy poured water into his mug and gave it a stir to get the tea bag working. Continuing his morning ritual, he went to his desk, tapped at his computer for no valid reason, and opened his paper to study the racing form. Like Charlie, he was seldom in the office before ten-thirty. In his late forties, he was stout with dark hair greased onto a head that was rather small for his hefty shoulders. His usual was a navy blazer with several pens in the breast pocket. The only time he used them was to write a slip at the bookies or an IOU after a lousy night of poker. He talked money; he talked horses, and he talked of his sexual conquests. Charlie reckoned Billy was impotent in all three departments.

Jill Barker, the advertising manager as she liked to be known, although she was merely the telesales clerk, was on the phone. All charm and blonde rinse, she was already in denial about her age and would only admit to being twenty-nine. Even Charlie, with a brain soused in vodka, could remember her first day three years ago when Trevor told him she was thirty-two. She had no time for the 'doffers in the office,' as she called them. Recently though, Charlie wondered if she would make a good soulmate since she was divorced, and he was involuntarily separated. He had asked her out for a drink after work and, to his surprise, she accepted. Three Bacardi Breezers did the trick.

'All men are pigs,' she'd slurred. But she was sober enough to swipe his hand from her black-stockinged thigh. 'My husband was a prat. No man will...' she said and passed out. At that point he had to pack her into his rattling Volkswagen Polo and drive her home. A night's sleep (alone) erased her memory.

Charlie gazed round the office. A miserable shower and yet he was the one stacking problems like tins of beans at ASDA. The unfinished article on his screen needed help, already too late for the coming week's issue. It was a story about a World War Two veteran celebrating sixty years of marriage. Trevor had said he didn't like the angle Charlie was taking. 'Bertie escaped from Stalag Luft VI, but he couldn't get away from Lilly,' was Charlie's approach. He was ordered to cut the cynicism and write an uplifting story of a local hero. Leaving the piece as it was, he wrote instead an editorial on the perils of eating fast-food, this inspired by the mystery of the sweet 'n' sour stain on his shirt and the poorly situated lamp post outside the Lotus Flower Takeaway.

By this stage of his daily boredom he would be gasping for a pint at The First & Last but not today. For some reason drink had lost its appeal. He thought of the farmhouse, the scrumptious breakfast, the clean sheets, of Herbie and Mrs Herbie, a vision of the afterlife. When they had assured him he wasn't dead, he'd thanked them for their hospitality and strolled down the lane with Herbie who was going to check on his cows.

Thinking again of the red-haired man in the pond, he found a pencil and began to write. He didn't recall if they had actually been spoken, or whether his subconscious was puking up, but somehow the words formed pictures, the pictures moved around, and bells started ringing.

'The voices,' he said, scribbling. '...knees...trees...Palmer...' He could see the red-haired man on his knees. There was shouting. A shot. The man was thrown into the pond. Palmer? What was he doing there? Was he merely thinking of the name because of his lunch at the Fir Tree Lodge? Palmer wasn't at the pond. But how would he know? All their faces were covered, except for the poor bloke who ended up a floater.

Jill, Carol and Billy stared at him. He might look a rambling idiot, but he was on to something.

'Did they say Palmer, or did I imagine it? Maybe there's more than one? Heaven forbid. What's Barbara going to say when she finds out her boyfriend is a murderer? Or what if Palmer was the victim? Maybe I'm not his only enemy?'

He tried not to rejoice in the notion that his rival was dead and what that would do for his chances of getting back with Barbara. Shot in the back and dumped in a pond. No one deserved that fate, not even Palmer.

'Charlie, are you all right?' said Carol. 'You're talking to yourself.'

'He must have money in the bank,' said Billy.

'Just thinking aloud.'

What should he do about it? The obvious answer was to call the police. But he'd been sozzled. Why should they believe him when, for sixteen hours, he'd thought he was living the heavenly good life? Not such a bright idea. Maybe he should go back to the pond. If he found a body then he could tell the police. On the other hand, better to forget all about it.

Chapter six

While Trevor was on holiday things did not run smoothly. On his second morning in charge Charlie had an argument with Jill when she confronted him with letters from two Chinese restaurants – complaints about his article on fast-food. Both restaurants, and two others, who voiced their opinions by telephone, had cancelled their advertising accounts with *The Explorer.*

'Explain that to Trevor when he gets back,' she said. Charlie couldn't afford to get on her wrong side. Two weeks was a long time to be in charge, and she could make his life hell with a mere flick of her tongue.

'Leave it with me, Jill; I'll make a few calls.'

'Hmmph!' She wasn't impressed.

After Barbara he'd love to have Jill, but after their recent date he'd realised that her high heels, tight skirts and sexy blouses were not for his benefit. He realised also, a second woman in his turbulent life was out of the question. Since his near-death, out-of-body experience a strange calmness had come over him. He hadn't seen or heard of Barbara or Palmer. He reckoned they were still chewing over the cud after his lunch at the Fir Tree Lodge. He hoped that was an end to talk of divorce and selling the house. Perhaps Malcolm would announce his impending death due to chronic addiction to nasal spray. Or maybe he would have the pleasure of reporting in *The Explorer* that Mr Palmer, property developer and wife-stealer, while sleeping, had choked on the huge marbles in his gob. Then at a stroke the last year, nine months, three weeks and six days would be washed away and his proper life restored: Barbara and him, a top journalist, retiring by the sea to pursue a career as a bestselling novelist, a fitting conclusion to his three-step plan.

So far he'd resisted the temptation to revisit the duck pond. He couldn't be sure of what happened that night. Some of it was fact, like his near drowning and Herbie fishing him out. But the red-haired man crashing into the water, a bullet in his back, now seemed the product of a drunken hallucination. The whole experience had left its mark. Since then he hadn't touched a drop of strong drink.

He tipped the remainder of his chicken chow mein into the bin. He wasn't really hungry and only bought it as a goodwill gesture in return for the owner of the Cantonese Garden continuing to advertise with *The Explorer*. He was chuffed at having saved two accounts, disappointed with the owner of a third and too frightened to go anywhere near the Lotus Flower after his comments regarding the artificial colours added to sweet 'n' sour sauce. He would tell Trevor he'd done his best, never mind what Jill said.

He had a pile of clothes to iron and an even bigger one to wash. The carpet needed vacuuming and several plastic bins needed dumping. But it had been a tiring day so he left the bags by the sink, the Hoover in the cupboard and flopped into the sofa.

He jabbed the remote at the TV and clicked open a can of Dutch lager, the cheapest he could find at Tesco. *Panorama* was just starting on BBC1. There was a report on property development in the south of England, how people could not afford to buy a house in their home village because blow-ins from the cities had increased demand and forced up prices. Unmoved, he switched to ITV and *Midsomer Murders*. Chief Inspector Barnaby was tripping over corpses in a picturesque village crammed with nasty suspects.

It started him thinking again about the body in the pond. Maybe he should tell the police? He could remain anonymous. Use the telephone. Leave a coded message, like a terrorist. Except he didn't have a code. Wasn't registered. Surely, you needed a standing account at the police station to leave a coded message? How else would the peelers know it was a code? He was supposed to be a journalist. He could be a journalist acting on a tip-off. A handkerchief over the phone, he could simply report the suspicious goings-on in Ballymenace Glen, hinting that a body lay at the bottom of the duck pond. Then again, didn't corpses in water rise to the surface after a few days? By now someone else may have found it. He grabbed his coat and rushed out.

Chapter seven

For nearly half an hour, he sat in the lay-by opposite the entrance to Ballymenace Glen. He'd locked his doors just in case. Whether to protect him from prowlers or to prevent a corpse hijacking the car, he couldn't say. When at last he'd summoned enough gumption to get out of the Polo and scurry across the road, another car came round the bend. He was a petrified rabbit caught in the headlights. *Bright Eyes* played in his head. A Subaru Impreza rolled to a halt behind his car. Two faces, girl and boy, glared at the stricken idiot in the middle of the road. It took all of three seconds for them to lose interest.

He couldn't decide what to do next, stay or go. Then a rare and sensible thought suddenly poked him. What if the body was floating on the pond right now and he'd run off? This pair of lovers might find it, jump to assumptions, and before he could say *bye-bye Barbara* he's on a twenty-year package deal to Maghaberry Prison. Decision made, he strode purposefully across the road and into the glen.

Although it was dusk, it was so much darker beneath the trees it felt like midnight. The evening was calm and warm, but he felt a chill in his bones. But for a solitary blackbird chirping in the trees, it was deathly quiet. Already he regretted coming, ever having a drink, and, at the age of four, asking his mother why boys were different from girls.

The pond lay further into the glen than he remembered, but eventually he reached the bridge and saw the broken railing, proof at least that he'd been there recently. The dark water looked cold and deep, but he knew that already. He shivered. Was that something beneath the surface? He stepped back. Nothing but trees and water all around him. He tried to recall the spot where he'd heard the voices. Another thought, several days late, suddenly entered his head. Had the red-haired man actually died? He might have been wounded and, when his attackers left, struggled out of the pond and made for the hospital. If so, then he was wasting his time here, giving himself the willies for nothing.

The chow mein wreaked havoc with his insides as he ventured over the bridge to the far shore of the pond. A bit of courage would be handy, but he was a journalist not a super sleuth. Reporting on the Allotment Society's Ugly Vegetable competition wasn't such a bad job. Instead, he was hanging around a forest, in the dark, waiting for a dead body to put in a guest appearance. He hoped corpses weren't like Metro buses and came along in threes.

Easily convinced there was nothing untoward in the glen, he trotted back to the path and away from the eerie silence of the pond. The sudden sound of a splash quickened his step. A piercing scream thrust him into overdrive. Even at thirty-four the human heart can only take so much. He'd covered a hundred yards before he stopped running. Couldn't have felt any worse with a feed of drink in him. Gasping, bent double, praying for a third lung, something inside him – a Department of Embarrassment in his conscience – suggested he go back to see what happened. Quietly, at least as quietly as a panting chest and a thumping heart can manage, he retraced his steps until he reached some rhododendron bushes between the pond and the pathway. Crawling beneath the foliage, bravely, yeah bravely, he stuck his head through a gap.

Lily-white and knee deep in the water, she faced him full frontal. Her breasts won hands-down for his attention, long strands of dark wet hair failing to cover the most vital points. Something floated between her legs. She screamed. He leapt from his hiding place ready to save her from the red-haired corpse. But she giggled as a youth rose to his feet, naked. Too late for Charlie; he'd reached the water's edge, his cover blown. The girl screamed again, grabbing hold of her boyfriend.

'Sorry. I thought you needed help.'

'Piss off, you pervert,' the lad shouted. The faces from the Subaru Impreza were now more than faces. 'You're the one who needs help, asshole.'

Charlie didn't stay for a chat.

Chapter eight

Wind and rain lashed the windscreen of the Polo as he drove the four hundred yards from the courthouse to the office. Despite an aching head and a fragile stomach, he made the effort to start work on time. He promised himself not to slip up again before Trevor returned from holiday. Two hours in court had produced little of interest, and so he was heading back to the office to take charge of the spread for the coming week's issue. He didn't want Ernie the printer injecting his muddled ideas or, even worse, for Jill to fiddle with his copy instead of paying attention to her one-page car sale, or the latest bargains at Wilson's Garden Centre.

Carol, Jill, Billy and Ernie glared at him with the same expression, amounting to:

'What time of day do you call this?'

'Another rough night?'

'You're really losing it, Charlie.'

He knew what they were thinking. At least, for a change, they were taking notice.

'I was in court this morning,' he said, dripping wet.

Disbelieving looks.

'You can check if you want.'

Jill was doing her business-with-glamour routine for Ernie, a jobsworth non-PC chauvinist, and *Explorer* veteran of thirty years. He leaned over her desk ogling her cleavage, while she explained the page layout. She wafted Yvresse; his overalls reeked of printing ink. Every week she flirted, giggling at his double entendres, as long as it meant she got her way with the layout.

'Any messages, Carol?' Charlie asked, more formally than usual.

'Just the one.' She handed him a Post-it.

Call Malcolm Palmer: 0248 664132.

Confirmation, he supposed, that Palmer was not the corpse who'd vanished from the duck pond. Mixed feelings about that. He scrunched the paper and shoved it in his pocket.

'Ernie, can we go over the layout now?'

'You're all right, Charlie. Jill's doing fine. Isn't that right, love?'

'If you say so, pet,' she replied.

Everyone resumed work. Charlie sat at his desk, retrieved the Post-it and stared at the name.

'Palmer,' he mumbled.

He thought of Barbara. He thought of Barbara with Palmer, speeding down country roads in his Aston Martin. Choosing furniture for their new home, Barbara choosing and Palmer signing the cheques. The pair of them snuggled up on their new sofa, drinking wine. Barbara showing off her new dress, Palmer unzipping it. He pictured the two of them skinny-dipping at the duck pond. A corpse with red hair floats by, and Palmer says, 'I'd forgotten about him.'

He tore into his drawers (the drawers of his desk). Papers, pens and coffee mug hit the floor. He tapped his keyboard; it beeped in protest. Beneath yesterday's *Daily Star* he found what he'd been looking for.

'Hold the bus. I want this on the front page.' He bounded over to Jill, waving crumpled sheets of A4 in the air.

'The front page has already been done,' she said. Ernie snatched the papers from Charlie's hand and began to read.

'This is more important than the plans for the old mill,' said Charlie.

'Trevor left instructions the old mill story should run on the front page,' said Jill. 'Do you want me to go against his wishes?'

'Don't you worry. Trevor will understand when he reads this. I'm in charge, for now, and my story goes on page one.'

Jill's face crimson, she shuffled uncomfortably in her seat, while Ernie laughed through his smoker's cough.

'A murder?' he said. 'In Ballymenace? I don't believe it.'

The others raised their heads.

'Who?' asked Billy. Ernie continued to read.

'Don't know. Says here it's a mystery. A man with bright red hair.'

'Rubbish,' said Billy. 'No one has ever been murdered in Ballymenace, not even during the Troubles. Terrorists couldn't be arsed planting a bomb here never mind bumping somebody off. Where did you hear about this, Charlie?'

'One of my sources.'

Billy laughed.

'Not another one of your make-'em-up stories? It's not *The Sunday Sport*, you know? Our news is supposed to have an element of truth.'

'That's choice coming from someone who reports the wrong football results, because he doesn't agree with the referee's penalty decisions. I don't care what you say. Do what you like to the rest of the paper, but I want my story on the front page. I'll take full responsibility. Just do it. Please.'

Charlie marched out, dizzy from stamping his authority, and climbed the stairs to Trevor's office where he could speak on the phone without being disturbed.

'Ah, Charlie,' said Palmer in the cheery tone Charlie had come to loathe. 'I wondered if you fancied another bite of lunch?'

He spoke as if their last meeting had been friendly, but Charlie refreshed his memory.

'What is it this time? You and Barbara want to move in with me until your new place is ready?'

'Have something for you, old bean. Might be of some help.'

'An invite to your wake?'

'Can you meet me today at my club?'

Was he going to ignore every jibe?

'What club?'

'Ballymenace Golf Club. You know it surely? It's just a kick over the hill. I'm about to tee-off, now the rain has cleared. Should be finished by two-thirty?'

'Whatever you say, Mal.'

'Must dash; have to work on the old handicap. You know how it is?'

'Yeah, I know how it is,' he said, although Palmer had rung off. 'Have something for you, old bean. Can you meet me at my club? Just a kick over the hill. OK if I have your wife? Sell your house? Ruin your entire life? Sure, no problem, Mal.'

Ernie and Jill stormed in arguing over the layout of the classifieds, demanding Charlie should referee. Thirty minutes later, he blunted both their swords by dropping two of his features to provide the extra space for Jill. Ernie twice threatened to down tools and head for home (as shop steward he had official union backing). Jill threatened to sue both men for harassment, following comments made in the frank exchange of views. Charlie was rather pleased at his diplomacy until they accused him of upsetting the balance of the paper with his, 'utterly ridiculous story,' as Jill put it. She wiggled her exquisite bottom from the office. Ernie and Charlie looked at each other.

'Worth the fight just to see that,' said Ernie with a sigh. 'You and I must be doing something wrong.'

'What are you talking about? You've been married for thirty years.'

'No harm in a bit of window shopping.'

When Ernie returned to his print shop, Charlie lingered at Trevor's desk wondering if he had done the right thing running the murder story. What would Barbara make of it? The scary part was the idea of his wife setting up home with a murderer.

Chapter nine

To the north side of Ballymenace Glen lay Herbie's farm, while sprawled over the hills to the south was Ballymenace Golf Club. The entrance was off a side road that ran from the town's bypass into the hills, dropping to Ballymenace on the other side. Perched at the highest point for miles around, the clubhouse overlooked every fairway. The building had suffered several attempts at modernisation, with a sun lounge and a flat-roofed annexe jutting from what once had been an attractive Victorian residence. In recent years, however, the architecture was more likely to get right up the nose of a certain Prince.

He hid the Polo between a sporty Mercedes and a racing-green Jaguar, not a sight to soothe one's inferiority complex.

'Lucky you wore a tie, Geddis,' he said, fiddling with the knot as he climbed the steps to the front door. 'You know how sticky these clubby types can be.' He brushed his jacket with his hand in the hope of sweeping away the creases, acquired from several nights of crashing out on his sofa.

The blood-red carpet of the foyer was threadbare and partially concealed under plastic runners. The main bar and restaurant was straight ahead, members lounge to the left, registration and changing to the right. Tempted by the first option, he chose instead the dark panelled corridor leading to the registration area. Dropping a short flight of steps into an annexe, he was greeted by a clubby type standing behind a sturdy counter.

'Good afternoon, sir.'

Sporting a navy blazer with club badge, and a club tie of green, red and gold, was a man close to seventy with a full head of wiry, grey hair. His half-rimmed glasses helped him look down his crinkled nose. Both hands fisted and placed assertively on the counter, he waited for the new arrival to speak. Charlie wasn't sure that he wanted to, feeling like an army recruit daring to ask the quartermaster if the uniform came in any colour but khaki. He looked up at the club official, who continued looking down at him. He cleared his throat and prepared to sound as authoritative as he could.

'I have an appointment with Malcolm Palmer. Is he still playing, or what?'

'One minute, sir, and I'll check.' He ran his finger down a column of the daybook, lifted a pair of binoculars, marched to the window and peered out. 'Hasn't made the fifteenth yet, sir. Could be another forty minutes.'

Charlie glanced at his watch. It was ten to two. Exactly forty minutes early. Palmer had everything down to a tee, he thought, excusing himself the pun.

'You could always wait in the bar, sir. It's back upstairs.'

The man turned his attention to four men wearing bright coloured jumpers, *Smarties*, about to set off on their round.

'Thanks very much.' Charlie felt dismissed.

'I'll just wait for him in the bar,' he said, climbing the stairs. 'Not yet on the fifteenth, sir, la-de-da!'

He ordered a pint of Guinness and sat by a huge window overlooking the eighteenth green. Arriving early was a bad idea. He felt anxious over what Palmer had to tell him. He wondered how it could be any worse than last time. Soon he ordered a second pint, this time with a whiskey chaser.

The lounge gradually cleared from the lunchtime rush of men conducting business and affluent housewives chatting after a morning round. He felt out of place here. Didn't have the confidence for sport or for moving in sporting society. Never even managed to score a winning goal for the school football team. His goal-scoring tally for his entire school career was three: two own goals and a fluky deflection. The ball struck him on the head when he bent over to tie his lace. It was disallowed for offside. He was cynical, too, of this lifestyle. A collection of successful men and women, or women espoused to successful men, yet with the time to linger over a game of golf and lunch thrown in. He glanced down the menu on the table. 'Inferiority complex with a side-salad please.' At least the young barman was friendly.

'Are you waiting for someone, sir?' he asked, handing Charlie the change from a tenner. No more than eighteen, he looked the type who'd stepped up to this level of career. Nevertheless, his manner was open and sincere.

'Malcolm Palmer, do you know him?' He may as well seize the chance to gather information, exercise his journalistic tendencies, if ever he had any.

'I do indeed, sir. Most people round here know Mr Palmer. He's on the committee.'

'Works hard for the club?'

'He's very involved with our move.'

'Your move?'

Why didn't he know about this? He was a reporter, for goodness sake. Why hadn't Billy told him? He was the sports editor.

'We're moving to a new site. Brand new championship course and a new club house.'

'And Malcolm is behind all this?'

'I heard him discussing it just last week.'

'What happens to this place?'

'I didn't hear that part.'

He moved away to serve a *Smartie*, leaving Charlie with some meat to chew on the Palmer bone.

Having skipped breakfast, and awaiting lunch, two pints and a whiskey chaser in twenty minutes had loosened his thoughts and fuelled a bout of anti-Palmer sentiment. He gazed through the window along the eighteenth fairway. Still no sign of Palmer. A walk would do him good and might clear his head.

Ignorant of golf club etiquette, he was intending to stroll down the middle of the fairway, but on the way he came across the club's tool shed. A ride on one of those lawnmowers would get him to Palmer a lot faster, he thought. No sign of any ground staff, he sat astride a big mower then immediately spotted a nice red tractor by the side of the shed. Like a kid in a fairground, who quickly susses out the best rides, he sprang from the lawnmower to the cab of the tractor. He found the key in the ignition, turned it, and the engine roared into life. Now he felt just like his new friend Herbie.

He shot forward with a jolt, but within a few yards he had the handle on it and set off along the eighteenth fairway. An elderly man chipping onto the green was a little put off, his ball opting for one of those bunker things. Four ladies, crossing a footbridge by the seventeenth, watched in horror as Charlie cut across the green, collecting the pin under the rear wheel. He gave them a cursory wave, and an open-mouthed lady felt compelled to return the gesture. Rounding a copse of trees beside the seventeenth tee, he spotted Palmer and friends playing onto a green. Foot down, he roared the machine to greater heights. It trundled up the hill, narrowly missing a bunker, and when he cut the engine the tractor came to rest in the middle of the green. Astonished faces looked on as he jumped from the cab.

'Hi, Malcolm. You did remember our appointment?'

Palmer's jaw dropped open.

'You damned fool,' shouted a ruddy-faced, wobbly man. 'Get that tractor off my green. Look at the damage.' With a wobbly hand, he pointed at the tyre marks on the grass. Not one to lack sympathy, Charlie followed the line of the man's wobbly finger.

'Oops!'

'It's OK, Myles,' said Palmer, recovering some composure. 'I'll deal with this. You play on from the seventeenth. I'll be along shortly.' Myles and two other companions bounded off to the next tee, muttering about vandalism and the decline of moral standards. 'You could have waited in the bar, Charlie,' said Palmer, stern yet composed.

'I couldn't wait to see what you had for me.'

'Let's walk. I'll have someone fetch the tractor.'

They set off along the edge of the next fairway.

'I think you and I have kicked off on the proverbial wrong foot,' said Palmer. 'We could be good friends once we settle our domestic arrangements.'

'Don't think so,' Charlie replied, but Palmer had more to spout.

'That's why I asked you here this afternoon. I thought perhaps if I was to start the ball rolling, get the nasty business out of the way, then we, and I'm including Barbara here, would feel the pressure lifted off.'

'You're wasting your breath.'

Palmer stopped and removed a folder from the pocket of his golf bag. It suddenly occurred to Charlie that the reason Palmer never seemed to get angry was because he didn't actually listen to a word being said. He was engrossed in his own little speeches, just like a politician, avoiding the issue by completely ignoring it then rabbiting on with his own agenda.

'Here you are,' he said, handing Charlie a slim white envelope. 'Barbara and I would like you to have this as a gesture of goodwill.'

Charlie tore it open to reveal a 'With Compliments' slip of paper with 'Palmer Property Services' printed in blue and gold. Attached by a paper clip was a cheque, payable to Mr Charles Geddis, for the sum of two hundred and seventy thousand pounds.

'What's this?'

'It's payment for your cottage on Lothian Avenue and then some. We thought you might appreciate the advance pending the sale. I valued the property at around 260K. Popped in an extra 10K as a token of our goodwill, a peace offering, that kind of thing.'

'I've already told you the house, *my house,* is not for sale. Not now, not ever.'

Charlie thought he detected a slight wince. He wondered if Palmer had listened at all, or would he launch into another delivery of bright futures, new beginnings, think of your wife routine? Then a scary thought. What if Palmer did intend to kill him? Would he end up like the man at the duck pond? Palmer could bump him off and still have time to cancel the cheque.

'Listen, old chap...'

'That's bloody choice,' said Charlie. 'You telling *me* to listen.'

There was no reaction, no retaliation. He couldn't believe it. The guy was cool; he had to say that.

'No matter what you say or do,' said Palmer. 'Barbara is leaving that cottage when our new home is ready. If you don't want to sell, that's your choice. The property will lie vacant...'

'Or I can move back.'

He definitely winced, twitched even.

'Yes, you can move back. But remember, if you decide to sell at a later date, you won't get what I'm offering you now. Barbara can rightly insist on having her share.'

Charlie wanted to lay one on him.

'That's blackmail.'

'No, Charlie. It's a genuine offer and against my good business sense. Think about it.'

He walked off in his good business sense manner, leaving Charlie spitting teeth.

'What happened to lunch then?' he called.

Palmer wasn't listening.

Chapter ten

'What the hell do you call that?' said Trevor, redness overcoming his tanned face. Charlie's bum hardly made it to the seat before Trevor shook the latest edition of *The Explorer* in front of him.

'What?' said Charlie, a half-decent attempt at innocence. The paper landed in his lap.

'That. That drivel. Murder at the duck pond? What kind of story is that? Agatha bloody Christie? Where's the report on the old mill?'

'Page six.'

'Great. Just great. I might have known. I might have bloody known.' Trevor tended to repeat himself in times of crisis.

Charlie thought it best to say nothing. Let Trevor vent his anger for a while and then he would explain. The office door was open wide, and he realised the others, a floor below, could hear the row. Right now, Jill would be swimming in a sea of arrogant vindication.

'And just for good measure you lose two accounts, rub Jill up the wrong way...' If only, Charlie thought. 'And every businessman in the town is a murder suspect. But, of course, there is no body. There isn't even a person in the area listed as missing. Thanks a heap, Charlie. Thanks a bloody heap. I need another holiday already.'

'But it's a good story, Trevor. It's true.'

Trevor gazed out the window, no doubt, hoping to spy the girl from the jeans shop. A glimpse of her shapely figure might ease his pain.

'Honestly, Trevor, a man was shot and his body dumped in the pond at Ballymenace Glen. My source was a witness.'

'He told you that?'

'Yes.'

'And you believed him?'

'Yes.'

'And the police found the body?'

'No.'

'Charlie, when are you ever going to wise up?'

'I'm not spoofing, Trevor. He told me that three men in balaclavas beat up this red-haired guy, and then they shot him. And while doing so they mentioned a prominent businessman.'

'Whose name is?'

'I can't tell you at the moment.'

'But you've passed the information to the police?'

'No.'

'Bloody hell, Charlie. You tell our readers a man was murdered, that he's floating on a duck pond, and it's got something to do with a local businessman? But you don't tell the police? Because of your story they're down there right now, with divers, TV cameras and dozens of people, waiting for a corpse to rise from the water like the bloody Loch Ness Monster. What are you trying to do? By this afternoon *The Explorer* will be the laughingstock of the whole country. And I'm the one who has to apologise for wasting police time. I've warned you before; if you can't find a decent story then don't make them up from your twisted head.'

'I'm not making it up, Trevor, honest.'

'Are you going to name your source?'

'No, but there's someone else who can prove I'm right.'

Trevor slumped into his chair, speechless.

'I'll take you to meet him, Trevor. I'll prove it's not a hoax. I'll–'

'You're certain about the body in the water?'

'Yes.'

'I'll go with you on two conditions.' He rubbed his face hard with both hands. 'Firstly, *if* there is a body in the pond, we tell the police about your witness.'

Charlie winced, raising a hand to protest, but Trevor jumped in loudly.

'And... if you're wrong about all this, promise me you'll get help, counselling, a doctor, or a frontal lobotomy?'

Chapter eleven

The lane was thick with mud from the recent heavy rain and well churned by the tyres of farm machinery. Oak, sycamore and horse chestnut were abundant with leaves and the fields rampant in grass, to the delight of Herbie's dairy cows. Charlie stopped the car in the lane beside a gate and pointed out to Trevor the duck pond in Ballymenace Glen. They walked through a large sloping field to a barbed wire fence that separated forest from pasture.

'Down here,' said Charlie, clambering over the wire. 'This is where it happened.'

Trevor didn't look impressed. The policemen didn't look chuffed either. They were packing their search equipment into a van, while a policewoman removed a cordon of incident tape from across the path that ran beside the pond. Two divers eased from their wetsuits and chatted with a senior officer. Charlie wanted to ask them if they'd found anything, but Trevor pulled him away.

'Stay out of it, Charlie. You've caused enough trouble already.'

'I thought maybe I could help. Tell them where it happened.'

'I think you should tell me first.' Trevor waited with arms folded.

'I was standing on the bridge, and I heard voices.'

'You? I thought you had a witness?'

Trevor looked ready to thump him. Charlie had to think quickly. For now the truth would do.

'OK, it was me. I was here. But I couldn't say that in *The Explorer*; people would think I was making the whole thing up.'

Trevor shook his head.

'How did you fall in?' he asked, when Charlie described his near-death experience.

'The railing broke.' He nodded towards the bridge.

'Looks like someone has repaired it,' Trevor said, biting his lip, resigned to yet another crack-pot yarn from his supposed news gatherer.

Charlie, dumfounded, stepped onto the bridge. He slid his hand over an intact railing looking as though it had been there for years, strong and sturdy. He pushed his hip against it, but there was no give. Trevor walked away.

'Come and see the farm,' Charlie said, chasing after him. 'I swear; it's like stepping back a century.'

Before they could drive up the lane, Trevor had to wipe his shoe in some long grass after a piece of cowpat stuck to his heel. Charlie saw it as a sign that his day was turning to manure. His head, he thought, was also full of it.

Ever hopeful, he pulled up in the farmyard delighted to see it exactly as he remembered.

'See,' he said with relief, 'I told you it's a time warp. Nothing has changed around here for years.'

'Except for that, maybe.'

Trevor pointed to a satellite dish fixed to the chimney of the cottage. Charlie didn't recall a television in the house, never mind Sky Digital. Feeling stressed, and under pressure to provide some credence to his story, he ushered Trevor to the front door.

'Wait till you see inside.' He knocked on the wood. 'The woman is a real old crock. Never smiles, hardly says a word...' The door opened.

'Oh hello again, Mr Geddis,' said a pleasant beaming woman. 'You're looking better today, are ye well?'

Some kind of pneumatic device was needed to close Charlie's mouth. Stout she was, but Old Mother Hubbard, plainly she was not. Bright flowery dress by Dorothy Perkins, neatly styled hair, a touch of rouge on her cheeks, she delivered a smile as warm as her pot of tea on that fateful night. Charlie didn't dare look at Trevor.

'Hello, Mrs Smyth,' he said at last. 'I just wanted Herbie to meet my boss. This is Trevor McLean, editor of *The Ballymenace Explorer*.'

Trevor smiled and said hello, and the woman nodded.

'Herbie's up the top field,' she said. 'Do you want to come in and wait? He should be down for his lunch shortly.'

'If you don't mind we will, Mrs Smyth,' Charlie replied, ever hopeful that Herbie, when he appeared, would seal his redemption.

'This is a beautiful room,' said Trevor politely, while firing hostile looks at Charlie.

'Thank you, Mr McLean. Would you care for some tea?'

'That would be very kind,' he answered for both of them. The woman went to her kitchen leaving Trevor to glare at Charlie his employee, assuming, by the end of the day, he remained so.

'I don't understand it, Trevor. It doesn't make sense.'

'You don't make sense,' Trevor hissed through gritted teeth.

Charlie repeated his story and offered apologies. Trevor seemed too exasperated to argue further. When Mrs Smyth returned with a tray of scones and a pot of tea, they passed themselves with trivial discussion about the weather, the prospects of a good crop, and the state of the nation.

Charlie couldn't face the scones. His stomach was a bubbling pool of lava about to erupt. He thought the tea might help, but it was too hot. Trevor had no problems and, after two scones with strawberry jam and clotted cream, he got to his feet and lied about having another appointment. Forsaking the tea, Charlie followed him to the door and, as the woman opened it, a huge John Deere tractor with springy wheels bounced into the yard. Herbie climbed from the cab looking every bit as old as Charlie remembered, but somehow more vibrant, more alive. Considering their first meeting, when Charlie presumed Herbie to be God's messenger, more alive was now a reasonable observation. He preferred the first Herbie, however. He glanced around the yard, looking for the rusty old tractor. There was something else different about rusty old Herbie, too. He still wore the flat cap, but the tatty suit was gone and in its place a pair of smart navy dungarees over a red chequered shirt.

'Hello there, young fella,' he said sprightly. Charlie blinked, praying it would all go away, wanting to run, wanting to hide. 'You look better than the last time I set eyes on ye. A lot drier anyhow.'

'This is my boss, Trevor McLean,' was all Charlie could manage to say.

'Another newspaper man,' said Herbie, shaking Trevor's hand.

'Pleased to meet you, Herbie. Charlie was telling me all about you.'

'Tell him about the man being shot,' said Charlie. 'And dumped in the pond?'

A wry grin swept over the old man's face.

'Tell him about me falling in and you dragging me out.'

Herbie kept hold of his grin. If his face weren't so wrinkled, Charlie would have said he looked a tad coy. But he was desperate. He needed confirmation of his story as Trevor continued to simmer. Herbie removed his cap and scratched the back of his head.

'Well now...' he began.

'Go on, Herbie.'

'The barley? Isn't that what you're gettin' at?'

'Yes that's it.' Charlie almost cried with relief.

'We had a fair drop that night. And a wee yarn or two.'

Charlie nodded eagerly. Now they were getting somewhere, and his ass was spared.

'But I warned ye, didn't I? I told ye it was powerful medicine.'

'Yes, but what about the red-haired man? Those guys in black?'

'You must've had more than I thought, young fella, talkin' such talk.'

'But it's true, Herbie. Remember I told you about it when you pulled me out of the pond? I wanted to go back to find the body.'

'You'd had a rough night in that shuck. Nearly met your maker.'

'But it's true, Herbie. I just want Trevor to hear it.'

'Just a bit of craic, son.'

'I think we've wasted enough of your time, Herbie,' said Trevor. 'Get in the car, Charlie.'

Farmer and wife waved as Charlie reversed in the yard and rolled into the lane. He glanced at Herbie in the mirror and could have sworn the old man winked at him. He wasn't sure of anything anymore, except that Trevor looked on the verge of blowing a gasket.

Chapter twelve

They were on the main road to town before either of them spoke, and then it was Trevor ordering Charlie to lower his window. The smell of manure from his shoe was rising, and it fuelled his foul mood.

'Pull over,' Trevor said. 'We need to talk.'

Charlie swung onto the hard shoulder. Trevor had to shout over the traffic whizzing by, although he was in the right mood for shouting anyway.

'What's the matter with you? I thought you would sort yourself out, while I was on holiday. Instead, you've lost me two clients and printed a blow-by-blow account of one of your drinking sessions. I'm your mate as well as your boss, Charlie, but you're not doing anything to help me.'

'It's Barbara,' Charlie replied. He had to say something. He'd no more idea of what was wrong in his life than Trevor had. 'I want her back. I want to go home.'

'Have you spoken to her? Told her how you feel?'

'It's not that simple. She's planning to shack up with Malcolm Palmer. They want to sell the house, *my house*. I don't know what to do, Trevor. Palmer is all wrong for her.'

'He is bloody loaded.'

'I know I can't compete, but I want her back. I realise now that I was stupid to have left her. At the time I just wanted some excitement in my life. I wanted to live a little, do things, be successful, but I've achieved nothing. My life is the absolute pits.'

'Take the day off. Go and see her. You never know, she might feel like giving it another go if you explain how you feel.'

'And what if she doesn't?'

'Then you might have to accept it's all over. It's worth a try. Joan and I would love to see you two get back together.'

Charlie grinned, knowing full well the only *back* Joan would like to see was his with a knife in it. She and Barbara were firm friends. It was only natural they should despise each other's husband. After all, they'd heard so much about them.

'Drop me off in town, and go see her,' said Trevor. He got out of the car then popped his head through the window. 'If it doesn't work out you can always settle for that Lisa. She's a babe.'

Lisa lived in the flat directly below Charlie's. They had each other's keys, useful for popping in to borrow the odd pint of milk, a slice of bread or, to lend a sympathetic ear. She was twenty-seven, tall, outgoing with a propensity for dating guys who used her and dumped her. At one time Charlie thought he could be the man who would take good care of her, who didn't want her merely for her legs and a couple of other features. To his surprise, Lisa seemed to agree with his thinking, but he soon realised that she saw him as a kindred spirit and not as a lover.

'Thanks, mate. You're in the wrong job, you know? Trevor, the marriage guidance counsellor has a certain ring to it.'

Wheels spinning, Charlie swerved onto the road. He had driven all the way home before realising that Trevor had only got out of the car to clean the dung from his shoe. He'd left him stranded.

Chapter thirteen

Depending on his mood and level of sobriety, Charlie swung from apathy to hatred in regard of his hometown. For him the only good thing about Ballymenace was driving out of it. At sixteen he became sole and founding member of the Ballymenace Escape Committee and spent days, weeks and months dreaming of London, New York, Ibiza and sin-drenched beaches.

Two years later, with one and a bit A levels, he seized his chance and escaped to the big smoke of Belfast, a mere ten miles up the road. He was about to set the world alight with his wit, charm and journalistic talent when he stumbled upon man's tendency to strike up a relationship with a pretty girl. The pair of them stumbled upon man (and woman's) tendency to fornicate without precautions, and a couple of months later someone older (her father) took him to the side and explained the meaning of the word responsibility. It was the twenty-first century, the noughties, fast living and shacking up without the need for an official document. Unfortunately, the girl of Charlie's dreams was the daughter of a Baptist preacher, recently returned from a stint of ministering in Alabama and very hot on wholesome family values. For some reason, Charlie pictured white hoods and burning crosses.

On the day of his wedding to Barbara, Charlie's father announced his retirement as the owner of the largest butcher shop in Ballymenace. To all but Charlie this appeared irrelevant, within the context of a shotgun wedding, until it was explained that Charlie's parents were retiring to a home by the sea, the Mediterranean Sea. As a wedding present, Barbara and Charlie were given number forty-seven Lothian Avenue, Ballymenace. One hundred and fourteen confetti throwers, tears welling in their eyes, saw a wonderful circling of life. How nice for the Geddises to gift their son and daughter-in-law the old family roost. Charlie saw the SS dragging him, kicking and screaming, all the way back to Colditz. To cap it all, Barbara's pregnancy was false, phantom, a cist or something of a female technical nature. It was the saddest news that he and Barbara had ever had to deal with.

Since then he'd clocked eight and a half years of marriage to Barbara, seven years congealed boredom at *The Ballymenace Explorer*, five years toying with his first novel, and four years paid-up contributions to the Ballymenace Pickle Your Own Liver Society. From eight and a half years marriage must be deducted one year, ten months, two weeks and five days spent in exile from the house at Lothian Avenue.

His home for the duration was a third-floor flat of a 1960s concrete masterpiece, within the Yonhill Estate, sprawled on the eastern outskirts of Ballymenace. Yonhill was a place of 'Special European Interest', a prime example of a failed social housing project. Special EU workshops on social services, hosted at Stormont, included visits to the estate. As delegates inspected the torn-up pavements, smashed bus shelters, bricked-up houses and the one remaining shop unit open for business, they were seen to nod in unison; all agreed that Yonhill Estate was not a template for successful community living. The specially orchestrated riot as delegates were driven away in a smashed-up coach ensured that a pot of European Peace Money found its way to the 'community projects' running on the estate.

'A tidy home is a tidy mind,' he told himself. 'Today's the day. Put the past behind you.'

Oasis blared from the stereo. A bit of air guitar.

Wipe the slate clean. Set a new course. Start as you mean to go on. All the clichés passed through his mind as he glided the Hoover over the tatty carpets.

When he'd finished with the Hoover, he dusted the bookshelves and washed a week's load of dishes. Trevor was right; he had to make an effort. He had to show Barbara that he could get his life together, that he could work hard, that he could be dependable, and that he was better for her than Malcolm Palmer.

Showered and changed into the only decent clothes he could find, jeans and polo shirt, he wished himself luck and set off.

Ten minutes later, the Polo, with a rattling exhaust, spluttered into Lothian Avenue. The houses at the lower end were old estate-worker terraces of rendered grey stone, but these gave on to modern semis built either side of what used to be called Priory Lane. At the top of the lane stood an old cottage with white-washed walls and a blue slate roof. Number forty-seven, the Geddis family seat, marked the dead end of Lothian Avenue. The poignancy had never been lost on Charlie. Two miles away, over the hills, the new bypass diverted traffic from the mundane delights of Ballymenace.

This was the night when he would apologise for going off the rails, overstepping the mark, and shunning his responsibilities. He was off on the clichés again. His whole life was a cliché. Of course, that, too, was a cliché.

'Stop talking to yourself, Geddis.'

The drizzle helped his disappointment fester as he gaped at the sign. Nailed to the gatepost was a blue and gold board: PPS, Palmer Property Services, telling the world that number forty-seven, Lothian Avenue, Ballymenace was for sale. Just for good measure, viewing was strictly by appointment.

The old place seemed forlorn. Window frames needed replacing, a couple of slates had slipped on the roof, but the house was sturdy. His parents had loved the place, its cosy rooms, the Aga simmering on freezing wintry nights, the roses and clematis smothering the trellis by the gable wall, and the tomatoes appearing each year in the greenhouse as if by magic. He knew what it meant for them to hand it over when they retired. To his shame, he never really expressed his appreciation of the gesture, never really said thanks. He'd grown up here, and yet, at eighteen, he couldn't wait to get away. And when he'd returned as a married man he couldn't wait to get away again. Strangely, now he wanted nothing more than to share those cosy rooms with Barbara.

He pulled a piece of crumpled paper from his pocket. Palmer's cheque. For a moment he stared at the figures written in the box. How much did this house really mean to him? Was he prepared to let it go? Would the sale mean closure on his marriage? The paper tore easily in half, then half again, and again. He tossed the pieces in the air and watched them flutter to the ground. He tried to use his key, but it didn't fit the lock. She'd had them changed since his last attempted homecoming. He rang the bell, knocked then kicked the door. No one home. He marched back to the car and was startled by the sound of his own voice.

'No way. No bloody way.'

He was beginning to sound like Trevor, repeating himself in a crisis. He opened the hatch and fumbled in the boot. Under a pile of old newspapers, he found his rarely used toolbox and pulled out a junior hacksaw. There was no one about the street. He didn't care. The wood cut easily, despite the rain, and halfway through, he pushed his shoulder at the post. The wood cracked as it split, and he wrenched it from the gatepost, his gatepost. Barely thinking ahead, he slid the sign into the back of the car and drove off.

He hadn't a clue where to go or what to do. He just drove in the rain, seething at Palmer's arrogance. By the time it was dark, he found himself on the other side of Ballymenace beside a modern, detached house displaying a 'For Sale' board of Palmer Property Services. There was no life about the house and no activity in the wide avenue. An idea was born in him. He knew what he had to do. The hacksaw was hardly needed for as he sawed at the post it loosened from its mooring in the lawn and fell over. Raising the hatch of the Polo he threaded the post between the seats. A glance around the avenue and he was off again. The next two signs were easier still, snatched from new unoccupied bungalows. He took three from a row of derelict terraces near the town centre, one from the old funeral parlour on Bridge Street and five from Palmer's latest development on the Belfast Road. He was soaked through, cold and angry, but it was great fun. Adrenalin for supper, yummy. Maybe, like Trevor, he'd chosen the wrong career. Spying, espionage, or down-to-earth burglary might be more his line.

With all the driving around town he'd given little thought of what to do with his booty. Then, fortuitously, he noticed the gates of Ballymenace Golf Club and skidded to a halt. His heart thumped. He gazed at the lights of the clubhouse. Judging by the number of parked cars, a lot of members were present. He started up the drive a few yards and with an impulsive flick of the steering wheel, veered onto the grass and down a hill. He cut his lights and, staying close to the trees, sneaked past the car park and clubhouse. Cruising along the second fairway, he narrowly missed a bunker as he rallied onto the green. Jumping out, he grabbed one of the signs and made for the pin. He pulled the flag from the hole and tossed it away. Then, like a bold mountaineer at the summit of Everest, he rammed home his symbol of conquest. Well chuffed, he jumped back in the car and hurried to the next green.

'Having fun, sir?' a voice said in the darkness.

Charlie stood at the twelfth green, last sign in hand, squinting into torchlight. He was more startled than frightened, as if he'd been shaken from a good night's sleep. Then he noticed the car, its blue flashing light, and a policeman astride a wire fence by the edge of the golf course.

'Care to explain what you're up to?' said the officer, the torch moving closer. Charlie cleared his throat.

'It's a long story, Constable.'

'Maybe you'd like to come to the station? My sergeant likes a good story. Might even stretch to a cup of cocoa. You can bring your friend with you,' he said, pointing at the sign.

'What about my car?'

'We'll sort that out later. You have more important things to worry about.'

Chapter fourteen

He dried his jeans by sitting close to a radiator. After a breath test and providing a urine sample, he was given hot tea without sugar in a polystyrene cup. The first sip scalded his tongue; he didn't bother with the rest. A young detective – younger than Charlie – arrived to conduct the interview. In five minutes, Charlie recounted the whole story: his marriage break-up, his dislike of Palmer, tearing down the 'For Sale' boards and planting them on the golf course. To add some background, he mentioned his boredom at *The Ballymenace Explorer,* his falling from a bridge and his belief that the body of a red-haired man lay in the duck pond at Ballymenace Glen.

Detective Inspector Des Watkins, a telegraph pole of a man, tall even for a policeman, didn't believe a word. He pointed out that he'd spent his entire day waiting by the pond in Ballymenace Glen, while two frogmen paddled in the water finding nothing. After sixteen hours on duty and now having met the root cause of his woeful day, his face was pleasant but not his manner.

'Cut the crap, Mr Geddis,' he said in a deep voice. 'It's very late, and you're wasting my time. Now let's start again.'

By the fourth telling of the story both men were less tolerant of the other. An hour later the tale was decidedly shorter. It was debatable whether Charlie thought it best to leave out the dead body, or Watkins had persuaded him that if he didn't change his story things would take a turn for the worse. When the matter was reduced to a simple act of wanton vandalism, Watkins ordered Charlie to a cell for the night. On the way he bumped into Malcolm Palmer, in dinner jacket, white shirt and bowtie. He was talking to the desk sergeant, getting all the facts on the evening's activity. His expression on seeing Charlie was a tad hostile, but he didn't get the chance to speak.

'What the hell are you playing at?'

'Barbara. What are you doing here?'

Feigning surprise was instinctive and, for the moment, Charlie's best option. He looked her up and down. She was ravishing. He looked her up and down again. Stunning was the word, but she was also angry. He had trouble keeping his eyes off her burgundy dress, lots of cleavage and hugging of breasts and, in the cold foyer, erect nipples straining the cloth. Her bare shoulders broke out in red blotches as her anger increased with his ogling. Judging by her new clothes, he reckoned he was paying too much in maintenance. Only then did it occur to him that she had come to the station with Palmer. They were together, of course, and Palmer was the reason for her elegant appearance.

'You can talk in there,' said the sergeant, indicating the room Charlie had just left.

'Give us a few minutes, Malcolm,' she said. She pulled a matching silk wrap around her shoulders, marched into the room and sat down. Charlie didn't get the chance.

'What's wrong with you, Charlie?'

They were alone, but for some reason she whispered. He stared at her hands on the table, her tiny freckles and her maroon nails skilfully tended. He was pleased to see she was still wearing her wedding ring. OK, it was on the wrong finger, but at least she hadn't thrown it away.

'I'm called down here at two in the morning, and you've nothing to say?'

His mouth was open, but not for talking. He was staring at her breasts again. It had been a long time.

'Why, Charlie?'

'I don't like him.'

'Pardon?'

'I don't like Palmer, and he's not going to sell my house.'

'The house you loved so much that you couldn't wait to get away? First as a child and then as a big kid?'

'It's still my house. It was our wedding present from my parents. There's no way Palmer is getting his hands on it.'

'But Malcolm paid you more than it's worth, and before he has even managed to sell it on.'

'I don't want his money. I don't like him, and I don't know what you see in him.'

'Now we're getting somewhere. You're jealous. You're trying to make trouble for us, aren't you?' She glared at him, her dark eyes piercing.

God, but she was lovely when she was angry, he thought. He stole another peak at her cleavage. She noticed and folded her arms.

'He's not right for you, Barbara.'

'And you are, I suppose? You're pretty quick telling me what *you* don't want, but what about me? Do I not have a say in running my own life?'

Despite her anger, he felt the urge to kiss her. Maybe if he had done so, one year, ten months, two weeks and five days ago, when she was throwing him out, he might not be in this mess.

'I want to come home, Barbara. I still love you. I know I've been a prat, but I've learned my lesson. I'm a changed man.'

'You've changed all right. First you destroyed our marriage, now you're destroying golf courses and spoiling the one chance for happiness I've had in the last two years. We are finished, Charlie. I'm happy with Malcolm, and when our new house is ready, we're moving in together whether you like it or not.'

'I promise I'll be good. I'll be reliable. I'll settle down, do my job-'

'That's a laugh. The only reason you still have a job is because I told Joan you have problems, and she has ordered Trevor not to sack you. Everyone is trying to help you, but you won't help yourself. Even Malcolm has been patient, and he doesn't owe you a thing.'

'I still don't like the guy.'

She was on her feet.

'Keep the damn house, Charlie.'

She made to walk away, but he caught her hand. A moment of weakness, perhaps, but she allowed him to take it.

'Barbara, there's something else I have to tell you. Something I've never told you before.'

'What?'

He caressed her hand in his and gazed into her sultry eyes. Before they were married, they used to hold hands at every opportunity. They walked down the street hand in hand, sat in the cinema, even during lectures at university, which was difficult at times because they weren't always seated next to each other. In the first few years of marriage they held hands in bed, in the shower and while she cooked breakfast on a Sunday morning. After eight years, however, Charlie had more often to use his hands to protect his head, while Barbara used hers to throw plates, vases and ornaments in his direction. Now, savouring her touch, he wondered if he should tell her about the red-haired man. She waited.

'Well? What have you got to tell me?'

'Your boobs look great in that dress.'

She jerked free and made for the door.

'If you don't get it together soon, I'll get a court order to keep you away from the house.'

Palmer opened the door. He looked sternly at Charlie then spoke to Barbara.

'It's all been sorted out. We can go now.'

'You can go as well, Geddis,' said Inspector Watkins. 'Mr Palmer has kindly agreed to forget the whole matter, provided you keep your nose clean in future.'

Barbara fired him a withering look and walked away.

'I hope that's an end to all this nonsense, Charlie,' said Palmer.

There was a hint of a warning in that upper-crust voice. Not just pissed off that his evening had been disrupted. It sounded more like a threat. A warning that Charlie was playing with fire, and that he would get more than his fingers burned. But he'd got Charlie's heckles up. Now he was determined to find the link between Palmer and the killing of the red-haired man. Barbara might not be so fond of him after that.

Chapter fifteen

It was probably exhaustion because he slept like the dead. His waking came gently, a succession of dozes and the odd blink of consciousness with portions of sweet dreams floating by. The dreams mingled with thought until reality got the upper hand, and finally he succumbed to a new day. By new he hoped different, happier and trouble-free. He lay on his back, hands behind his head, staring at the yellowed ceiling, pondering his next move. He'd be delighted if it had something to do with Barbara and Palmer, but it was too early. He was merely deciding whether to go for a pee or to roll over and go back to sleep. But time is a great leveller. Ten minutes later his bladder could take no more, and he rushed to the bathroom.

His next problem arrived shortly after the bladder issue was put to rights. What day was it? Was it a workday, or could he really go back to sleep? Why couldn't life be more like a computer? If he didn't want to log on first thing in the morning he didn't have to. A secure password and no one could access his day. He snuggled under his Manchester United duvet, a giant screen saver, hiding him from the world.

He did a quick recap of the last few days: golf courses, Palmer, Jill, Trevor, Inspector Watkins and, most importantly, Barbara. At least four days' worth of trouble.

By that calculation it should be a Friday, or perhaps Thursday. In truth, he hadn't a clue what day it was. If it was a weekday then he was already late for work. If it was Saturday or Sunday, then what's the rush?

Any morning routine he ever espoused to was left behind at Lothian Avenue, one year, ten months, two weeks and six days ago. He had no enthusiasm for the day ahead. Didn't matter which day. Cosy beneath his duvet was the most he could expect from his life. Eventually, guilt over-powering reluctance, he rolled from his bed, sleepy and naked. He gathered his jeans off the floor and found a clean pair of boxers in the top drawer of the dresser. Yesterday's socks would have to do. He donned the boxers, pulled on the jeans, the socks and a pair of trainers. He had a faint recollection of two ironed shirts hanging in the wardrobe. The old wood creaked with the effort as he opened the door. He was dead right. Two shirts were hanging inside.

'Whoa!'

He reeled backwards, but it caught him in the privates. Sprawling on the floor, face up, he met a red head between his legs, face down. At first glance it resembled a raunchy homosexual act except the redhead was quite dead, incapable of anything regardless of sexual preference. Panic fuelled his strength. He wrestled free and scuttled to the far side of his bed, shaking. Suddenly the room was freezing cold, and there was him without a shirt. Scrunching his nose at the stench, he glanced at his visitor then rolled away in horror. If life was indeed like a computer, somebody up there knew his password. He'd just been hacked.

'What do I do?' He stole another glimpse of the body.

'Maybe it'll go away. Better still, it's not really here. I'm asleep, dreaming. Not pleasant but hey it's better than being awake.' He checked again but the body was still there.

'I'll phone the police. Yeah, I'll call the peelers. They'll get rid of it. They'll know what to do.'

His breathing was loud and troubled, but at least *he was* breathing. That thing on the other side of his bed was in *his* flat, lying on *his* floor, and it didn't have the good manners to take the odd breath. He hadn't even begun to tackle the myriad of questions that came with it. He knew it was the red-haired man from the glen. Had to be. How many red-haired men are going around at the moment, particularly dead ones? And why did he have bright red hair? How did he get into his flat? That was a biggie. Why was he here? An even bigger biggie. Why was he dead? That, surely, was the mother of all biggies. Charlie fought hard against his fear. To continue skulking on his bed, scared shitless, meant he couldn't get help or even a clean shirt. He crawled over the mattress and forced himself to look at the poor sod on the floor. The body was wrapped in black polythene and tied with blue nylon ropes, one at the feet, one at the knees, and one around the arms and torso, from the waist to the shoulders. It was mummification on the cheap. The head was the only body part exposed. Thankfully, the red and heavily matted hair covered most of the blackened and decaying face.

Scurrying to the living room he found his Bon Jovi World Tour T-shirt lying in a ball on the sofa. Pulling it on, he grabbed the telephone and dialled 999. A female voice responded instantly. He hung up.

'What am I going to say? Here's the guy I've been telling you about. I brought him home for safe keeping. Hasn't said much. Seemed happy enough in my wardrobe.'

He lifted the phone again and redialled. This time he got as far as Police Control. When a serious male voice asked for his name, he put the phone down again. He would have to think about it for a while longer. Maybe

Trevor would know what to do? Yeah, it was time for work.

He was halfway down the stairs at quite a lick, when another vision of horror struck. He ran back to the flat. His Manchester United duvet would have to do. Sweeping it off the bed, he draped it over the corpse. Somehow the image was less frightening. Now it was merely a red duvet with a few humps. The Shroud of Old Trafford, you might say. He couldn't wait to tell Trevor about his visitor. His boss would have to apologise and so would Barbara. Maybe Jill, too, if he was lucky. He could invite them over to witness the police removing the body and, when he made his statement, he could drop Malcolm Palmer's name right in it.

Chapter sixteen

'The Don Paco looks nice,' said Carol, more to herself than to Jill or Charlie. They had already switched off to her holiday deliberations. 'But it's too far from the centre of San Antonio.' She leafed through one of the brochures piled on her desk. 'I want to be close to the nightlife.' She'd done little work, apart from answering the phone and making coffee. 'What do you think of Minorca?'

No reply.

'Or Rhodes?' She munched another finger of KitKat, indecision a good excuse for chocolate. 'Jill?'

Jill was the only person engrossed in proper work.

'What do you think of Minorca?' Carol repeated.

'Too quiet for the likes of you.'

'I don't know where to go. I've been to Magaluf for the past three years. I need a change.'

She looked at Charlie for some input. He was much too busy. His natural level of indecision had been restored. So far he'd told no one about his plastic-coated friend. Not everyone had a dead body come to stay without so much as an invitation. Somebody was taking him for a fool, and the one name that sprang to mind was Malcolm Palmer. But why have a man shot, thrown in a pond, fished out, wrapped in a bin bag and stuffed in a wardrobe? What sort of game was he playing? Hide the stiff? This was murder, and all Charlie could see was him copping the blame. How could he get someone to believe his version of events?

'Charlie,' Carol shouted.

He jumped, spilling coffee over the centre spread in *The Sun.*

'Is there anybody there?' she said. 'Any chance of intelligent conversation round here?'

'Jill, tell Carol about your diarrhoea,' he said.

'Don't be disgusting,' said Jill.

'But that story could just run and run.'

'Now there's a thing,' said Carol. 'My friend Wendy and her boyfriend went to Kenya last year on safari. Do you know how they spent their entire holiday?'

Jill stopped work to listen.

'Sitting on the toilet and puking in the wash basin.'

'Oh, Carol, for goodness sake. Do you have to follow Charlie's disgusting mind all the way to the sewer?'

'Food poisoning,' said Carol.

In vain, Charlie tried to think of something other than death. Instead of red-haired polythene mummies, skulking beneath a Man United duvet, he drifted off. There wasn't much to choose between his life and the gastric eruptions of two people on holiday. 'Mia, nineteen, from Essex' went in and out of focus on the centre pages as he toyed with the options for disposal of a dead body.

Number one: his wheelie bin, or, even better, Palmer's wheelie bin. He couldn't decide on the blue bin for recycling, the brown for composting or the grey for landfill. Dump the stiff in the wrong bin and the council could refuse to accept it. For number two there was burial: a shallow grave in the forest, with the body covered in leaves. Throwing him back in the duck pond was option three. Let someone else take the credit for finding him. In future, he should pay more attention to *Midsomer Murders*: fabulous tips for doing away with people. Finally, a procedure he'd once read about and not without a certain appeal. Apparently, a dead body placed in a septic tank with the right ingredients added to start the decay process, say a dead sheep, would dissolve completely in five years. Gone without a trace. Probably wise to remove the plastic wrapping first. But why should he help Palmer by disposing of incriminating evidence? If Palmer was out to frame him, he should be trying to frame him back. That was the answer. Put the body in Palmer's wardrobe and see how he likes it.

'Who's Palmer?' Carol asked, interrupting his plan to steal Palmer's Aston Martin, stuff the body inside and push it off a cliff.

'Why are you asking?'

'You've been muttering the name for the past ten minutes.'

Leaning back in his chair, arms open wide, he yawned then let out a disheartened sigh. One sock was brown and the other, navy blue. Living alone was taking its toll, but it was marginally better than sharing a flat with a corpse.

'Malcolm Palmer is the guy who is ruining my life. He has everything you could possibly want – fast car, successful business, lots of money – and now he has Barbara.'

'Sounds like stiff competition,' said Carol. He shivered at the word stiff. 'Do you think it's serious?'

'They're having a new house built in Cultra, and Barbara wants a divorce. No, I don't think it's anything to worry about.'

'What are you going to do?'

'Not much I can do. Palmer is rich, successful, and I can't stand him. He's Mr Bloody Perfect. If only I could find some dirt on him, something to convince Barbara that underneath that debonair exterior he's really an asshole.'

For a moment he was tempted to share his secret. He needed to tell someone. Listen girls, there was a dead body in my flat this morning, and I think Palmer had something to do with it. Should I call the police? Hand him in to lost property? Sure, they were bound to believe him.

'Is that Malcolm Palmer, the estate agent, you're talking about?' said Jill, for once looking up from her screen.

'Yes, Jill? What's it to you?'

Charlie and Jill had hardly spoken since their quarrel over losing the Chinese restaurant clients. Added to that, he didn't think his family traumas would be of the slightest interest to her.

'If you're going to take that tone just forget it,' she said, resuming her work.

Carol shot him a look and, nodding in Jill's direction, suggested he should apologise. Charlie rolled his eyes. Carol rolled hers. He shrugged. She pursed her lips. Charlie gave in.

'I'm sorry, Jill. What were you going to say?'

'Forget it. Doesn't matter. You're obviously not interested in anything I have to say.'

Carol urged him on with another look. Charlie made a face, and she bettered it. It was a cross between a poker game and the national gurning championships. Remaining seated, he rolled his chair across the office to Jill. She continued typing. He rested his arms on her desk.

'Jill, I'm really sorry. I'm very touchy at the moment. While Palmer is on the scene, I've no chance of getting back with Barbara. He's up to something, and I'd like to find out what it is.' He could have told her Palmer was up to his neck in rotting corpses but thought better of it. 'I know I've been a fool, but I'm going to fight for my wife. I want her back for good.' Wasn't that a line from a song?

Her eyes, wide and a steely blue, softened with tears. Then she smiled.

'Uncle Dickie,' she said.

'Uncle Dickie?'

'My Uncle Dickie knows a thing or two about your Mr Palmer.'

'What sort of things?'

'How he swindled him out of land and money.' Charlie's heart quickened. So many questions. His tongue began to swell.

'How much? Why? When?' All good journalistic inquiries.

'I don't know all the ins and outs, but I'm sure he'd be happy to tell you.'

'Great, when can I see him?'

She checked her watch.

'Now, if you like. He's not far from here.'

He was already heading for the door, searching his pockets for car keys.

'You can buy me lunch on the way,' she said, pulling on her coat and gathering her handbag.

There was little he could do to hurry her. He would have to be patient and suffer her company over lunch.

'Sure, my pleasure,' he said through gritted teeth.

'But not Chinese,' she said as they stepped into the street. Charlie laughed, then realised she was deadly serious.

Chapter seventeen

A McChicken sandwich was all Jill got, because Charlie couldn't settle until he'd heard what Uncle Dickie had to say. To keep her sweet, he promised a slap-up dinner after work.

Uncle Dickie's farm was not far from Ballymenace, but far enough to lie on the edge of Belfast's urban sprawl. The so-called 'Official Stop Line' that signified the end of the city and the beginning of the country had been breached some years ago. An ancient country lane was now all that separated Uncle Dickie's land from a thousand homes. Only five years ago his neighbours had been the McCandless family, poultry farmers and potato growers. Now he was blessed with a whole bunch of white collars, bankers, solicitors, teachers, police officers, young IT professionals with their 4x4s, touring caravans, leylandii and conservatories. Progress had to be a good thing.

As they pulled into the yard Dickie Marshall, a burly man of sixty-two, was closing the gate leading to a field of sprouts and cabbages.

'Hello, Uncle Dickie,' Jill called out as if to allay his fear at the sight of an unidentified battered Polo stopping in the farmyard.

He wore navy dungarees and Wellingtons that looked too big even for his hefty frame. His once black hair had turned silver at the temples, his face blotchy-red from the outdoor life. There was genuine warmth in the greeting for his niece, and he nodded to Charlie even before Jill introduced them. They shook hands, Dickie's grip strong and firm. Charlie felt comfortable with it.

'We were wondering if you could tell us about your dealings with Palmer Property?' said Jill. 'Charlie is doing some research.' She winked at Charlie, her colleague.

'For the newspaper?' said Dickie.

'It might be,' said Charlie.

Dickie pulled a watch, with half of the strap missing, from his pocket.

'It's time for tea,' he said. 'Come on inside, and I'll gladly tell you all about Mr Palmer.'

The two men sat at a solid oak table in the kitchen, while Jill made the tea. Their voices and the rattling of crockery echoed in the sparse room. It lacked warmth, quite the opposite of Uncle Dickie, who seemed a jovial man. Added to Charlie's recent experience of Herbie Smyth he now imagined all farmers were made the same way. Jill set three mugs filled with strong tea and a plate of Rich Tea biscuits on the table. The arrival of the tea ushered Uncle Dickie into his story.

'We tried to sell up, me and the wife,' he began, in a loud voice. 'Five years ago it was.'

He stopped to slurp the tea and munch a biscuit.

'Kitty and I were getting on in years. Both our daughters were married and not to farmers, either. They weren't interested in running this place after I'd slipped off the old milking stool. So we decided to sell the land except for the top field. I was going to build us a nice wee bungalow up there, nothing too fancy.'

His face reddened as the tea took effect, and he started another biscuit.

'The money from the sale would keep us comfy, and there'd be enough for the girls when we were gone. I put the farm up for sale, and Palmer Property Services were the agents. Nowadays most of the land round here is sold for housing, being so close to the city, but I wanted to sell the farm as a going concern. Three months passed, but there was no sign of a buyer.'

'But you would make more money selling the land for development?' said Charlie.

'We didn't want a whole crop of houses right beside our new bungalow. Spoil the view, wouldn't it? We wanted the place to look as it always had.'

He lifted a third biscuit, not that Charlie was counting.

'Eventually, Palmer comes wondering along to see me. He's a fancy man, big car and a mouth to match.'

'I know what you mean,' said Charlie.

'Palmer suggested I sell my land to him or to one of his companies, Palmer Developments. I told him I didn't want a cart load of houses next to me, but he was adamant the land could not be sold as a farm. Then he suggested I sell one or two fields at first. He had an idea for building a hotel and golf course. I refused, and suddenly he ups the price by five thousand an acre.'

Uncle Dickie sat back in his chair, mug in hand, as if he were absorbing the offer all over again. Charlie recalled his conversation with the barman at Ballymenace Golf Club and wondered if Dickie's farm was the intended site for the new course.

'What did you do?' he asked.

'Kitty and I talked it over, and finally we agreed to sell the two fields at the bottom of the hill, fourteen acres in all. Palmer said it was sufficient for the hotel, and we could discuss land for the golf course at another time.'

He rose from the table and opened the back door.

'Come and see,' he said.

They crossed the yard and, beyond a hay shed, came to a gate. Dickie pointed downhill toward the Belfast Road.

'Look there.'

'Houses,' said Charlie.

They gazed at the haphazard arrangement of dozens of detached, semis and town houses, squeezed into fourteen acres.

'What happened?' asked Jill.

'Palmer was to pay for the land in two stages, eighty percent up front and twenty when planning was approved for the hotel and the work had begun. Planning permission was a mere formality, he told me. Four months after I'd made the deal there was no news or money. So I gave him a call. He avoided me for a week then told me the council had rejected the plans for the hotel. "Don't worry, Dickie," he said. "Everything's under control. I'll make a few adjustments to the plans and resubmit in a couple of months."'

Dickie paused; his face looked saddened. Charlie couldn't get the story quickly enough.

'Then what?' he said. Jill glared at him.

'Is there something wrong, Uncle Dickie?' she asked, placing her hand on his shoulder.

'I'm all right, love. It's just that Kitty passed away at that time.'

'Uncle Dickie, I'm so sorry. I should have realised. We've heard enough; we'll go now and give you some peace.'

Charlie looked crestfallen. He was dying for the whole story, and it was just getting to the good part. But to his relief Uncle Dickie spoke up.

'It's all right, Jill. I'll tell Charlie the rest.'

He pulled a handkerchief from his pocket and blew his nose.

'After Kitty died I wasn't thinking much about the farm or Palmer. But within a few months I decided to sell up completely. I had no need of a new bungalow anymore. Better that I moved away from this place. Too many memories. My plan was to buy somewhere close to my daughters and grandchildren. I was about to call Palmer when I looked out from this very spot. Half a dozen JCBs, dumper trucks and lorries, carrying pipes and bricks. I thought work had started on the hotel, so I called Palmer. Four weeks the swindler avoided me. By that time any fool could see there was no hotel. Planning had been refused a second time, he told me. Instead of a hotel he'd started building eighty-four houses. I told him I didn't want houses on my land. It was not what we had agreed. He said it was too late. It wasn't my land anymore. I asked for the rest of my money. He told me he'd knocked twenty percent off the original price. Since he was no longer building a hotel, I was not entitled to the original amount.'

'Did you take him to court?' said Charlie.

'My solicitor told me that because the building of a hotel was not specifically written into the sale I would have a difficult and expensive time arguing otherwise. My Kitty was gone; I had no stomach for a fight.'

'How did he build all those houses without planning permission?' Jill asked.

'Some members of the council wanted to haul him through the courts, but Palmer had just as many friends who made sure that didn't happen.'

'He bribed them?'

'A hard thing to prove, Charlie. A friend, who works for the council, told me several councillors enjoyed Caribbean cruises that year and came home to relax in their new conservatories. Nothing to do with Palmer, of course.'

'The crafty bugger,' said Charlie.

'Well at least he didn't get his hands on the rest of your land,' said Jill.

'And he won't. Not while I have a breath in me.'

Charlie thanked Uncle Dickie for telling his story. They left him tending to his cows in a field above the Belfast Road and the houses he never wanted.

Chapter eighteen

Charlie squirmed when he realised Jill was holding him to his promise of dinner. For one thing, they couldn't go to a restaurant with him dressed like a roadie for a rock superstar. He needed to shower, and he needed to lose the Bon Jovi T-shirt. He would have to go home, but that meant dealing with the Shroud of Old Trafford. He'd run out of bright ideas for disposal. Besides, he doubted that he had the strength to move a dead weight from his bedroom, never mind down two flights of stairs and into the boot of a Volkswagen Polo.

Who could he tell about his visitor, and what was he going to say? He was a journalist for goodness sake; surely he could make up something? Play the innocent, the wronged party, and the police were bound to believe him. But then a series of dreadful thoughts flashed through his head, and any notion of calling the police scarpered. Whoever put the body in his wardrobe had done so for a reason. OK, that much was obvious. Were they trying to frame him? Or did they merely need somewhere handy to keep it for a while? They must have dragged the man from the pond on the night they killed him or at least before the police carried out their search. But why stash it in his wardrobe? Had they tipped off the police? If so, then by now his flat was a crime scene, with scores of detectives and forensic scientists sifting through his worldly possessions. Worse still, he would be their prime suspect. They would be looking for Charlie Geddis. And another thing. Why did the man have bright red hair? Was his bizarre appearance enough to get him killed? Better dead than red?

Weighing up the options, he decided not to go home. Instead, he bought an olive-green shirt from Morrow's Menswear in Ballymenace and called at the office to wash and change. Whatever lay in store at home would have to wait until he could figure out what to do.

He was glad he'd made an effort to look presentable, at least from the waist up. His shirt looked smart; his well-worn jeans looked well-worn and his socks still didn't match. Jill arrived at Villa Milano in stunning form. She'd cast off the pretentious businesswoman look she wore at the office. She sparkled; her winsome face was relaxed and smiling, her blonde hair less controlled, freshly washed and blow-dried. Being a red-blooded male of the horny variety, he had trouble taking his eyes off her legs in a rather short skirt, black lace tights and enormously high heels.

'Is there something wrong?' she said.

From the legs to her tiny round face, he was hooked. She was a thirty-something Barbie with attitude.

'No, absolutely not. It's just that you look...'

'What?'

'Fantastic.'

His eyes moved to her black bustier, as she slipped her leather jacket to the back of the chair.

'I suppose I should take that as a compliment.' She watched him staring at her bare shoulders. 'Are you sure you're all right?'

'I'm fine,' he said. 'I was just thinking. What should we have to eat?'

Could hardly tell her the truth. Having her on the table before they'd even ordered. Forcing his eyes to the menu, he fought to keep them there. He kept telling himself that this was not a date. Anyway, he and Jill didn't get on. His three-step plan was to win back his wife. There was no room for further romantic complications. Besides, he had a dead body waiting for him at home, sufficient to quell any notion that might stir in his loins.

They ordered seafood linguini and a green leaf salad, not his favourite, but he wanted to appear magnanimous. He recognised the fact that Jill had given him his first real lead on Malcolm Palmer. From the wine list he chose a thirty quid bottle of Lambrusco. He liked to think he had a working knowledge of wine, considering the investment he'd made over the years in the world of drink. He could see the waiter was unimpressed. Probably thought he was a smart-ass, who didn't know his aligoté from his nebbiolo.

'I don't do this very often,' she said, when the waiter had gone.

'Do what?'

'Get dressed up to have dinner with a man, a married one at that.'

'Nowadays it seems I'm only married in the technical sense.'

Couldn't have marriage as an issue, not now, not tonight. Too many hormones in the air. He tried to concentrate on the corpse in a bag.

'Are you happy with that?' she asked.

'Far from it.'

Time to change the subject, he thought, or else his tendency to flirt would kick in and she would have no chance.

'Thanks for today,' he said.

'You're welcome. At least I'm getting dinner out of it.'

During the meal she listened to his sorry tale and his three-step plan for getting back with Barbara. He thought it best to leave out the part about the Shroud of Old Trafford. Spoil the mood, wouldn't it? The more they talked the more he found himself opening up to her, something he hadn't thought possible with the Jill he knew at work. With all the chat, he hardly noticed he was on to a second bottle of wine. Visions of corpses and duvets were greatly suppressed.

'So tell me about your life?' he asked.

For a moment she seemed hesitant and began fidgeting with her left earring.

'There's nothing much to tell really.'

'A beautiful woman like you must have a man in her life?'

Her response showed how far their relationship had improved in a single day. If he'd posed the same question yesterday, she would have torn him limb from limb with a blink of her daring eyes.

'Not at the moment,' she said, sliding a finger around the rim of her glass. 'I suppose I'm a bit fussy when it comes to men. I've always been attracted to the rich and successful kind. The only trouble is they're the type that turn out to be such a disappointment. I was married once, you know?'

He recalled their previous 'date' when he got her drunk. Clearly she did not share that memory.

'Only lasted two years, but it served me right.'

'What do you mean?'

'I had a job as PA to a company director who sold bathroom suites. He was successful, very handsome and very married. The first time he appeared tempted I made it easy for him. Six months of love in places you wouldn't believe, and finally he leaves his wife and two kids. We'd been married nearly two years, very happily I thought, and then history repeated itself. He ran off with a nineteen-year-old model, who'd draped herself over one of his Jacuzzis for a photo shoot. Next thing I know they're trying out his latest range in hot tubs.'

She took a sip of her wine and smiled at Charlie. He was having trouble with his eyes again. They were ready to close. The past few days' activities and two bottles of wine were taking their toll.

'And that's my last experience of men. If there is ever going to be another, he'll be different.'

He was different, surely?

'I want a man who's going to drag me off to somewhere exciting.'

He could manage that, exciting was good.

'Up the Amazon, trekking in the Himalayas, across Russia on a train, fishing blue marlin in the Caribbean, the bull run in Pamplona...'

Steady on, don't get carried away. He liked excitement as much as the next man, but after all that he wouldn't be fit for anything else. Even now, all he could do was nod and sway.

'You should read Hemingway. Saves all the hassle of travelling, visas, tetanus jabs, delays at the airport.'

Smiling, she put her hand on his and gently squeezed his fingers.

'I need excitement, Charlie. I hate my life. You know me at work, and you don't like me, no one does.'

'After today I think we understand each other a little better. Come on, I'll take you home.'

They stepped into the night air chilled by a stiffening breeze. He fumbled in his pocket for his car keys.

'Oh no you don't,' she said, taking him by the arm. 'You're not driving; you've had too much wine. I'll drive; you can stay at my place.'

Dessert, he thought. He pictured himself undoing her bustier in a way he had still to figure out, feasting on her perfume, and placing his hand gently on her...

Chapter nineteen

'Here we are,' she said, parking her Mini in a space directly below the window of her flat.

'We're here already?'

'You fell asleep.'

He followed her up the steps, fighting the urge to put his hands on her delicious bottom. Ignoring the light in the hallway, she switched on a lamp beside the sofa in the lounge. Tossing her jacket on a chair, she went to the kitchen, separated from the living room only by a breakfast bar. Charlie's eyes remained fixed on the mysteries of her bustier. If only his hands were on it too. He'd lost all sense of his quest for Barbara and his concerns for unidentified objects lying on his bedroom floor.

'Tea or coffee?'

'Coffee's fine,' he said, flopping into the sofa, resigned to the idea that coffee probably meant coffee and nothing else.

'Pleasant surprise' understates the tingling in his groin when she plonked herself beside him. They sipped their coffee in silence, trading the odd smile, searching for something meaningful to say. Her left leg brushed his right leg. His tingling became a swelling.

'Thank you for tonight, Charlie. It was good sharing thoughts with someone who cares enough to listen.'

'I know how you feel. I enjoyed it too.'

She smiled, and her eyes twinkled. Without a thought of what he was doing, he stroked her bare shoulder with the back of his hand. She didn't resist. He set down his coffee and moved closer. Either she was waiting for his next move, or he was on a booze cruise of the mind. He kissed her gently, yet briefly. She didn't pull away. The next one lasted seconds, before it all went French. Then to her neck, getting high on her perfume and sucking her wonderfully soft skin. She moaned, and her arms encircled him. She giggled when he reached her cleavage. No buttons on her bustier. He fumbled for clasps at the back. Nothing there either. God knows it should have been easy; he'd been staring at it all night. Faking patience, he kissed her again. His hands were all over the place, trying to unlock the secret of her clothing. And your man thought he had problems cracking the Da Vinci Code? He gave up on the bustier and headed south, but without warning she pushed him off and got to her feet.

Mystery solved, as she moved away she ran down the zip at the side of the bustier.

'I won't be a minute,' she whispered, slipping into her bedroom. With lightning speed he was down to his boxers. He was stuffing his odd-coloured socks into his trainers, when she called.

'Charlie?'

'Yeah?'

'You're determined to get back with Barbara, aren't you?'

Strange question at a time like this.

'Yes,' he said, pulling down his boxers and chucking all of his clothes over the back of the sofa.

'That's what I thought.' She reappeared in a bathrobe and clutching a flowery duvet with matching pillow. 'Make yourself comfortable on the sofa. I'll see you in the morning.'

He watched her fighting back the giggles, stealing a peek at his little soldier standing to attention.

'But I thought...'

'Night night, Charlie.' The door closed behind her.

What a woman, he thought flopping on the sofa. It wasn't long before he was fast asleep.

Chapter twenty

He awoke, stiff-necked, to the heart-warming smell of bacon frying and coffee percolating. Cinderella was back in the navy suit, her pretty face looking serious. Business as usual.

'Breakfast is ready,' she said, when she noticed him stirring. 'I'm late, so I'll leave you to it. Don't worry about clearing up. I'll do it later.'

He sat up, wiping sleep from his eyes and, at the same time, trying to stretch. Difficult.

'What are you doing this morning?' she asked, spooning scrambled egg onto a plate beside three rashers of bacon and a grilled tomato.

'Don't know,' he said with a yawn, but already he was thinking of his dead body problem.

'Are you coming to work?'

'I thought I might call with Barbara; tell her all about her beloved Malcolm.'

'Do you think that's wise, Charlie?'

'I suppose not, but I'm going to do it anyway. It's not like me to do the sensible thing.'

She came over and sat beside him on the sofa. She wasn't put off by his lack of clothing.

'You know, Charlie, I had a wonderful time last night.'

'Me too.'

'If you're really serious about getting back with Barbara, I'd like to help you. What I mean is we can be friends. I'm here for you, if you need me.'

'Friends.' He got the hint. No hanky-panky. 'I'd like that,' he said.

'Go have breakfast, and feel free to have a shower. I'll have to fly.'

'I'll be in by lunchtime, if Trevor is asking,' he said.

She kissed him on the cheek.

'Be careful today.'

She was out the door, while he stood caressing the spot on his face where she'd kissed him.

He devoured every mouthful of breakfast as if it were the latest craze to hit suburban living. It was right up there with Mrs Smyth and her farmhouse special, although Jill nudged it on looks. After two mugs of strong coffee, he tidied up around the kitchen with some ulterior motive that she would be impressed.

Her apartment lay close to the centre of Ballymenace, not far from the main road leading to the bypass. A few yards from Jill's place he caught a bus to the centre of Belfast and then another which left him outside Villa Milano on the Lisburn Road. Thankfully, he found the Polo exactly where he'd left it in a side street. Even joy riders had their pride.

On the way to his flat he tuned in to the news but heard nothing to suggest the police had launched a nationwide hunt for a psychopath, following the discovery of a red-haired corpse, wrapped in bin liners and cosy beneath a Man United duvet. As his head cleared, he came up with a plan, and what he hoped was a plausible excuse for the police, about the body in his bedroom. Considering his recent experience of Detective Inspector Watkins, he reduced the story to the literal facts. The body fell out of his wardrobe; that was the truth. The precise time he found it, surely, was unimportant? The simple truth would go down well with the police, and he had no further information to assist their inquiries. Until he knew more, he would leave Palmer out of the reckoning.

His building looked deserted; no other cars parked outside. He wondered if his neighbours had seen anything suspicious. The delivery of a large parcel, for instance? Besides Lisa, there was a female chef who lived alone and worked shifts, a Polish couple, both waiters, and a French guy of about thirty, who was into photography (or maybe pornography) and heavy metal. He decided that even if a corpse was paraded past their door none of them, except Lisa, would care enough to get involved.

A cold nausea gripped him as he climbed the concrete stairs, the scrumptious breakfast in his stomach reminding him it was still there. He pressed his keys into his fist, his left hand on his new mobile with a flat battery ready to call for help. His old mobile hadn't survived its swim at the duck pond. Slipping the key in the lock, he pushed the door open and leapt behind the wall. Maybe the corpse would make a run for it?

He forced himself to peer inside. All was quiet. Feeling a tad braver, he crossed the threshold and tiptoed to the bedroom door. No need to go in there. He could phone the police from his living room and wait outside. A sudden thought struck him. He couldn't leave the duvet over the body. What would the cops make of that? A ritual murder where the killer likes to leave his victim nice and cosy? He would have to remove it. Deep breath. He kicked the door open and stormed in.

Chapter twenty-one

Seriously, his drinking would have to stop. He stood over an empty space on the bedroom floor. There was no red hair, no plastic wrapping and no body. If the police had already taken it away surely there would be a chalk drawing on the carpet, blue-and-white incident tape in the driveway, a mobile HQ parked in the road and at least fifty peelers digging up the lawn.

He did a retake of the past twenty-four hours. Was it all a dream, like the incident at the duck pond? No body there either. Drink was really messing with his head. He needed help. These hallucinations were lasting much longer now.

But wait a minute. He glanced about the room. His bed was missing something. OK, so he may have imagined the killing at the pond and the stiff in his wardrobe. But he did not dream up a Man United duvet. It was his duvet. Barbara gave it to him in one of her more compassionate moments, after she'd thrown him out. The body was gone, and so was the Shroud of Old Trafford.

He opened the wardrobe, empty except for two clean shirts. He was spooked, seriously spooked. He felt worse now than when he and the body first got acquainted. Now he had all of the trauma but none of the evidence. Somebody was messing with his head, someone who didn't like him very much. That could be Palmer, or even Detective Inspector Watkins. He had certainly annoyed both of them in recent days. He supposed he was happy the corpse had gone and relieved that he didn't have to call the police. But what if it came back? It could show up while he was asleep in bed with no duvet, or DHL could knock on the door during *Coronation Street*, and he would have to sign for a stiff parcel. He would be the sad winner of a custody battle. Maybe the killers would seek visitation rights. Could he sue for maintenance? He was losing the will to live, at least the will to do anything more than breathe. For him to realise that was the most frightening thing of all.

Chapter twenty-two

On the way to Lothian Avenue, he rehearsed the story he would tell to Barbara. He couldn't disguise his delight at digging the dirt on Palmer so easily. After all, he *was* a journalist. He had one misgiving though. Should he mention the corpse? Somehow it didn't add much credibility to the idea of Palmer as a property swindler.

The frosted glass of the door hit him on the nose. Pity he hadn't put his foot in the way like a Jehovah's Witness. No doubt she would have slammed it all the harder.

'I don't f****** care how he runs his business,' she shouted, dismissing Charlie's efforts to explain.

'I'm just trying to show you he's not the Mr Nice Guy you think he is.'

In all their years of marriage, and even in the troubled times since, she had never used such foul language. Five minutes, with his face pressed to the door, convinced him she would not reopen it. A love note, he thought, might help ease the tension.

> *Dear Barbara,*
> *Despite your recent outburst, I still love you,*
> *and I want to come home.*
> *Charlie.*
> *PS. I trust you don't use such language in*
> *public.*

He slipped the note through the letter box and backed away from the door, hoping she would rush out and jump into his arms, and they could get back to the way they used to be. After waiting for nearly an hour, with not even a ruffle of curtain at the window, he gave up and drove to the office.

* * *

Trevor was in a foul mood.

'Where the hell were you?' he said.

Charlie gazed at Jill for inspiration. She smiled but said nothing.

'I was working on a story, you might say.'

'What story?'

'Planning. I'm investigating local planning arrangements. Got to check out the council. There are a lot of disgruntled ratepayers out there, you know.'

Trevor was signing letters for Carol. He hadn't listened to a word.

'Right, fine,' he said on his way out the door.

'Thanks for breakfast,' Charlie whispered over Jill's shoulder. 'It was lovely.'

'Shush! Don't let the whole world know.'

Carol looked over, no doubt wondering why they needed to whisper.

'Are you free this afternoon?' he asked, feigning interest in the words on her screen.

'I've got to work. Haven't you?'

'I'm going to the council office, to see what I can dig up. From what Uncle Dickie said, I'm sure Palmer has connections with most of the boroughs in Northern Ireland. It might be worth making a list of the building projects he has in the offing. Why don't you come with me?'

'I can't,' she said, indicating the work in front of her.

Carol was looking on again. They both forced a smile, and she returned to her PC.

'Tell Trevor you have a meeting,' said Charlie.

She looked doubtful.

'Go on. Think of it as the start of that great adventure you were talking about.'

'It's hardly an assault on Everest, but what the hell?'

Chapter twenty-three

The Ballymenace Council office was a drab 1960s, two-storey concrete block with an array of square, tinted windows. No one could see in. It was doubtful that anyone inside cared to see out. Those who did were met with a view of the car park and the chicken processing factory across the road.

He circled, searching for a parking space. He was about to abandon the Polo at the front door, when a metallic-blue car pulled out of a space and roared to the exit. He sunk his foot on the accelerator and followed.

'What are you doing? There was a space free.'

'And that, Jill dear, is our Mr Palmer. Excellent timing, I wonder where he's off to?'

'What about the council?'

'It can wait.'

The Aston Martin pulled onto the road. Charlie waited for a second then followed at a distance. They were headed out of town, past Jill's flat, on the road to Belfast.

Some would say the make of car reflects the character of the driver. Palmer was a wheeler-dealer, a real go-getter. Charlie was not. Little wonder the Polo whined as it shadowed four hundred and thirty brake horsepower of sleek British engineering along the dual carriageway. Fortunately, Palmer kept his speed down giving Charlie the chance to follow without several pistons going AWOL. Eventually, having negotiated traffic, road junctions and school crossings he rattled to a halt opposite the Ormeau Road branch of Palmer Property Services. He and Jill were just in time to see Palmer going inside. The Aston, parked by the door, gleamed as if it were *Thomas the Tank Engine* waiting proudly for the *Fat Controller*.

'We might have a long wait,' said Jill.

'It may just be a passing call. I don't think this is head office.'

Jill was right. An hour passed and no sign of Palmer. She left Charlie to buy a copy of *Hello* and a packet of mints from the newsagents a few doors along from Palmer Property Services. Charlie was disgusted. Sod's Law told him that that would be the moment when Palmer would reappear. What Sod's Law didn't tell him was that Jill would be the first to notice.

'Go, Charlie, for goodness sake. He's getting away.' She flung open the door and jumped in.

'Easy on, it's not *Fast and Furious III,* you know.'

The Aston was out of sight by the time they entered the stream of traffic.

'Go! You're losing him.'

She thumped the dashboard, but it didn't help their speed. They caught sight of him a hundred yards further on. He turned into Sunnyside Street and headed downhill onto the Annadale Embankment beside the River Lagan. Suddenly, at a wide point in the road, he did a U-ey. Charlie was impressed with Palmer's slick handling of the car, spinning round, and avoiding all the traffic, while talking on his mobile. He tried the spinning round thing too, and would have managed it but for a lorry, coming in the opposite direction, piled high with wooden pallets.

Charlie didn't see it at first, as the driver tried to avoid them. The lorry swerved left; its load swerved right, and a dozen pallets clattered over the road. Charlie floored the pedal to get away, and somehow the Polo escaped. In the mirror he saw a chubby frame scrambling from the lorry, now embedded in the railings by the river. He saw the big man thundering after them, shaking his fist. Palmer, by this time, was out of sight.

'You're hopeless, Charlie. Why don't you let me drive?'

'You're a woman.'

'Sexist pig.'

'Where to now?'

'I really don't care. Just take me home.'

'Jill, don't be like that.'

'Like what?'

'Like the batteries are done on your vibrator.'

'Charlie Geddis, you are the rudest man I've ever met. I don't know what I was thinking, coming out here with you. Offering to help you. Why should I care about your problems?'

It seemed they had lost him. With Jill in a huff, Charlie gave up and headed back along the road to Ballymenace. They were on the outskirts of the town when Jill screamed.

'Look! There he is.'

She pointed to the entrance of a building site, and Charlie slowed down as they rolled by. There were twelve houses at various stages of construction dotted around the site. Strangely, there didn't seem to be any builders around the place.

'Exclusive family homes, set in a private rural location,' said Jill, reading the sign.

'Maple Grove. I'll bet they cost a bob or two,' said Charlie.

'Four or five bedrooms, three reception rooms, integral garage, luxury kitchen, very nice,' said Jill.

He stopped the car on a grass verge twenty yards beyond the entrance to the site. The Aston was parked on stony ground opposite the one house that seemed completed. A sign on the wall marked it as the 'Maple Grove Furnished Show House, Sherwood Bungalow Design'.

'Now what?' asked Jill, apparently over her bout of stuffiness.

'We wait.'

'For what?'

'I don't know. Maybe you're right, and we're wasting our time.' They looked at each other and smiled. 'I'm sorry for being a prat,' he said.

'Oh.' She pinched his cheek and wiggled it. 'You can be a nice man, sometimes.'

He adjusted the rear-view mirror to observe the house and slid down in his seat. Jill took to humming and reading *Hello*. Scarcely a minute passed before Charlie could take no more of the *Eastenders* theme. He was about to tell her in his usual manner when a car came towards them, braking hard to make the entrance to the site. The grey Volvo Estate pulled up behind the Aston Martin, and a woman of slight build, dark hair and wearing a purple skirt and jacket hurried towards the house. Palmer met her at the front door, and she stepped inside. After a brief glance around the site, he closed the door behind them.

'Well, well, well. What have we here?' said Jill.

'Probably one of his 'three o'clocks' as Palmer would put it. A branch manager, or a secretary, getting her orders for the week.'

'She may be a secretary, but I don't think she's here for a list of orders.'

'What do you mean?'

'Oh, Charlie, for goodness sake. Surely, with your filthy mind, you can tell when a woman is up for a bit of afternoon delight.'

'With Palmer? But he's seeing Barbara. The dirty rotten, two-timing ass–'

'Would you prefer that he was faithful to your Barbara?'

'No, I mean yes, I mean the dirty sod.'

Charlie got out of the car.

'Come on; let's take a look at Big Mal on the job. Might take a few snaps.'

He checked there was sufficient charge on his mobile.

'Charlie, you can't take photographs. It's illegal.'

'No it's not; the guys at *The Sun* do it all the time. Public interest and all that. Come on; I need your phone; my battery's dead.'

They hurried through the gate then veered right to the rear of the show house. On the way he jotted down the registration of the Volvo, proof he wasn't a totally inept journalist.

One of the features of this housing development was the surrounding trees and shrubbery. They took advantage of them as a hiding place.

'What do you think?' he whispered.

Jill was tiptoeing through the mud.

'I've just broken a heel. And don't think I'm crawling under a bush with you. I can't lie there in this skirt.'

'Quick! Someone's at the window.' Charlie broke her fall as she hit the ground.

'Oh no.'

'What's wrong now?'

'I've laddered my tights. Is that OK with you? Are you happy now?'

Charlie clicked the camera on Jill's mobile.

'Did you see something?'

'Just a shot of the house. It might come in useful.'

She looked disgusted, easing her body onto the mud. From under the bush they could see the kitchen of the house, one of the bedrooms and a set of patio doors that opened from what they assumed to be a dining or family room. There was no sign of movement inside.

'Charlie? How long are we going to lie here?'

'Until we get a good picture, why?'

'This is a furnished show house. It said so on the sign.'

'So?'

'If they're doing it, they're probably in bed. We're not going to see very much from here.'

'Let's take a peek through the window.'

He crawled over the muck towards the house. But like all good war movies, when the soldiers storm the enemy position, some poor soul always gets stranded in no man's land.

'Charlie,' Jill whispered and pointed at the patio doors.

Charlie was that soldier. Stuck in the mud. They were bound to spot him. He tried to blend into a pile of bricks, but he needn't have bothered. They were far too busy.

A pair of buttocks pressed against the patio doors. The purple suit was gone. The woman was down to a black thong, bra and suspenders; Palmer wore nothing but his shirt. In all the excitement Charlie clicked the camera several times without checking if he had a good shot. Seconds later, the woman wrapped her legs round Palmer's waist, and they shuffled to another room. Charlie couldn't believe they hadn't spotted him. Extracting himself from the mud and bricks, he clumped to the wall and crouched below the kitchen window. He waved for Jill to follow. Strange that speed tiptoeing hadn't made the Olympics. Jill would've been a rare British success, gold medallist and world record holder.

'If we ever get out of this alive, Charlie Geddis, you have some serious sucking up to do. Look at my suit.'

'You're loving it. I could tell by the way you hurdled those bricks. You're a natural.'

She thumped his arm, and he nearly dropped the mobile.

'I want to make these shots count,' he said. 'You take a peek through the window and tell me what you see. I'll reel off the snaps, and we'll scarper.'

'We better move to the bedroom.' She waved him on. They crawled along the narrow skirting of concrete to the next window.

'Right,' he said.

'Right,' she repeated.

'Well go on, take a look.'

Fuming, she raised her head to the corner of the window and peered into the room.

'Whoa!' She dropped to the ground.

'What?'

'He's talking on his mobile.'

'Is that all? What's she doing?'

'You could say her mouth was full.'

'What?'

'Just take the damn picture, Charlie.'

He raised the mobile to the windowsill, and fired off three shots. He was happy to wait for another, but Jill dragged him away.

'Get me out of here, Charlie. I want to go home.'

'I thought you wanted some excitement in your life?'

'I don't want it all in one day.'

Chapter twenty-four

He struggled with the pasta. He'd already burnt the sauce and had forgotten to heat the garlic bread.

'How's it going?' Jill called from her bath.

'Fine,' he replied for the umpteenth time, biting his lip.

Time to cut his losses. He binned the sauce and the mush that had been spaghetti and grabbed the telephone. By the time she emerged from the bathroom, smelling vivacious, he'd ordered pizza and poured two glasses of red.

'Where's my dinner?'

'On its way,' he said glibly.

When the food eventually arrived she tucked in, but his appetite and his thoughts were somewhere else.

'Hello? Anybody in there?' she said.

'I was just thinking.'

'That much was obvious. What are you going to do about our Mr Palmer after today's episode?'

'I've talked myself out of telling Barbara. After last time, I doubt if she would even open the door. I can't understand why Palmer is screwing around. He must realise that if Barbara found out she wouldn't stand for it. Looks like she's bagged herself another unreliable man.'

'At least you weren't unfaithful.'

'But she won't believe a word I say. Do you think I'm wasting my time digging the dirt on Palmer?'

'Apart from his affair, with woman unknown, and his shabby treatment of Uncle Dickie, you don't have much to go on.'

'I wouldn't mind nailing the slimy git anyway, just for being a slimy git.'

'Maybe we should take a more official line. Go back to the council offices, look into his building plans, see if we can find evidence of shady deals, or more victims like Uncle Dickie.'

'I suppose you're right, but I'd also like to print the photos and try to find the woman with the nice bum.'

'Down boy,' she said.

* * *

They spent the next two afternoons at local and neighbouring council offices, inquiring about Palmer's current building projects. Very few people were prepared to disclose any details of Palmer's activities, never mind providing information Charlie and Jill could use for their cause. Charlie then persuaded Jill to visit the Ormeau Road branch of Palmer Property Services to gather brochures on new housing developments and to try to winkle information from the staff, in the hope that an unwary assistant revealed more than they should. Jill could hardly refuse since it was her idea to pursue this line of inquiry as opposed to Charlie's more sordid approach.

By the weekend they knew Palmer had at least fifteen building projects on the go, three of which were in and around Ballymenace. A chatty assistant in Palmer's commercial department told Jill that planning was underway for an out-of-town shopping centre, but she didn't name the town. Charlie, once again, recalled his day at the golf club when the barman told him of the proposed new course and how Palmer had a lot to do with it. Was he planning a new shopping centre on the site of the present golf club?

Eventually, the work they were paid for reared its head in the form of Trevor-the-exasperated-editor.

'I don't know what the two of you are up to,' he said. 'I don't want to know, because it'll piss me off so much, I'll want to sack both of you. But if it doesn't interfere too much with your grand scheme, it would be nice to have something to print in our next issue.'

Charlie tried to look as though he cared. Jill, on the other hand, was affronted that Trevor had criticised her work, or rather the lack of it.

'I'm really sorry, Trevor,' she said, firing pained looks at Charlie. 'I won't let it happen again.'

'See that it doesn't,' said Trevor.

He strutted from the office, no doubt thrilled at his assertiveness. Flap over, Charlie was already pondering his next move, while Jill, her cheeks still burning, was embroiled in the weekly ads.

'And another thing, Charlie,' said Trevor, peering round the door. 'Get your ass over to the Parish Hall this evening.'

'What for?'

'Remember the old mill? You know, the story you're supposed to have followed for the past three months? The one you relegated to page six and replaced with a yarn about a floater at the duck pond? There's a public meeting tonight with councillors and the developers of the site. It might get overheated if the public get a chance to have their say. I want all the details. And, Charlie, I want sensitivity, understand?'

'Of course,' said Charlie, palms open wide as if Trevor should dare expect anything less.

Chapter twenty-five

They arrived shortly after seven and slipped in at the back of the hall, the meeting having already begun. Jill had been reluctant to come along until Charlie explained that the developer of the old mill was none other than Malcolm Palmer. This he discovered when skimming through his notes from his first story on the mill, three months ago.

St. Matthew's Parish Hall, situated in the most ancient district of Ballymenace, was even older than the building to be discussed. It stood on Upper Market Street adjacent to its church and opposite the derelict mill. The long room, with cream-painted walls and huge radiators, had a fusty smell of wooden floors and scout tents.

At the front, seated behind a long trestle table, a silver-haired man with a chubby face and glasses recorded the minutes of the meeting. A confident-looking woman, dressed in a dark grey business suit and white blouse, sat to his right. She scanned the room as if taking mental pictures of everyone present. Beside her, a dapper young professional in a smart pinstriped suit and moussed hair fiddled with his laptop. A third man, on his feet, addressed the twenty people dotted about the rows of fold-up chairs. According to a printed paper sign on the table, the bald man with bulging frame and droning voice was Councillor Jim Farrington. This was a stroke of luck,

Charlie reckoned, because Farrington, a former deputy mayor, was the present chairman of the Ballymenace Council Planning Committee. He was reading from his notes.

'...I would like to say on behalf of the council that the preservation of Howard's Mill is assured by the plans to be presented here this evening. And now I would like to introduce Michelle Eastman who is PR executive for Palmer Property Developments.'

'Thank you, Jim,' said the girl in the business suit rising to her feet.

Farrington sat down, eyes glued to her shapely figure. Young enough to be his daughter, with enough confidence to have him for breakfast, Michelle Eastman oozed ambition. Her clothes said, 'I'm going places', her short blonde highlights said, 'I could eat you whole' and the warmth in her voice said, 'but I want to be your friend'.

Over the next ten minutes, Charlie wondered if Miss Eastman had once captained her school debating team. Her presentation was glowing, her visual displays immaculate. She explained how the old mill would be lovingly restored yet transformed into an apartment complex of the twenty-first century. The main building would convert to a block of twenty-five apartments served by six outbuildings, providing such amenities as a mini-market and coffee shop.

'A sense of old community can return to this neglected area,' she said. 'Imagine the convenience of ye olde corner shop for all those late-night luxuries and the wonderful aroma of espresso and fresh-baked croissants, first thing in the morning. Each apartment on the south-side will have an elegant balcony, with views over the drumlins of County Down and the splendour of the Kingdom of Mourne beyond. Picture the idyllic breakfasts, in the tranquillity, before one goes forth to the bustling city for a hard day's work and the exquisite joy of your return in the evening sun. We continue our sense of community by incorporating an area for social interaction: a place for exchange, for introduction, and who knows? For a little romance?'

She smiled and seemed to drift off on the thought.

'Of course, our community will be a place befitting the modern era: a gymnasium, a swimming pool with spa, and not forgetting our wine bar. And finally, what better way to preserve the old-world charm than by keeping the original name. That is why, ladies and gentlemen, the Mill Complex, or MC as we like to call it, will be *the* place for the modern generation. Thank you for allowing me to share the dream.'

Charlie reckoned that Miss Eastman, who remained on her feet, was expecting a standing ovation. No one even bothered to applaud. Only a few mumbled expletives, shaking of heads, tuts and an air of indifference. Farrington rose to thank her and then invited comments from the floor.

'Old-world charm? The place is a bloody eyesore,' said an elderly man in a raincoat. 'Should've been knocked down years ago. A park is what we need. Somewhere to walk the dog.'

Michelle Eastman smiled but said nothing. Next up was the Rector of St. Matthew's, a tall silver-haired man with a friendly, diplomatic face.

'I must confess I am a little disappointed that the old mill cannot be used as a centre to serve the local community. A place to keep the young off our streets, a day-nursery, or a drop-in centre for the elderly.'

His comments were met by resounding cheers from many of the audience, including Jill. Michelle Eastman smiled again, or maybe winced.

'Not an economically sound option, Rector,' said Jeremy Bolton, the dapper with the laptop.

He grinned sardonically at those who booed. A short, plumpish girl, with penny-glasses and brown hair in a bowl-cut style, got to her feet. She wore a multicoloured hooped jumper over black leggings, flat heeled boots, with a denim satchel hanging diagonally across her chest. She stood out from the others in the hall, yet she had to wave her arms at the table to gain Farrington's attention.

'I believe,' she began, in a shaky voice but determined to be heard above the hisses fired at Bolton and continued, 'that the old mill is a memorial to the oppressed worker. In the nineteenth century, hundreds of men, women *and* children were used as slave labour to line the pockets of capitalist factory owners. They worked long hours in filthy and dangerous conditions and were paid paltry sums for their efforts.'

'Good for you, luv,' an elderly woman in a headscarf called out.

'Many lives were shortened for having to work in such places,' the girl continued. 'I believe the mill should stand as a reminder to all of us of the plight of the ordinary worker in the battle for social justice–'

She was interrupted by Jeremy Bolton.

'Sounds like you want to reopen the mill as it was a hundred years ago.'

Everyone laughed.

'My comrades and I will not stand for thoughtless abuse of our environment. We shall resist the planners, who fornicate with developers, whose lust for money is stripping the land of its innocence. No longer will they plunge their manly power into the virgin cavities of our countryside, raping and forever scarring its beauty.'

Red-faced and panting, she looked as though she needed a good smoke. Her efforts were completely ignored by the panel.

'If there are no further comments,' said Farrington, 'it only remains for me to thank everyone for attending. You have the council's assurance that all views will be given due consideration, and we will endeavour to provide a facility at the mill, which has the best interests of the community at heart.'

As the audience shuffled to the door, screams erupted from the top table. Michelle Eastman's white blouse exploded in red. The clerk, rushing to help her, took a hit on the forehead. The girl responsible for the passionate speech was now coolly lobbing little paper bombs, filled with what appeared to be tomato ketchup, at the officials.

Chairs went flying. Jeremy Bolton lunged at the girl. Farrington tried to follow but was halted by two well-aimed volleys. As Bolton made a grab for the girl, she calmly stepped to the right, and he crashed into a row of chairs. People rushed back inside the hall to witness the commotion. They jeered at the sight of Bolton sprawled on the floor and the others plastered in red gunge. With her ammunition dispensed, the girl closed her satchel and waddled to the door, ignoring the jibes and laughter.

'Capitalist dogs,' she said then hurried away.

Michelle Eastman resembled a victim in a gratuitously violent movie. Assisted by the elderly woman in the headscarf, she retreated to the ladies. Several other women, armed with paper tissues, came to the rescue of Councillor Farrington and his clerk. Jeremy Bolton dusted himself down and salvaged his laptop from the scene of battle. Charlie seized the chance to have a word with Councillor Farrington.

'What's the current relationship between the council and Malcolm Palmer?'

'I don't know what you're talking about,' he said, red-faced from anger and Heinz sauce.

'You scratch my back and I'll scratch yours. Is that it, Councillor?'

'Nonsense. Who are you anyway?'

'*Ballymenace Explorer*,' said Charlie. 'He never has any trouble with planning permission in this town, does he, Councillor?'

Farrington barged past Charlie and Jill, heading for the door.

'Buddy buddies, eh, Councillor?'

'No comment,' he said over his shoulder. Once outside, Charlie let him go.

'What have we here?' said Jill impishly, tugging at Charlie's sleeve. Charlie, waiting to have a chat with the other officials as they left the hall, hadn't noticed what Jill found so interesting.

'The car Farrington's getting into. It's a grey Volvo, and there's a familiar face behind the wheel.'

'Don't remember much about her face,' said Charlie, gazing at the dark-haired woman. Jill nudged him in the ribs as the car sped off.

'Small world, Charlie?'

'Perhaps we should pay Mrs Farrington a visit, if that's who she is. We might bring one or two pictures of familiar places. What do you say?'

'You have a nasty mind, Mr Geddis.'

'And you only want me for my body, Miss Barker.'

'In your dreams.'

Chapter twenty-six

He parked the car in a tree-lined road, opposite a modern red-brick, double-fronted house with bay windows, a huge conservatory on the side, neatly mown lawns and a sweeping drive. If Ballymenace could ever be said to have an elegant district it was Regency Park. For twenty minutes, slouched in his seat, he watched for signs of life about the house. He noted the grey Volvo outside the double garage and cross-checked the registration with the one he'd written in his notebook. Definitely the same car they had seen at the building site.

Earlier in the morning, he'd telephoned Ballymenace Office Equipment to confirm that the managing director, Councillor Jim Farrington, was at work. Assuming any little Farringtons would be at school or college, the lady of the house might be home alone. When he'd gathered some nerve he ventured into the drive, a large brown envelope tucked under his arm. He rang the doorbell and stepped back, pacing up and down like a nervous actor on his opening night. The solid-wood door swung open, and there stood a tanned, dark-haired woman of about forty. She wore an emerald-green jogging suit, but he couldn't help thinking of the bra and suspenders she'd displayed at the building site. She'd brought a whole new meaning to the term show house. Quickly shaking off that vision, he had no doubt it was the same woman. Her dark eyes seemed friendly enough, and she smiled briefly.

'Mrs Farrington?' he said politely, something of a novelty for him.

'Yes.'

He flashed her a brief glimpse of his press card and slid his foot onto the doorstep.

'Charles Ge– Goodman,' he said, suddenly thinking it wise to use a false name. '*Sunday News*. Would you mind answering a few questions?'

'Questions?'

'Your husband is Councillor Jim Farrington, is that correct?'

'Why do you ask?'

'And he is the managing director of Ballymenace Office Equipment?'

'What is this about?' She sounded indignant, but he was just rising to a decent stride.

'How does your husband get on with Malcolm Palmer?'

She turned pale. The door was closing.

'I don't know of any Malcolm Palmer.'

'Surely you've heard of Palmer Property Services? Palmer Developments? Palmer Conservatories? Palmer Timeshare?'

'I don't know of any connection with my husband.'

'You're sure?'

'Yes, of course I'm sure.'

'And what about you, Mrs Farrington? What's your relationship with Malcolm?'

'I beg your pardon?'

'Come now, Mrs Farrington.'

'If you don't mind, I'm rather busy.'

'Aaagh!'

He'd never tried it before, never would again. His foot was stuck as Mrs Farrington applied her weight to the door.

'Go away or I'll call the police, you horrible man.'

'I can't, you silly cow. My foot's caught in your door.'

She pushed all the harder. He slammed his shoulder, Milkybar-Kid style, against the door. It burst open, and the woman bounced down the hall crashing into a large vase that shattered on the wooden floor. Charlie, down on one knee, caressed his throbbing foot, while she hurled chunks of pottery.

'Get out. I'm calling the police.'

'You won't need to, missus, I'm sure they can hear you.'

She scrambled to her feet, backing down the hall and still chucking pottery.

'Help! Rape!'

'Steady on. Who said anything about rape?'

She reached her telephone.

'I'm not leaving till you see these,' Charlie said.

She punched in the digits. He pulled a large photograph from the envelope and rushed towards her. The handset clattered on the floor.

'Oh my God.' Her hands gripped her face. 'Oh my God.'

She rocked on her feet, staring at the image of her on her knees attending to Palmer's desires, while he chatted on his mobile. Charlie didn't bother with the rest. One picture, one-nil to him.

'What do you want?' she asked deflated, her gaze beginning to register the debris on the floor.

'I just want to ask you about Malcolm Palmer.'

'Please, put that away. You'd better come in.'

He limped over the broken pottery.

'Sorry about the vase, but you *were* crushing my foot.'

She ignored the apology and led him to a sitting room. The house was rich in style, oak panelling in the hall, deep pile carpet and stately leather armchairs in the lounge. A sturdy coffee table, with carved legs, sat in front of a marble fireplace. She lifted a pack of cigarettes and a gold lighter from the mantelpiece and lit up. Her hand shook as she drew on the cigarette.

'What are you intending to do with that?' She indicated the picture in Charlie's hand.

He had absolutely no idea. Have it printed in *The Explorer*? Trevor would never allow it. It was simply his way of getting to Mrs Farrington. So far, so good.

'Mr Palmer is a well-known businessman,' he said. 'It's in the public interest to reveal his affair with the wife of a well-known councillor.'

'Oh my God.' She coughed on her cigarette, nearly choked actually. 'You mean you're going to print that?'

'And there's more.' He pulled several other photos from the envelope. He was pleased they had turned out so well.

'Oh my God,' she said again.

The picture of her bottom pressed to the glass of the patio door, he thought, was tastefully erotic. But it only fired her rage.

'I know what you're up to, but you won't get away with it. I'll get an injunction. I'll go to the police.'

'And tell them what exactly?'

'That you have invaded my privacy.'

'Mrs Farrington, you were having sex at the window of a show house on a building site in broad daylight. Obviously, you weren't too concerned about your privacy.'

'You're trying to blackmail me.'

'No I'm not,' he said, alarmed. He really hadn't considered that possibility. 'I only wanted to ask you some questions. You weren't interested, so I used the pictures to get your attention.'

She pressed the cigarette into an ashtray, lit another, and dropped into a sofa.

'What do you want to know?'

He had a mental list, but the order had got muddled in the heat of the fight.

'Tell me about your husband.'

'Jim?' she said, raising an eyebrow. 'I thought you wanted to know about Malcolm? I mean Mr Palmer.'

'OK, what goes on between Jim and Malcolm?'

'I really don't care for your flippant attitude, Mr...?'

'Green, the name's Green.' He couldn't remember the one he'd used earlier. She didn't seem to notice.

'Jim supplies office equipment. Malcolm is a client. His company buys desks, photocopiers, that sort of thing.'

'Is that it?'

'What do you mean, *is that it?*'

'No other contact with Palmer? What about your husband's role in the council? He *is* chairman of the planning committee.'

'So?'

'Has he done Palmer any favours?'

She cocked her head, looking confused.

'For instance, when Malcolm needs planning approval for a new building project, does Jim hurry things along?'

111

'I really have no idea.'

Being such a fine judge of character, Charlie decided she was either lying brilliantly or telling the truth badly. In other words, he didn't believe her. Time to get nosey.

'How did you and Malcolm get together?'

'He came to the house a few times to see Jim. They play golf occasionally. He called me one day when Jim was at work and things developed from there.'

Her voice tailed off, embarrassment perhaps, or the idea of talking to a sleazy reporter wasn't to her taste.

'How long has this been going on?'

'Nearly three years.'

'And Jim doesn't know?'

'Jim and I go our separate ways. I tell him very little of what I do, he tells me even less.' She leapt from her seat. 'I really don't care if you tell Jim about Malcolm. I should've done it ages ago. It no longer matters. As soon as Malcolm completes this last deal we're leaving.'

'What deal?'

'I don't know, a building project. When it's finished, he'll leave the business here to his charges. We're going to Spain to manage his timeshare company.'

Charlie suddenly thought of Barbara and how she was in for a shock when Palmer took off with Mrs Farrington.

'Do you know what this project involves?'

'No I don't,' she said. 'If there are no further questions I think you should leave. I have a mess to clear up before I go out, and there is a nasty smell in my sitting room.'

She moved to the door. He sniffed his armpits and checked his shoes for dog poo.

'Is your husband helping Palmer with this deal?'

'I have no idea.'

They stared each other out. He would have expected a woman whose affair had just been rumbled to look defeated but, despite her initial shock, she seemed in control. Her eyes looked keen and lively. It was a convincing performance. She snatched the envelope from his hand.

'I'll hang on to these if you don't mind.'

Stepping outside, he turned to bid her goodbye.

'Thanks very much, Mrs Farrington. Very nice to meet you, put the name to the face.'

'Sorry I can't say the same.' She tore the envelope apart.

'I wouldn't bother with those,' he said. 'I've plenty more.'

The door slammed.

Chapter twenty-seven

It was late, well after eleven, when he rang the bell at Jill's apartment. He'd been driving around most of the night trying to make sense of his recent experiences. He would love to see Palmer vanish in his own fart, but he doubted that even that bizarre fantasy would get him back with Barbara. Maybe Trevor was right? He should cut his losses and make a fresh start or, at least, a fresh start without clichés. He and Jill were growing close. But he couldn't take her friendship for granted. That had been his downfall with Barbara. If he'd treated her as a partner, and not a coat hook, they might still be together.

Jill was surprised to see him.

'I'm sorry it's so late, but I could do with a friendly face.'

She was dressed in a white bathrobe, her head wrapped in a white towel and her face smothered in moisturising cream. All in white like an angel.

'You'd better come in then,' she said with an understanding smile. 'I'll put the kettle on.'

Charlie slumped on the sofa, exhausted.

'I went to see Barbara, to tell her about Palmer and the Farrington woman, but she wasn't home.'

'What about the Farrington woman?'

'I paid her a visit, took some pictures with me.'

'Charlie, you didn't?'

'It was the best chance I had to find out what's going on.'

Over coffee he told her about Mrs Farrington, and how she and Palmer were planning to do a runner.

'Poor Barbara. What'll happen to her?'

'Hopefully we'll get back together,' he said. 'That's why I've been doing this.'

'Yes, of course it is. I'm sorry. What are you going to do next?'

'I don't know.'

'Why don't you leave things as they are, at least for a while? If Palmer skips the country with Mrs Farrington then Barbara will find out what a cad he really is. She'll realise you've been right. You'll have a better chance of getting back together. Let things take their course, Charlie. It'll keep you out of trouble too.'

'There is one other thing I haven't told you.'

'And what's that?'

'I think Palmer is a murderer.'

'What? How do you know? That story you wrote in the paper? Was that about Palmer? He's just a crooked estate agent; surely he wouldn't go so far as to kill someone?' Each question jumped an octave before her better judgement cut in. 'Charlie.' Her voice deepened. 'Are you sure about this? You're not making it up?'

'Thanks for your support, Jill.'

'I'm sorry. But you have been acting a bit strange lately. All this chasing after Palmer, peeping into houses...'

'You have to believe me, Jill. You're the only person I can trust. I know I was drunk that night, but I'm telling the truth. I was standing on the bridge in Ballymenace Glen and I heard voices. I saw these hooded figures. They fired a shot, and a man fell into the water. The body turned up at my flat.'

'When? How? Did you call the police?'

'Last week. It fell out of my wardrobe. And no, I didn't tell the police.'

'But, Charlie you have to.'

'I can't.'

'Why not?'

'The damn thing disappeared again.'

He could tell by her face, struggling to hold back a smile, she had trouble with this fact.

'I spent the night here with you, and next morning, when I got home, it was gone. And so was my Man United duvet.'

'Your duvet?'

'I covered the body with it.'

This time the laughter came, and she failed miserably to stifle it with a hand over her mouth.

'It's not funny, Jill. I liked that duvet.'

'I'm sorry, Charlie, but you have to tell the police.'

'I can't. They'd laugh in my face, after the trouble I caused for them. Because of my story in *The Explorer* they had to search the duck pond for a body. Then they arrested me for planting 'For Sale' boards on the golf course. I can't tell them about the dead man in my wardrobe; I have nothing to show them. They'd charge me for wasting police time and for possession of two clean shirts.'

'But if Palmer is really a murderer he won't think twice about doing it again. What if he comes after you?'

'Then I'll have to get him before he gets me. I've got to find out what he's up to. It must be a huge deal if he's leaving the country when it's finished.'

'Maybe it's the old mill development?'

'Not big enough. Has to be worth a fortune if he's prepared to string two women along, kill somebody, and leave the country. But why complicate things by promising Barbara a new life, when he's been shagging Mrs Farrington for three years?'

'Maybe he needs Barbara for part of his scheme?'

'Or he needs Mrs Farrington. Neither one is likely to tell me anything.'

'Then how do we find out more about this deal?'

'Well,' said Charlie, about to drop a big one. 'I've been thinking.'

'Yes?'

'We could take a peek in his office.'

'We?' she said. 'We?'

'Don't worry, I have a plan.'

'I'm sure you do.'

'Don't give up on me now, Jill. You said you want excitement in your life, remember?'

'Let's hear it.'

'Palmer's private office is on the first floor of the Holywood Road branch of Palmer Property Services in Belfast. We wait until he goes out then we pop in and have a look around.'

'Just like that?'

'We might need a diversion, to get past the staff.' He sat back in the sofa, satisfied with his plan.

'What sort of diversion?' Jill asked.

Lost for words, he felt his face glowing.

'I thought you might have an idea for that part.'

Chapter twenty-eight

Palmer was eager to meet him. For once that was great news, because Charlie couldn't wait to have a good snoop around Palmer's office.

'So how is the budding Lord Lichfield?' Palmer asked, when Charlie telephoned to arrange their bogus appointment. 'Running out of housewives to harass, are we?'

'Only if you're running out of women to shag,' said Charlie.

'Are you going to tell me why you've called, or is it merely to inquire whether Sheila has told me of your photographic exploits?'

'Nothing fazes you, does it, Palmer? Aren't you even worried what Barbara will do when I tell her about Sheila Farrington?'

'I know you won't do that, Charlie. You don't really want to spoil Barbara's chances of a new life?'

'A new life with you?' Charlie was dying to call him a murdering, cheating scumbag, but Jill advised him that it was best if Palmer didn't know they suspected him of murder. 'You cheating scumbag.'

'Charlie, you don't understand. Sheila is yesterday's news. That little episode you captured on camera was our last. Should have ended it months ago, but it's over now. I had to tie up the loose ends. I don't like to leave a mess.

Sheila will understand. She and Jim are really quite devoted.'

'You have one major brass neck, Palmer.'

'If there's nothing else, Charlie, I have a tight schedule today.'

'Just one thing,' said Charlie, coming over all friendly. 'Are you still interested in selling my house?'

There was a pause before Palmer answered.

'What do you have in mind?'

'Can you meet me tomorrow, twelve o'clock, at the Fir Tree Lodge?'

'I suppose I could manage that. I'll see you there.'

Finding tatty clothes wasn't difficult considering the state of his wardrobe. Apart from the recent purchase of a green shirt, he couldn't recall buying any clothes since Barbara threw him out: one year, ten months, two weeks and three days ago.

* * *

He hung around at the corner of a side street in sight of Palmer's office on the Holywood Road, waiting for him to leave for their bogus lunch date. His jeans were ripped at the knees, stained with paint and that smelly stuff for preserving wood. He wore a brown woollen jumper, unravelling, no shirt or socks, and a pair of trainers split across the soles. Hair uncombed, he hadn't bothered to shave. The anorak Barbara gave him on his last birthday was the only decent thing he wore, although he'd creased it so it didn't spoil the look. He'd gargled a few mouthfuls of Drambuie and sprinkled some over his clothes. It was the only bottle of drink left in his flat. No great loss, he hated the stuff. Heavy rain, seeping into his trainers, was a more unwelcome aid to the disguise.

He took shelter in a doorway of a betting shop, and twenty minutes later he watched Palmer dashing from his office and speeding off in the Aston Martin. Staying in character, Charlie sang and staggered to the door of

Palmer Property Services. Face pressed to the window, he caught the attention of a young girl working inside. Lips sucking the glass, he waved a grubby hand. She dropped her head in fright or disgust. He spotted Jill at the back of the office sitting opposite a grey-haired lady, who was chatting away and smiling a lot. Throwing his weight against the door, it hit the wall with a bang. Everyone jumped: the two staff, Jill and a woman in a long coat, who was browsing over houses for sale.

'Mornin', ladies!'

Rolling in, he collided with a stand displaying leaflets of the Palmer organisation. He faked a trip and fell into the arms of the woman in the long coat.

'Oops! Sorry, missus.'

She pushed him away and continued studying the variety of properties for sale in East Belfast and North Down. Charlie mimicked her interest and for a moment took note. He had no idea about the price of houses. Having been gifted his parents' home he had never actually bought one. They cost an awful lot of money. Perhaps selling number forty-seven wasn't such a bad idea, especially if Palmer was offering way over the going rate.

He saw only two staff in the office, the young girl, and the grey-haired lady chatting with Jill. Palmer was bound to have a secretary working upstairs, but before he could get up there he had to lose the woman in the long coat. She looked about forty-five and struck Charlie as well off. That brown coat was expensive and so were the houses she was looking at.

'Buyin' a house, luv?' he said, edging closer.

'Go away, you horrible man,' she said with middle class derision.

'Only being friendly like. Fancy comin' down the pub with me?'

He offered her the bottle of Drambuie. She tried ignoring him. He slipped an arm round her shoulder; she swiped it off. But it was enough. At last, Charlie saw the resignation in her face. Barging him aside, she made for the door as he collided again with the displays. Didn't know her own strength, that one, he thought.

The grey-haired lady, a tall woman approaching sixty, wearing a grey suit, rose from her desk and bounded towards him. She had a face sagging with make-up and swamped by a frown. Her eyes looked angry behind the glasses resting on her nose.

'Will you please leave, or I will call the police. You are destroying private property and upsetting my clients.'

She was quite formidable on very high heels, hands on bulging hips like a scolding matron, her blouse strained across a large bosom. The metal badge on her lapel had the name, Angela.

Charlie farted, long, rasping and loud. Didn't mean to, last night's chicken korma, but it was in keeping with the character. He tried a gormless smile. Fanning herself, the woman drew back.

'Get out of my office.'

'Have a wee drink, Angela.' He offered the bottle.

'Claire, help me get this filthy man out of here.'

The young assistant hurried from her desk. No more than eighteen, thin and pale, with only the sense to do as she was bid. The pair of them grabbed Charlie by the arms.

'Ow!' Jill cried out.

'Ow! Ow!'

'Is something wrong?' said Angela.

'Ow!'

'What is wrong, dear?'

Jill slowly turned around. Charlie's eyes widened.

'It's my baby,' she said. 'I think my baby's coming.'

She rubbed her hands across a huge stomach. Both women sprang to her aid, while Charlie stifled laughter. Until that moment he had no idea what Jill had planned for her part in the diversion. She'd stubbornly refused to tell him.

'Take it easy, dear. Try to relax,' said Angela, crouching beside her.

'I want to push.'

They helped her to a sofa, laying her down and propping up her head with a cushion. 'Claire, get Margaret.' The young girl looked in a daze. 'Now,' Angela bellowed.

Claire hurried up the spiral staircase at the back of the office and, seconds later, reappeared with a stunning woman, Charlie presumed to be Margaret. She could have been another Jill: twenty years older, perhaps, a little taller and not pregnant. Barbie's Mum.

'What's going on?' she asked above Jill's cries of pain. It was clear that Margaret was used to taking control in a crisis. She clocked the situation in a second.

'Claire, get a cold wet towel.' Bending over, Margaret took Jill's hand. 'You're going to be fine, dear. How far apart are the contractions?'

Jill rolled her head from side to side.

'Oh, I don't know. I'm not due for another two weeks, but oh!'

She glanced at Charlie. He was entranced by her performance. But her eyes were telling him to get a bloody move on. No one noticed him sliding by and taking to the stairs.

'Let's time your contractions then before we do anything else,' said Margaret.

'But I want to push again.'

'Deep breaths, deep breaths,' said Angela.

'Claire, phone for an ambulance,' said Margaret, now with less confidence.

Charlie left them to it and, moving upstairs, found himself in a spacious room with a desk in the middle, six filing cabinets against one wall and a huge window looking onto the road. Fortunately, there was no one else around.

A door to the right was ajar leading to what he assumed was Palmer's private office. He barged inside.

Furnished in black granite and chrome, there was a black leather settee and granite coffee table. Another huge window looked down on Holywood Road, awash with rain and traffic. He glanced around for something obvious, something that might reveal all about Palmer and his crooked business. He reckoned he was safe for as long as Jill continued to scream. Two filing cabinets were locked. He diverted to the desk, where a computer was switched off. An in-tray overflowed with invoices and company brochures, but nothing drew his attention. The out-tray had a few sheets of A4, mostly printed emails addressed to staff. One was notice of a golf outing to Donegal, another, a note to local managers regarding opening times for show houses in the new developments. Charlie went through the drawers. Pens, pencils, staplers, company-headed paper, nothing.

He remembered the filing cabinets in the secretary's office, was making for the door, then turned and reached again for a drawer in the desk. He removed sheets of the company-headed paper, a variety of A4 and A5 with logos of each of the Palmer companies. Palmer Property Services, Palmer Developments, Palmer Commercial, Palmer Financial & Mortgage Advisors, Palmer Investments, Palmer Timeshare and Palmer Conservatories: each one showing address, telephone number, website, email, and a list of company directors. There was something strange printed at the foot of a page relating to Palmer Timeshare. Pulse racing and eyes bulging, he scanned the list of directors and managers. Two names, Hobson and Blake, both divisional managers, he recognised from his research. But there, right beside M. Palmer, Managing Director, was another M. Palmer. A misprint? More than one Palmer? Heaven forbid. He flicked through the other sheets. It appeared again only on Palmer Investments.

He stuffed the papers back in the drawer, hurried to the secretary's office, and flitted from one filing cabinet to the next. Jill screamed again, and he heard a siren. He was taking far too long. There were too many files for him to browse in the cabinets. Client lists, brochures of property sold, ledgers and financial accounts. He rifled through a folder containing minutes of board meetings. He couldn't read fast enough, yet nothing leapt from the page to confirm even one suspicion. That was all Charlie had: suspicions, curiosity, nothing of substance.

He replaced the folders in the cabinet and, standing in the middle of the room, he had a last look around. In the corner, beside the door, he noticed a table covered with a dustsheet. Peering underneath, his eyes widened and he peeled off the cover. Within a few seconds he realised he was looking at a scale model of what appeared to be an enormous building plan. There were neat rows of tiny houses, just like in *Monopoly*, only hundreds of them. Roads, dual carriageways and roundabouts were expertly created around what seemed to be industrial parks and shopping centres. In the bottom left-hand corner an inscription on a copper plate read, 'PALMERSTOWN, TOTAL AREA: 9.6 SQUARE KILOMETRES'.

'Help me,' Jill screamed.

'It's all right, dear,' Margaret was saying. 'We'll soon have you in hospital; here's the ambulance now.'

Charlie searched for something familiar in the model, a building, or landmark, anything to identify the location. He'd never heard of the place. Maybe it was in England. Could it be a completely new town? But it was time to go. Stooping to gather the dustsheet from the floor, he discovered a shelf under the table, holding about a dozen scrolls of paper. Choosing one at random, he rolled it open.

The heading at the top of the map read, 'Chart No.4, Grid Ref. 091624-095700'. Instantly, he recognised a portion of road that lay to the south of Ballymenace. He chose another scroll and rolled it over the first. His hands trembled, his breathing strained. Down the left-hand side of the map he located the centre of Ballymenace. A red felt pen had been used to draw a line around an area southwest of the town. Printed within was the name, 'Palmerstown'. He traced the red line with his finger, his brain soaking up the detail, his local knowledge shoving questions before him. He noted the bypass, but where was the golf club? Where was the farmland?

'The glen? Herbie's farm?'

'Charlie, where the hell are you?' Jill shouted.

'Is Charlie your husband?' Margaret asked. 'Can I call him for you? Get him to meet you at the hospital?'

'No. It's OK.'

'Where's my house?' Charlie whispered in disbelief.

His finger swept across the chart. There was a road, marked in black pen, running from the bypass through this Palmerstown area, over the hills and down to the centre of Ballymenace. He pushed the maps aside and studied the model. Now he recognised the bypass and Ballymenace town centre and the new road he'd noted from the maps: a dual carriageway running between the two. He returned to the map and found Lothian Avenue exactly where it should be. Tracing the black line of the road, it ran from the town centre to the dead end, where Lothian Avenue became Priory Lane, exactly where number forty-seven stood. Back to the model. There was no lane, no Lothian Avenue and definitely no number forty-seven. Scary thoughts tumbled, one disturbing vision after another.

'Leave me alone.'

'The paramedics are trying to help you, dear,' said Angela.

Jill was in trouble, and Charlie heard someone on the stairs. Tossing the sheet over the table, he staggered from the room.

'What on earth?' said Margaret, confronted by Charlie the vagrant.

'Hello, luv. Wanna wee drink?'

'Get out of here before I call the police.'

Despite her being rather tasty, older yet tasty, this time Charlie was glad to oblige and went singing down the stairs.

'Bye bye, luv,' he said.

Chapter twenty-nine

A paramedic was talking to Claire, the young office girl.

'You meet some strange people in this job,' he said, closing the rear door of the ambulance, after Charlie had a peek to see if Jill was inside. They looked him up and down and laughed. Feeling at a loss, quite the tramp, he watched the ambulance drive off in the lunchtime traffic, without Jill.

A revving engine suddenly drowned all other noise in the road. A horn sounded in long urgent bursts. She waved at him, but she did not look happy.

'Charlie Geddis, don't you ever do that to me again,' she said as he joined her in the car. With a sharp flick of the wheel she launched them into a gap in the traffic.

'Do what?'

'You left me stranded. I was nearly carted off to the Ulster Maternity. How could I explain two cushions and a corset? I had to kick that poor ambulance driver to get away. Pregnant women just don't do that, Charlie.'

'You're not pregnant.'

'Those women in the office thought I was in labour. I left them trying to phone my husband using the false number I gave them. That's it, Charlie, I'm never doing that again.'

'You won't have to. I got what we needed. I know what Palmer's up to.'

'You didn't? Tell me then.'

'Slow down. Pregnant women shouldn't be driving so fast.'

She eased off the throttle and settled to driving on the inside lane towards Ballymenace.

'He's building a whole new town, Jill, and he's naming it after himself, pretentious git.'

'Pardon?'

'It's not called pretentious git. He *is* a pretentious git. He's calling it Palmerstown. It's big, really big.'

'Where is it?'

'Right on top of 47 Lothian Avenue, Ballymenace.'

'But that's...'

'My house, Barbara's house. Palmerstown will cover all the land between Ballymenace and the bypass. The golf club, Ballymenace Glen, Herbie Smyth's farm, the lot. And a new dual carriageway will go right through my living room.'

'Oh my God. That's why Palmer's been seeing Barbara.'

'Exactly. He needs *our* house so he can build a connecting road from Ballymenace, through his new town to the bypass. And he's prepared to pay a fortune to get his hands on it. He's volunteering to be the agent for selling my house, when really he's the buyer. I've got to tell Barbara.'

'That's not such a good idea, Charlie. You know that she won't believe you.'

'I can't wait any longer. She needs to know what Palmer is up to. This time I will have to make her listen or she's going to lose her home.'

Charlie insisted that Jill drive them to his house on Lothian Avenue.

* * *

The door opened, and Barbara stepped back in horror. Charlie was quite shocked, too. Standing behind her was a valiant-looking Malcolm Palmer.

'Hi, Charlie,' he said smugly. 'I've been waiting for you. I thought you might show up here when you didn't keep our appointment.'

Ignoring him, Charlie turned to his wife.

'Barbara, we need to talk.'

She hardly needed to sniff the air, but she did.

'You're drunk.'

'No I'm not. I can explain. I know what he's up to.'

Palmer laughed, his hands resting protectively on Barbara's shoulders.

'You're in a bad way, old chap. I've told Barbara all about our meeting. We can see why you didn't show up. No need for you to bother now, not in your state.'

'Don't listen to him, Barbara. I'm not drunk.'

'Look at you. I'm surprised Jill has anything to do with you. Oh my God,' she said, staring beyond him, a hand over her mouth. 'She's pregnant.'

Jill was out of the car. Hands on hips, arching her back, she thrust her appendage outwards. She hadn't had time to remove the false pregnancy, not with fighting off the paramedic, dashing to the car, collecting Charlie and speeding off.

'No she's not.' Charlie tried to explain, but he sensed Barbara was far beyond excuses.

'Joan told me you'd been seeing a lot of Jill, but she didn't mention this.'

Her eyes filled with tears. Charlie wanted to wipe them away, tell her the truth, make her understand, but Palmer eased her back inside.

'You've caused more than enough trouble for one day,' he said, his arm around her shoulders.

127

'Why, Charlie?' Barbara said weakly, gazing at Jill, who was caressing her bump and probably wondering how it felt to be pregnant for real, oblivious to the confusion she'd caused.

'Please let me explain.'

'You could have told me!'

Palmer was closing the door.

'I never want to see you again,' she said finally as the door shut.

He should write an article on slamming doors. Conduct a survey perhaps, measure the noise emitted from doors closing, the optimum force required to achieve slam, the emotional trauma of slamming victims. He could deliver the keynote address at the World Symposium on Doorstep Disputes, 'Charlie Geddis, the flat-nosed doorstop: a case study,' or, 'When one door closes, you're bloody well locked out.'

Chapter thirty

He tossed an empty can across the room. It hit the previous one and rolled under the table. He reached for a full one. His hand moved around the settee, his eyes fixed on the television and the match on BBC2.

'Bugger.'

The last can of Heineken gone and still sober. Four days since his row with Barbara, four days to run out of beer. He'd heard how angry she'd been, when Trevor told her that Jill's pregnancy was phantom with a capital P. But she refused to see Charlie. He took to quiet contemplation of the drunken variety, alone in the dingy flat, dishes piling up in the sink and milk going sour in the fridge. He struggled to write an exposé of Palmer's activities. But with time to think, he decided he didn't want to hurt Barbara anymore. He was convinced that when it suited him Palmer would dispose of her and run off to Spain with Sheila Farrington. He could only hope she would then see things differently, and maybe they could make a fresh start. Or maybe Palmer would dispose of Sheila and run off to Spain with Barbara, and he would never see her again. Either way he was completely helpless. For now, his journalistic *pièce de résistance* could lie on the floor and gather dust.

Not a drop of beer left and he couldn't be arsed going out for more. England's second test with Sri Lanka was reaching a decisive stage. He didn't know what that meant. Never understood cricket. How could two teams play for five days, England scoring 586 over two innings with Sri Lanka on a total so far of 322, and yet the match was headed for a draw? Had to be something wrong with the maths. He dragged himself to the fridge just as somebody hit a six. An hour's viewing for a single piece of action and he'd missed it.

'Crap.' A reference to the state of play or to the contents of his fridge? What did it matter? It was one word that summed up his life perfectly.

He knocked on Lisa's door and waited. He wondered if she was busy with yet another boyfriend who would love her and leave her. He pressed his ear to the door and listened. Right on cue it swung open.

'Hi, Charlie.'

She was dressed in her hotel receptionist's uniform, cream blouse and blue skirt, her brown hair up but trying its best to make its way down. If Jill and Barbara were cute pretty, then Lisa was more catwalk pretty, slim, smouldering pout, big eyes and long legs.

'Coming or going?' he asked.

'Home for tonight. I've been on the eight-to-six shift. I'm absolutely whacked. Fancy a coffee?'

'Great,' he said. It wasn't beer, but he reckoned her company might do him some good, and he followed her inside. 'I just called to see how you were?' It sounded better than saying he only came to scrounge drink.

'Well, I've broken up with Darren. Didn't want things getting too heavy. Been out a couple of times with Sean from work, but I think he's gay. We have a new assistant manager called Phil. He seems nice, but I think he has a girlfriend. And French guy downstairs spoke to me this morning for the first time.'

'The photographer?'

'Is that what he does? He did ask me if I did modelling.'

That was Lisa: ever hopeful, ever trusting.

'Isn't life complicated, Charlie?'

If only you knew, he thought.

'How are things with Barbara?'

'You want it in Centigrade or Fahrenheit?'

'Oops, sorry I asked.'

Suddenly there was a banging outside at the front door followed by dull thuds and a rush of feet on the stairs.

'What was that?'

'Don't know,' said Charlie, making for the door.

He heard footsteps stomping by, moving on to the next flight of stairs. Easing the door open slightly, he peered out. Three figures, in balaclavas and wielding baseball bats, were heading for his flat. One moved more slowly than the other two. It was difficult using a Zimmer on stairs. Another bang and he realised they'd broken through his door. If only they'd turned the knob, it wasn't locked. He closed Lisa's door and stood with his back against it. He began to shake, his hands seeping sweat. They'd come for him. He was about to end up like the red-haired man.

'What's wrong?'

'Hide me.'

Banging, clattering and garbled voices came from upstairs.

'Somebody's in your flat.' She looked to the ceiling. 'What's going on?'

They passed each other, Lisa heading for the door, Charlie diving behind her sofa.

'Don't go out there,' he whispered, too late as she stepped into the landing. He heard her gasp of horror and, peering round the sofa, he saw two of the hoods barging past on their way down. The slow one stopped in front of Lisa.

''Scuse me, luv,' said the hard, real hard, voice behind the mask. 'Don't know where I'd find Charlie Geddis, do ya?'

Charlie squirmed in his pants and couldn't help a slight release of wind. He prayed it wasn't too loud.

'Um, no I don't,' Lisa replied. 'I haven't seen him.'

The man foisted his baseball bat in front of her, and she backed away.

'Lucky for him.'

'What has he done?' Lisa asked nervously.

'Nothin' we can't put him straight on.'

He glanced inside the flat then looked her up and down. The eyes continued to stare, but Lisa couldn't move any further away, her back against the wall. Charlie could hear the man breathe. He willed Lisa to shut the bloody door. The man lingered, tapping the bat in his hand.

'Lovely blouse,' he said.

'Pardon?'

He reached out and touched her arm, feeling the material. Rooted to the spot, Lisa watched his stubby fingers moving over her cream blouse.

'Silk?' he said. 'Where'd you get it?'

'House of Fraser.'

'Haven't been there lately. I could do with some new clothes though.'

She nodded as if she understood perfectly.

Peering round the sofa, Charlie studied him: black boots, black jeans, black jumper and black hood. New clothes? He wasn't kidding.

'I'm not always like this, you know?' said the hood, his voice softening.

Charlie wondered what was going on. One minute the guy wants to beat him to a pulp, the next he's discussing *haute couture* with Lisa.

'I like clothes,' he said. 'Women's clothes.'

Lisa managed to nod.

'You see, I'm really a woman trapped in a man's body.'

A hard man's body, Charlie thought. A hard man in need of a Zimmer. The boots, Charlie realised on second glance, were of the stiletto-heel variety.

'I'm gonna have the op, you know? Already taking the drugs. I can't keep on living a lie. Soon as I get shot of this.' He, or she, indicated the Zimmer frame.

'What happened?'

'Fell off a pair of seven-inch heels. Broke both ankles.'

Lisa's involuntary nodding continued. She peered into the room and, for a second, Charlie thought he'd been rumbled.

'Tracy?' a shout came from downstairs. 'Let's get outta here.'

'Thanks, luv,' said the man, or woman. 'Sorry to bother you.'

Lisa nodded, speechless.

'House of Fraser, you said?' She nodded again. 'I'll remember that. And if you see Geddis, tell him we'll break his fucking legs when we get him.'

He, or she, shuffled away, struggling to hold their baseball bat and Zimmer as they went down the stairs. A minute later the front door slammed behind them.

Charlie guided Lisa back inside. She looked dazed, her hair, having fallen loose, covered her face as she continued to nod.

'Who were they, Charlie? And why are they looking for you?'

'I don't know exactly, but I've a fair idea who sent them.' He settled her in a chair and coaxed her to drink some coffee.

'Maybe we should call the police in case they come back?' she said.

'No need, everything's fine. Those guys hadn't two brain cells to rub together. Tomorrow I'll have a word with their master.'

'Charlie, your flat!'

She hurried upstairs, with Charlie following behind. They stepped into the wreckage that was his living room.

'Oh, Charlie. They've trashed the place.'

Actually, it wasn't that bad. A few plates broken, television smashed, beer cans lying on the floor. Apart from the television most of it was down to him.

'Bloody hooligans,' he said. She gave him a big hug.

Chapter thirty-one

The turbulent sky reflected his mood, a threat of rain and no prospect of sunshine. Standing on the bridge, he peered into the dark water of the duck pond now, incidentally, devoid of ducks. He should have drowned in the murky water that night. Who would have cared? Not Jill. Back then she was the last person he would have imagined as a good friend. Maybe Lisa? Too many boy troubles of her own. Trevor? Not a chance. He wouldn't waste any time replacing him at *The Explorer*. Barbara?

She would have mourned for a while, the loss of an estranged husband. But sooner or later she would have moved on. In fact she had moved on without him, and he wasn't dead. Two or three more whiskeys would have done the trick. But instead of his demise here he was convinced his wife's lover was trying to swindle them out of their family home. Worse still, Palmer had gained Barbara's trust. He was deceiving her, and now he was about to hoodwink the entire population of Charlie's hometown.

Didn't anyone realise what Palmer was up to? An entire new town plonked on Ballymenace. More people, more traffic, more noise and a huge swathe of countryside swallowed up. And it seemed that Palmer would do anything to ensure the project went ahead. One poor soul had died already; he could be next. He looked to the heavens for inspiration.

'Feel free to join in, up there. Answers on a postcard?'

Call it divine interruption, but there was a noise, bleeping music, the *Match of the Day* theme. He gazed into the woods then remembered the new mobile he'd recharged the night before.

'Hello?' he said tentatively.

'Charlie,' said the cheerful voice. 'Malcolm, here. Thought perhaps I owed you a call.'

'Whaddya want, Palmer? I'm busy.'

'Sure you are. I was wondering if you've had a change of heart regarding number forty-seven?'

'My God, I take my hat off to you. Either you've cornered the world's supply of barefaced cheek, or you have a dose of cranial diarrhoea. I know exactly what you're up to, Palmer. Do you think I'd be daft enough to sell my house to you now?'

'Did you enjoy your tour of my office the other day?'

'I don't know what you're on about.'

'Well, Charlie, let's just say, hypothetically, you had a good look over my plans and decide to broadcast them using that rag you call a newspaper. May I remind you that everything is legal and above board. The plans are lodged with the council. I have bought the land, incidentally, making several farmers very happy and very rich. There are no secrets. I have only to tell the public, and I can't see them getting too upset. Barbara isn't interested in what you say; why should Joe Public even raise an eyebrow?'

'If you're so squeaky clean, why send your heavies round to give me a kicking?'

Palmer chuckled.

'I don't know what you're on about, old bean.'

'And what about the poor sod you had killed?'

'You have a vivid imagination, Charlie. Ever try writing a novel?'

'Go pickle your balls, Palmer.'

'Now now, no need for insults, Charlie. Not when I've tried to help you out.'

'Help me out?'

'I want to offer you a better deal on the house.'

'You need it badly, don't you?'

'Five hundred thousand, Charlie. That's twice its value.'

'Not to you it isn't.'

'I've been reasonable up to now. I've offered you good money for the house. I'm taking care of Barbara. She will have a new home, and you can walk away comfortably off. I've tried to be friendly, and that's not easy with you.'

'Aw shucks, you're all heart.'

'This is your last chance. Do we have a deal?'

Charlie gazed at the still water, dreaming of Barbara and him living blissfully at Herbie's farmhouse. He wished it were true.

'I'll tell you what, Palmer. My price is a million, and there's one condition.'

'Which is?'

'You tell Barbara the truth.'

'You're a facetious little man, Charlie.' The line went dead.

'And you're an asshole, a toerag, a pompous murdering git...' He banged the mobile off his head. It was bloody sore.

'Afternoon, young fella.' Herbie appeared from behind a large oak. Flat cap down over his right eye, he puffed his pipe and sported an amused grin. 'I heard the voice. It sounded pained.'

'It is pained, Herbie. I'm at the end of my tether.'

Herbie sighed and nodded as if he understood. Amid the cloud of tobacco smoke, Charlie noticed the old man's crooked smile.

'Come up to the house. We can share a yarn and some lunch. The woman's carving a nice ham shank, and she's baked some wheaten.'

'No thanks, Herbie. I'd better head off to work before I get into more trouble.'

'Will ye join me in a drink then?' he said, producing a hip flask from his tatty pinstriped jacket.

'It's not that rocket fuel, is it?'

Herbie chuckled.

Regardless, Charlie accepted the flask, took a swig, coughed and spluttered.

'Jeez, you could run your tractor on that stuff.'

'Aye.' Herbie agreed with a look that suggested he did, took a drink and wiped his mouth with a wrinkled hand. Leaning on the railing of the bridge, he joined Charlie in gazing into the pond. 'And what brings ye to these parts, young fella?'

'Just passing. Good a place as any to stop and have a think.'

'And what troubles ye?'

'Everything. My life is a mess, and when I try to change it, things just get worse. I'm having trouble with my wife's new boyfriend.'

'Sounds like trouble, alright.'

'Have you ever been approached by a company called Palmer Property Services?'

'Indeed I have,' said Herbie, drawing a deep, whistling breath.

'Are you aware of Palmer's plans for this glen? He's building a new town. It's going to stretch from the bypass, across the golf course, through here and over the hill to Ballymenace.'

'That'll be the reason he's offered to buy me farm, lock, stock and barrel. That's why most of me neighbours are selling up.'

Charlie could hardly contain himself. His brain crashed through the sound barrier, while his mouth played catch-up. All this time, and the answers he'd been searching for were right here with Herbie Smyth.

'They're making it easy for him? Surely you're not selling up, Herbie?'

'Not me, young fella. He'll not lay his fancy bricks on my soil. Three times the worth of the place he offered me, but I gave him short shrift. Coming to my door in his fancy motor and smart clothes, waving his cheque book in front of the woman. That's no way for a gentleman to behave. He was none too pleased, I can tell ye.'

It was the first time Charlie had seen the old man's grin slide from his face.

'Has anyone else refused to sell?'

'Look yonder,' Herbie said, pointing with his pipe. 'The fields that ye can see are all mine, and that's how they'll stay. But the land below mine, close to yon bypass road, that's Tom Dawson's. At least it was till Palmer came along. Tom, his Patsy and four daughters, a finer family you'll not see this side of history, bought for thirty pieces. Movin' to one of them villa-type places in Spain. And then there's the land o'er the hill, near the town...'

'Archie Butler's place?' said Charlie, again recalling childhood run-ins with the nasty farmer and his big stick.

'That Mr Palmer has made old Archie a very rich man. Bought his Jessie a fur coat and jewellery to go with it.'

Herbie waved his hand in the air as if to indicate the rest of the world. For a moment Charlie wondered about the fur coat, recalling the mink rearing on Archie's farm.

'Everybody is selling up. No money in farmin', they say. At least there's dignity in it, I say.' He pointed at the trees in the glen, to the golf club, and shook his head. 'Men like Palmer are wiping every last ounce of green from the land, and for what? To line their pockets.'

At that point Charlie added a little slice of detestation. He told him about Palmer deceiving Barbara and his attempts to buy the Geddis family home.

'The trouble is Barbara won't believe a word. She thinks I'm trying to split them up because I'm jealous.'

Herbie offered the flask, and Charlie took another swig. It went straight to the back of his throat. His eyes watered, and he coughed as shivers ran down his back.

'I'm beating my head against a brick wall. I don't know what to do anymore.'

Herbie sighed. It sounded sympathetic. Tilting his cap backwards, he looked over the pond at the dragonflies hovering above the water.

'I once knew two young lads,' he began. 'Neither one blessed with a full barrel of wit but hard-working nonetheless. They farmed the land as their fathers and grandfathers had done before them. Dawn to dusk, they ploughed, sowed, reaped, mended walls, and milked the cows. One of them was poor and laboured with his hands and what measly tools his father had used. His one concern, every hour of every day, was to keep his farm goin'. He ploughed the fields, sowed the barley, and he brought home the harvest.'

Charlie wished he'd taken a few more swigs from the flask.

'Now the other boy had better land, rich soil, well drained, and the best farmin' contraptions money could buy. Big tractors, excavators, combine harvester, everything he needed to make a good livin'. You'd think it was easier for him to sow the barley and reap the harvest.'

Charlie agreed; it was a doddle.

'But for one thing.' Herbie wagged his pipe back and forth. 'And both those boys knew it well.' His voice faded to a whisper as if to share the secret only with Charlie. 'You need the seasons, the warmth of Spring with ample rain and a dry spell for the harvest. One year, no matter how they toiled in the fields, by horse plough or Massey Ferguson, they couldn't get the harvest they desired. The rains came but not in spring. All through August and September it poured from the heavens. The barley was all but lost. Not a thing they could do about it.'

Herbie tipped his head back and took another drink from the flask. Charlie waited for the punchline, the moral of the tale, the intervention of a leprechaun to save the harvest, or even a banshee to make for a tragic ending. Nothing of the sort. Herbie was silent.

'Well?' said Charlie, hands open wide.

'Well what?'

'What happened to the boys?'

'They lost their crops.'

'The fairies didn't save them? The farmer's union didn't have a whip round?'

Herbie laughed.

'Nothin' like that, young fella. Both men worked hard to bring home a good harvest. But there are other forces at work in this world, things that men cannot control. No matter what we do, or wish others to do, something beyond our power, beyond our understanding, will have the final say. I'll be away now, young fella,' said Herbie, another hint of a wink in his eye. 'There's a fence in the top field won't mend itself.'

'Are you telling me I should do whatever I think is right? And let fate take its course?'

'Aye.' It was more an intake of breath than a reply as the old boy disappeared in the dark green of the woods.

'See ya, Herbie.'

'Aye.'

Chapter thirty-two

'Trevor wants to see you,' said Carol, tapping at her PC and as usual barely lifting her head to acknowledge him. Jill was her conscientious self, on the phone with a client, her eyes fixed on some infinite point beyond the window. Even Billy, somehow, looked busy. In his case, busy meant he didn't have a mug of tea in his hand and the day's racing spread before him. Billy was actually typing something on his computer, and for once the computer wasn't crying back in anger. The whole scene made Charlie feel queasy. He wondered if something were about to happen. Worse still, was it going to happen to him? Judging by the atmosphere at ten-thirty on a Wednesday morning it already had, and none of his esteemed colleagues had the guts to tell him.

'I'd better see what the big boss wants,' he said, tossing his jacket on the chair and heading for the door.

No one bothered to reply. He had an eerie feeling his exit should be accompanied by a roll on the drums, as if he were on a circus high wire or had an appointment with a guillotine.

'How's it going, Trev?' he said marching in as the drumming stopped.

Trevor was standing by his window, Arsenal mug in hand, staring into the street. No change there then.

'Ah, Charlie,' he said in a startled voice. Charlie managed a grin. Trevor seemed flustered, caught once again eyeing up the girl from the jeans shop.

'Carol said you wanted to see me.' He reckoned Trevor needed reminding of why he was there.

'I do, I do,' he said, taking to his chair.

Charlie sat down and waited, while Trevor leafed through his diary, arranged his pencils, folded *The Sun*, rubbed his face with both hands, yawned and cleared his throat. Stalling tactics, any fool could see it.

'Why aren't you in court this morning?' he said at last.

'I checked earlier,' Charlie lied. 'Nothing much happening.'

'I may as well come straight to the point.' Another clearing of his throat and a sip of coffee. 'I want to make a few changes around here. See if we can't spice up our lives a little. Sweep the place clean. Put a fresh perspective on things.'

It seemed Trevor was coming down with a dose of hackneyitus.

'Sounds ominous,' said Charlie. 'What do you have in mind?'

'Jill and Carol, for instance. I thought perhaps they could swap roles for a while. Let Carol handle the advertising accounts, see if she can add a few ideas. I want Jill to take more responsibility for the office, maybe try her hand at writing features.'

Charlie agreed, although he didn't, for one minute, believe it was the reason why Trevor wanted to see him. He rose to leave, and Trevor started to fidget again. Another clearing of his throat erupted to a full-blown cough.

'I want you to swap places with Billy,' he said.

'You're joking?'

'The change will be good for you, Charlie. It's only for a while, to see how things go.'

'But I'm the senior reporter. What does Billy know about news gathering? I know sod all about sport, except football. Tell me this is a wind-up?'

'I'm perfectly serious. I want Billy to take over your role from next week. I've already spoken to him, and he's willing to give it a try.'

'That's awfully nice of him. I suppose you had to up his pay? How's he going to lift his fat arse out of the chair to get a story? I'm not doing it, Trevor. I'll go to the union, I'll–'

'Charlie, you don't have a choice. You either do it, or you're out.'

'Now I get it. This is your way of getting me out. You haven't got the balls to sack me.'

'No, it's not like that. I just want to make some changes for the well-being of everyone at the paper.'

'There's more to it than that.' Charlie kicked the desk, and Trevor jumped.

'All right, I'll tell you,' Trevor shouted back. 'But you still won't like it. You see, Charlie, lately you've been a real pain. You come in late; you clear off early, taking another member of staff with you. Your output is down; your stories are claptrap. I should have sacked you months ago, but you're supposed to be a mate. We were close friends before you split from Barbara. She and Joan prattled on about holidays, furniture and the kids, while we pissed off to the match. I know you've had a hard time since then, so I cut you some slack.' His face coloured, and beads of sweat appeared on his forehead. He got to his feet, hands flailing. 'But now you're annoying other people. People in high places, and they don't like it.'

'That's what journalists do: seek the truth, print the news. And who are we talking about exactly?'

'It doesn't matter.'

'Yes it bloody does.'

'Your beef with Malcolm Palmer,' said Trevor.

'He's putting the frighteners on you?'

'Not personally but he has connections. People who pull strings for other people, funny handshakes and all that shit. Before you know it, we'd be cashing our dole cheques down The First & Last. Now do you get it?' Looking worn out, Trevor slumped in his chair. 'If you don't fall in line then all of us get the heave-ho. Sports reporter is the only way I can keep an eye on you, that's if you still want your job.'

'You're all heart, Trevor. Does this mean I can go to the World Cup?'

'No, but you're invited to mine this Sunday. Joan is having a grand opening of our new conservatory. We guys can watch the grand prix.'

'Gee thanks. Looking forward to it already.'

* * *

Not that he was counting but by two o'clock he'd had a pint of Guinness, seven vodkas and a dodgy pork pie, and was clinging to the bar for support. He grinned proudly at anyone who cared to notice. Monica, the barmaid, shapely but getting on a bit, provided him with something to look at. Her black skirt barely fulfilled EU criteria to be classed as such, and her white T-shirt was see-through to the extent that her Wonderbra had its work cut out for it. Watching her move on high heels, her long black ponytail bouncing and daring to touch her bottom, had kept him occupied since opening time. She called him love and honey. Charlie was amused and excited, a tonic for his ego as well as his vodka.

After the lunchtime rush the city centre pub had a steady coming and going all afternoon, and by six o'clock the place was full again. Two barmen joined Monica to keep pace with the demand for drink.

'What'sa big rush tonight?' he said, swaying with his glass. 'I can hardly move in here.'

'They're watching the match, love.'

'Whish mash?'

'Oh, I don't know, honey. Manchester United in the World Cup or something.'

'I forgot about that. Giz anor drink.'

'Time you had a wee break, honey?'

'Jus one more before the mash shtarts. Put anor vodka in there.' He offered the glass, but she ignored it, and instead pulled a half-pint of lager and set it in front of him.

'That's all you're getting for a while, love. You'd better make it last.' She took the empty glass and moved on to another customer.

He tried to focus on the TV, perched high in the corner of the room (not him, the TV). He strained his ears to listen. In the end all he could do was tag along with the other punters. He clapped when they clapped, cheered when they cheered, swore when they swore, and at half-time he passed out all on his own. When Manchester United went three-nil down against Barcelona in the Champion's League, he was vaguely aware of his body parting company with the bar.

Chapter thirty-three

Monica stepped from the pond, her nipples threatening to burst through her Wonderbra. Barbara played football with Herbie, while Trevor held his hand and poured beer over his trousers.

'You're all wet, honey,' he kept saying.

Then Barbara scored a goal and swapped shirts with Herbie, but now Herbie was Jill, and she and Lisa argued over who had the cutest breasts. Then hundreds of Palmers on Zimmer frames and wielding baseball bats invaded the pitch and beat the crap out of Trevor.

'Ugh!' He needed to puke. Out of bed, to the bathroom, he turned on the tap at the basin and drew breath. It was his tap, his bathroom, his stomach heaving. He was home. He heard a noise coming from the living room and plodded to the door, scratching his head.

'Ah, you've surfaced?'

'Barbara!'

She looked him up and down in a way that made him realise he was naked. Herbie, Monica, Jill and Palmer were all a dream, an awfully long, twisted and cruel nightmare. But he was fine now. He was home with his wife, everything the way it was supposed to be.

'Charlie, are you all right?'

The flat? They were standing in his grotty flat. Was it not a part of the wicked dream?

'How did I get here?' he said, wiping sleep from his eyes and drool from his mouth.

'Someone called Monica sent you home in a taxi. Lisa found you halfway up the stairs, or halfway down. Take your pick.'

'Lisa?'

'Yes. Lisa. She called me, said you were in a terrible state.'

'Lisa?'

'Yes. Lisa. Are you with me at all, Charlie?'

So it wasn't a dream. Lisa, Palmer, Barbara and Jill playing football with Herbie. It actually happened? If he weren't so wide awake, he'd swear he'd been on the razzle.

'You were delirious, crying my name and making wild threats against Trevor. You frightened her, Charlie. That's why she called me. You were an absolute sight when I got here. You're not much better now. Go and get cleaned up and put some clothes on. I'll make you some breakfast before I go.'

'Don't go. I need to talk to you.'

'Then you'd better get a move on.'

He shivered under a cold shower and managed a quick shave. Then he dressed in a T-shirt and jeans, which he found ironed and laid out on the chair beside his bed. It didn't occur to him that he could not have put them there.

She sat at the table nursing a mug of coffee in her hands. A plate of fried bread, egg, sausage, bacon and tomato awaited him. Didn't think he could stomach it, but he didn't want to hurt her feelings. After all, this was the first meal she'd cooked for him since his departure from the family roost. Maybe it was the start of something, a mending of all the hurt between them. He recalled his three-step plan and pondered his progress so far. Gazing at the egg on his plate, he fell into the symbolism of how the yolk, delicate but secure within the white, depicted the fragility of marriage. The shrivelled bacon embodied his sordid past, old and decrepit. The slices of fried bread, a strong foundation for their future, and the sausage...

'Are you not going to eat?' said Barbara.

He took a sip of coffee, sprinkled salt over the egg, and stuck his fork into the yolk, the fluid seeping across the plate. He couldn't get his throbbing head round the symbolism, but it wasn't a good omen.

'Feeling better?'

'A little,' he said. 'Sorry for putting you to all this trouble.'

'I'm well used to it.'

Plenty of acid in that, he thought, pretending to concentrate on the food.

'So who is Monica?' she asked, sounding neither annoyed nor amused.

His mouth full of fried bread gave him time to think, not that it made much difference. He hadn't a baldy notion about Monica, except she had a starring role in his dream team.

'Just a girl I met,' he replied, like an adolescent to a nosy mother. He could tell she didn't believe him by the way she smirked, her mouth hidden behind the coffee mug. Stupidly, he felt the need to explain as if one lie was more convincing paired with another. 'Actually, we've been going out for a while.' She didn't seem bothered. Not surprised, not angry, not amused and not jealous. Indifferent.

'What have you done with the duvet I gave you?'

He thought for a moment. The Shroud of Old Trafford story wouldn't ring true.

'It's in the laundry.'

'What did you want to talk about?'

'I need to explain about Palmer, why I'm investigating him.'

'I'm not discussing Malcolm. You're wrong about him, and you're only causing trouble with this stupid obsession.'

'But, Barbara–'

'No, Charlie!'

He'd never heard her explode with such force. The mug slammed on the table, coffee splashing over his breakfast. They glared at each other, one angry, the other shocked.

'I'm sorry,' he said. 'I won't mention him again.'

She fetched a cloth from the sink to soak up the mess.

'I've got to go. I've been here all night. Mummy's been staying with me. She'll be wondering if something's wrong.'

Barbara was set on leaving for whatever reason. Now it was clear to Charlie that she couldn't bear to talk with him, when all he wanted to do was slag off Palmer.

'I'll see you, Charlie. Take better care of yourself, please.'

She kissed him on the forehead then gathered her coat from the sofa. He sat with knife in one hand and fork in the other, gazing at his sodden breakfast.

'Barbara?'

'What now?' She was by the door, putting on her coat.

'Can I come home please? I want to be with you.'

'Charlie, don't start this again.'

'I'm a changed man, honest. I'm working hard. I'm more reliable than I used to be. Ask Trevor if you don't believe me. I'll come home when I'm supposed to; I'll help you round the house. No more daft ideas about writing novels or working for *The Sun*. I'll forget about Palmer. I'll behave.'

Leaning against the door, she looked as if his pleading had just bowled over nine of her pins to leave only one standing, the one that held all her sensible thinking. He came towards her, hoping she would suddenly throw her arms around him and tell him that everything was going to be OK. He was still holding the knife and fork.

'Charlie, we both know you haven't changed from the day you walked out.'

'You threw me out.'

'No, I suggested you left for a while to do some of the living you claimed that I, your job and Ballymenace were depriving you of. You weren't bothered about coming home until I started a new life for myself.'

'With poncy-faced Palmer and his money.'

'Yes, with Malcolm. What's so terrible about that? He is my choice, and you don't have a say in it. You gave up that right when you cleared off. And what have you done with all your precious time? Two years, and you haven't changed. If you had, I wouldn't be here this morning nursing you through another hangover. Go ask your friend Monica what you're like.'

'I don't know anyone called Monica.'

'Need I say anymore?' She opened the door.

'I still love you, Barbara.' He touched her hand, soft and warm, but she quickly withdrew it.

'Bye, Charlie,' she called from the stairs.

He called over the banister.

'Tell me you don't love me, and I'll never mention it again.'

'Bye, Charlie,' she said from the next landing.

'Tell me you don't?'

'Bye.' The front door closed behind her.

'Brilliant.' Fists clenched in triumph, a knife in one, fork in the other. 'She still loves me.' He rushed back inside, past his breakfast, heading for the toilet. Unfortunately, the contents of his stomach got there before he did.

He didn't make it to work. Instead he lay under a blanket on the sofa watching his new portable TV, borrowed from Lisa. He couldn't give a toss about installing a water feature in the garden. Didn't care much about relocating to New South Wales. Definitely had no interest in digging up a field to search for an Anglo-Saxon kitchen. Even *Top Gear* had lost its appeal as The Stig continued to show off in the latest Aston Martin. Charlie was thinking. All afternoon, nursing a delicate tummy, he tried to organise his thoughts within a vodka-soaked brain.

It wasn't a eureka moment. He certainly didn't leap in the air; his body couldn't stand the height. But after a few hours he had a plan. Expose Palmer. That was the plan. But he needed someone to put the little snippets of thought together. He needed someone to fill in the details, colour the picture, chart the right course, someone to help him avoid clichés. He needed Jill.

Chapter thirty-four

All day Friday he continued to need Jill. He had things, important things, to discuss with her. His plan to expose Palmer needed something, like substance, for example. He hoped she could provide a few ideas. Gaining her attention, never mind asking for input to the 'shaft Palmer enterprise', was proving difficult. She and Carol had made a start on the job-swap initiative and had no time to pander to his insecurities. All morning he'd witnessed their comings and goings across the office, helping each other and giving advice.

'I usually write it this way,' Jill said.

'I keep this list of addresses; it comes in handy,' said Carol.

'Do you want to swap desks?'

'We need to keep our own computers.'

They spent an hour and a half moving all their bits and pieces across the room. The whole time incessant chatter, advice, warnings, anecdotes and shortcuts were lobbed back and forth. It was like sitting by the net on Centre Court at Wimbledon, or getting caught in the crossfire as Tom Hanks and his buddies stormed a German bunker in *Saving Private Ryan*. Right now, he could do with somebody storming the office to save him from two chattering women.

He tried to suss out what Billy really thought of their job swap. Billy, however, was deeply engrossed in the racing at Ascot, placing bets with an online bookie. Charlie smirked with satisfaction. By next week he would be writing only the sports, and Billy would be studying the form. Who was going to write the news? That, of course, was Trevor's problem.

The relationship between Jill and Carol had always been one of polite tolerance. Their jobs overlapped at the edges, they chatted during tea breaks, and occasionally went out to lunch. Carol was only nineteen, much younger than Jill whatever her admitted age, but they got on reasonably well despite having little in common. Their job swap had taken place in a friendly and courteous manner. By three o'clock they were settled to their new roles, and all was quiet. Charlie was just about to ask Jill for help with Palmer, when there was a flurry of conversation.

'Jill?' said Carol from her new position.

'Yes, Carol?'

'It's three o'clock.'

Charlie's head shot up like a stoat. He sniffed danger.

'It's just that...' Carol hesitated. Jill wasn't looking.

'Yes, Carol, what is it?'

'It's three o'clock.'

'I know what time it is.'

It was *Private Ryan* again. Charlie wanted to stick his fingers in his ears. He knew there was a big bang coming.

'It's tea time,' said Carol.

'So it is.'

'We have swapped jobs.'

Jill glared across the room. Carol opened fire. Charlie was tempted to dive under his desk.

'You should be making the tea now instead of me.'

'Oh no, I don't think so. Trevor didn't mean for us to change that role,' said Jill.

'Yes he did,' said Carol.

The argument raged. Bravely, Charlie went to the kitchen.

'Here you are ladies,' he said, a few minutes later, holding two mugs of tea. 'My treat.'

He set one in front of Carol, who looked too stunned for words, and with a charitable smile handed the other to Jill. She wasn't impressed either.

'I'll make the tea for a while,' he said. 'You girls have a break.'

'Is this the Charlie Geddis we know and love?' said Carol, unwrapping a KitKat. Her latest diet had just been ditched.

'The Charlie Geddis I know and love only does something like this when he wants something in return,' said Jill.

'Jill, I didn't know you loved me.'

'I didn't mean it like that.'

'Now you're breaking my heart.'

'Where's my tea?' Billy asked, glued to his screen.

'Get it yourself,' said Charlie.

'Sucking up to the women, eh? Very sad.'

Charlie returned to his desk, and a relaxed mood once again settled in the office. He watched Jill reading her screen and sipping tea. Now was his chance. He launched his chair across the floor.

'Can I have a word?' he whispered.

'Yes, Charlie, what is it?'

'I mean a big word, a conversation. I've been dying to get you alone all day.'

Her cheeks glowed red, her eyes widened, her expression daring him to continue. He suddenly realised that he'd sounded bold. Not that he usually cared. Definitely a first that he considered her feelings at all.

'Sorry, what I mean is, I need your help. I have a plan to get Palmer.'

'I hope there's more to it than the last one,' she said. 'And I'm not getting pregnant again.'

Carol's eyes shot up from her screen. Charlie faked a smile at her, while Jill blushed.

'I need to run it by you, iron out the details.'

'After work?'

'I'll buy you dinner.'

She looked sheepish. Her eyes darted about the room then back to Charlie. Carol and Billy were staring. To both of them, Jill and Charlie must have seemed a bizarre couple.

* * *

Dinner was cod and chips at The Jolly Friar, two doors down from the office. It didn't take long to regret the idea. Firstly, the chips were greasy and the cod expertly concealed in thick batter. Secondly, the meeting ran off in Jill's direction with her bubbling from excitement about her debut article for *The Explorer*. Resigned to a slice of bread and butter, and a few mushy peas, Charlie listened to a detailed report of the new aromatherapy class at Ballymenace College of Further Education. Instant boredom. The only essential oil he knew of was Castrol GTX. His chips were probably fried in the stuff. But Jill was such an enthusiastic wee soul; when she got talking, he didn't have the heart to interrupt. Maybe he could channel her enthusiasm into planning a strategy for taking on Palmer. After all, it was her pregnancy scam that provided the chance to look around his office and uncover the plans for Palmerstown.

Charlie nodded agreement, smiled and even attempted the odd question, just to keep her bubbling. After dinner, and still talking, she invited him to her flat for coffee. On the journey, aromatherapy was dropped in favour of the wider issue of writing, and did he think she had potential as a novelist? He would have gladly enrolled in the aromatherapy course rather than listen to another word about how her English teacher at school told her she had an intriguing style. In fact, a massage would go down nicely. He followed her up the steps, picturing smellies and a rub-down, while she talked a load of Catherine Cookson.

She opened the door, and they stepped into the hall. Jill screamed as Charlie slumped to the floor.

Chapter thirty-five

Somebody pulled him to his feet. He couldn't stand but staggered gently on the spot. There were dark shapes, balaclavas and rough voices. It felt like waking from a general anaesthetic: muddled thoughts, not sure how to move in case it hurt. He was dragged to the kitchen and his head forced under the cold tap. The water didn't help the pain.

'You'd better dry yourself,' said a woman, handing him a towel.

He wiped his face and breathed deeply; his eyes closed. When he felt strong enough to look again, he studied the woman standing before him. Black leather jacket, black leather jeans and black boots. Her hair was black with the fringe resting on her dark glasses. It felt like the dark ages.

'Hello, Sheila, fancy meeting you here,' he said with forced bravado.

'Charlie Geddis, you're a hard man to track down,' she said.

Because of her dark glasses, his eyes were drawn to her mouth, small and pouting. Her lips were thin and sported a purple lipstick. She was very attractive, but under the make-up he could see the touches of age emerging, the tiny creases around her mouth. Muted cries came from the living room. Jill was in the grip of a tall figure, a gloved hand over her mouth, an arm around her waist. She struggled, but it didn't trouble him. Two figures stood either side of Sheila Farrington, one of them supported by a Zimmer frame. It was clear who was in charge.

'Let her go,' said Sheila. 'As long as she keeps her mouth shut.'

The man relaxed his grip, and Jill made a run for the door. The other big guy shoved her onto the sofa.

'Get off me,' she said, trying to get up.

'Sit down,' said Sheila. 'Sit down, shut up and you won't get hurt.'

'You've seen too many gangster movies, Sheila love.'

'No, Charlie, this is definitely real life.'

She motioned for him to sit beside Jill. One of the men drew the curtains, and the room fell into semi-darkness. Sheila paced up and down in front of them.

'What do you want?' Jill asked.

'Well, Miss Barker, I would have thought the answer to your question is obvious. I gather you're not the least bit shy when it comes to invading someone's privacy?'

Jill gulped, speechless, a petrified gaze in her eyes.

Charlie was impressed by Sheila Farrington. This was not the trembling woman who'd been so horrified at the sight of her bare bottom in print. Tonight she was confident, controlled, relaxed even. It was sharp-tongued Jill who withered under the strain.

'So big Mal sent you to do his dirty work?' Charlie said, immersing himself in the gangster ambience.

'I can deal with the likes of you without Malcolm's say-so. He knows nothing about it.' She stood over him, staring down. 'I think we have some unfinished business?'

'What would that be?'

'The pictures you and Lois Lane went to the trouble of taking. I want them.'

'What's the deal?'

'No deal, Charlie. Either you give me the pictures, or I cut my friends loose.'

There was a loud smash, and Jill screamed. A baseball bat had swiped her flatscreen TV off its stand.

'Easy on, Tracy,' said Charlie.

'How did you know my name?' said the hood. She wielded her bat in the air with one hand, gripping the Zimmer with the other. Charlie smirked bravely.

'Shut up, Tracy,' said Sheila. 'I don't have time for tantrums. Now, Charlie, the pictures please?'

'No can do. They're my insurance policy in case things don't go my way. But don't worry, Sheila. I won't use them to hurt you. I've nothing against you personally.'

'That's very sweet, but I need more than your assurances. Besides, things aren't exactly going your way at the moment.'

'Life's tough, Sheila.'

'Malcolm and I will be leaving the country when he completes this deal you seem intent on destroying. I can't allow you to do that.'

'Maybe you and Malcolm aren't really suited? Could be he has someone else in mind.'

She laughed.

'I wondered when you'd get to that. You mean Barbara, of course? I don't think so. I'm sure she's a nice girl but hardly Malcolm's type.'

'He's going to a lot of trouble on her behalf, building a new house in Cultra.'

Sheila didn't even flinch at the suggestion.

'I'm really disappointed,' she said. 'I've overestimated your intelligence. I thought you had everything figured out. But let me put you straight. Malcolm has a building project, the details of which I know little and care even less. We are leaving for Spain when it's finished. Malcolm also needs your precious Barbara. When the deal is over, she's history. What he doesn't need right now is you,

156

poking your nose into his business. Are we clear on that, Charlie?'

He got to his feet and stood face to face with Sheila Farrington.

'I'm glad you have complete trust in him,' he said.

Tracy proved to be handy with the baseball bat, despite her incapacity. Charlie dropped to the floor. Jill screamed until one of the hoods smothered her face with his hand. The throbbing across Charlie's back collided with the ache in his head. He drifted off for a second, but Sheila's voice drew him back.

'You are not a very clever man, Charlie. Why try to act like one?'

Sheila paced about the room, studying Jill's family photos and the crystal ornaments on the bookcase. She didn't seem bothered by Charlie's attempts to rile her.

'Please be careful with those,' said Jill, released again from the grip of the hood.

A small vase smashed on the wooden floor.

'Sorry,' said Sheila.

Tracy laughed, and her mates joined in.

'Shut up, Tracy,' said Charlie.

In a flash the other two hoods hauled him to his feet, and Tracy grabbed him by the throat. Charlie began to choke. Sheila stepped closer to his throbbing face.

'You seem to have a knack at upsetting people.'

Charlie gurgled a reply, while Jill struggled to pull Tracy's hands from his throat.

'Let him go,' Jill said.

'Enough, Tracy,' said Sheila.

Charlie landed in a heap on the sofa.

'Now the pictures?'

'Oh, Charlie, just give her the damned things, and get her out of here,' said Jill.

'Sorry, no can do.'

A nod from Sheila and Charlie was launched across the room. The assistant hoods splayed his left hand on the breakfast bar, and Tracy shuffled over and let rip with her bat. Charlie yelped, and as they released him, he slid to the floor.

'Had a change of heart, Charlie?'

'Digital,' he groaned. 'Memory card. It was a digital camera.'

Sitting up, Charlie attempted a smug grin but thought better of it. He wasn't about to surrender Jill's mobile phone. Better for Sheila to believe that he'd used a camera.

'I would guess that your lovely body is stored on at least five hard drives; the pictures make a great screensaver, and I've added quite a few names to my address book. One email and half the country will see how well you give head. Then there's always Facebook and YouTube.'

Sheila went to the kitchen returning moments later with a large handbag, also in black. Even a tough image requires matching accessories.

'In that case I will also need an insurance policy,' she said, producing her mobile from the bag. 'These shots will be more convincing if you are both naked.'

'What?' said Jill.

'Get your clothes off, all of them.' The hoods stepped forward to emphasise the order.

Charlie made heavy work of removing his jacket and shoes. His left hand surpassed his head and back on the throbbing scale. Despite the injuries, and with added threats from Tracy, he was down to pants and socks in a few seconds. Jill refused to remove any clothes in the presence of three strange men. It was something of a compliment, Charlie thought, that she hadn't included him.

'I'm not doing anything in front of these perverts.'

'Do as you're told, or we'll be here all night,' said Charlie.

She fired him an icy look.

'This is all your fault, Charlie Geddis. Why did I ever listen to you?'

'Stop moaning,' he said. Why did women always think they could improve a bad situation by going on and on about it, he thought.

Reluctantly, Jill undid the buttons of her pink blouse. Sheila watched impassively until she was down to her knickers.

'That'll do,' she told her. 'We're not here to give Charlie a cheap thrill.'

'I am not cheap, Mrs Farrington,' Jill replied with a scowl.

'Of course you're not, dear.' Turning to Charlie, standing ever-hopeful in his pants and socks, she said, 'All of it, Charlie.'

It gave the hoods something to laugh about. Jill looked disgusted, her hands shielding her naked breasts.

'Seems you have a slight confidence problem, Charlie,' said Sheila, looking him up and down.

'Very funny.'

'Why are you doing this?' Jill asked in a trembling voice.

'You're not very bright, are you, dear? You keep asking questions with such obvious answers.'

Charlie puffed, losing patience. Was Sheila going to spend all bloody night giving a blow-by-blow account of her stupid antics? She could be home by now, with a nice cup of tea and a chocolate biscuit, and he could be in the six-hour queue at A&E.

'You see, Miss Barker,' Sheila continued, 'I have it on good authority that Charlie is desperate to be reunited with his wife. What is poor wee Barbara going to think when she is presented with mucky photographs of you and Charlie?'

'You bitch,' said Jill.

'I don't think you'd be too keen for your pale flesh to appear in the local paper either. On the other hand, if you and Charlie are prepared to walk away from all this then the photographs will never see the light of day. Does that answer your question, Miss Barker?'

Jill huffed and said nothing.

'I trust we can use a little imagination to get the best out of you?' said Sheila. 'Let's start with a kiss.'

Jill was rigid. Tracy prodded Charlie on the shoulder with her bat. He pecked Jill on the cheek. She pulled away in disgust.

'I think we can do better than that,' said Sheila.

They held a kiss, and the camera clicked.

'Now a little embrace.'

They hugged, and the camera clicked.

'On the sofa.'

They sat down, and the camera clicked.

'Good, very good. How about lying down?'

Jill lay down. Charlie flopped on top of her. The camera clicked.

'Charlie, you're a real tiger,' said Sheila.

The camera clicked several times as they wriggled to escape each other.

'Right, tie them up,' Sheila said at last.

Tracy removed the laces from Charlie's shoes and used them to tie Jill's hands together. Then she tied Charlie's hands to Jill's. Another hood produced a bag of cable ties and some string from the kitchen and bound their feet. By the time they'd finished, Jill was sandwiched between Charlie and the back of the sofa. They were bound together at their hands, hips and feet. Tracy, with her glove removed, lifted Jill's bra off the floor and dangled it over them. Then she felt the edge of Jill's white knickers between her finger and thumb.

'That's a lovely set,' she said quietly, as her mates headed for the door.

'Pervert,' said Jill.

'I meant your bra and knickers, they're very nice.'

Charlie whispered a brief explanation in her ear.

'Oh, I'm sorry,' she said.

'What for?'

'I don't em...'

'She didn't mean to offend you,' said Charlie, 'since you're about to have the operation.'

'How did you know?'

'I can tell these things. I can sense when a man is not happy in his body. I can see you're trying to reach the woman inside you, the woman who needs to reveal herself to the world.'

'You can tell all that just by looking at me?'

Charlie could see that under her leather jacket Tracy wore a black satin blouse. When she leaned over to check their hands were securely tied, Charlie saw the cups of a bra. Tracy was less than graceful, however, in a pair of ladies boots similar to Sheila's but five sizes bigger. The Zimmer did nothing for the image.

'I hope our little get-together has given you food for thought,' said Sheila. 'Next time I won't stop Tracy tearing you limb from limb.' The front door slammed.

Frantic struggling ensued as they tried to free themselves.

'Hold on, Jill. Take it easy, calm down.'

'Calm down? Look at the state of us. Is this what normal people do on a Friday night?' Charlie raised an eyebrow. 'Don't answer that. Just tell me how we're ever going to get free?'

Chapter thirty-six

'Are you expecting anyone tonight?'

'No, but Mummy will be here first thing. We always go shopping on Saturday mornings. She has a key. Oh God! I can't let her see us like this. The shock will kill her.'

Their hands were trapped between their bodies. They tried to ease one free, but they were held firm and, judging by the pain, Charlie reckoned his left was broken. Each time he looked down he met Jill's naked breasts.

'Can't you look somewhere else?' she said.

'I'm trying to untie the knot.'

'Charlie, this is hopeless. What are we going to do?'

'Do you mean right now? Or do you mean, what are we going to do about Palmer?'

'I don't care about Palmer anymore. I wish I'd never got involved in your silly schemes. Look where we've ended up. When we get out of this mess we're going straight to the police.'

'And they'll solve everything, will they?'

'But this has gone too far; someone is going to get hurt. These people will stop at nothing to get their way. Why don't you let them finish their business? You heard what Sheila Farrington said. When it's over they're off to Spain. You'll have a better chance of getting back with Barbara when Palmer is gone.'

'And what if he's taking Barbara to Spain and not Sheila Farrington? What will I do then? Besides, some poor sod has already been murdered, and I'm not exactly in tip-top shape; my hand is killing me.'

The thought that they could have been killed shut them up. They lay still in the darkness for what seemed like hours. Charlie wondered if Sheila Farrington had played a part in the murder of the red-haired man. Did she love Palmer enough to kill for him? Were they the same hoods he'd seen at the duck pond? Did they deposit the body in his flat? Why steal it back again? Did Barbara care enough for Palmer to turn a blind eye? Was Palmer planning to bump him off? With all these questions bouncing round his throbbing head, he tried again to break free. When he thought Jill seemed more relaxed, he raised the subject again.

'We can't let this stop us from getting Palmer. There's too much at stake.'

She stared him in the eyes, a look that said, 'I may as well listen, I'm not going anywhere'.

'What was your plan?'

'Plan?'

'You said you had a plan you wanted to discuss with me. That's why we had dinner, remember?'

'After tonight it needs a rethink.'

'What did you have in mind?'

'Well em... I want to, you know?'

'Charlie Geddis, you haven't the faintest idea what to do next. I don't think you ever had a plan.'

'Yes I did. We need to expose Palmer's crooked deals and find out why a man was murdered.'

'They killed him because he knew all about Palmerstown?'

'We know about Palmerstown, but they didn't kill us.'

'If Sheila was behind it then maybe it's related to Councillor Farrington and the planning committee.'

163

'It must go higher than Farrington. Getting the necessary approval hasn't stopped Palmer in the past. Usually he starts building on a site first and then seeks permission. If it's not contested by Joe Bloggs in the street, he gets it passed easily. That's what happened to your Uncle Dickie. If it is contested, and it goes to court, Palmer spins the judge a sob story about providing much-needed employment in the construction industry and how a marvellous set of town houses in a country field will boost the local economy. With all the publicity, the houses get built, sell like hotcakes, and he's quids in.'

'If he isn't bothered about planning permission,' said Jill, 'why has Sheila tried to scare us off?'

'She's just spooked. Shock of her life, me turning up on her doorstep with those snaps. She's protecting herself from her husband as much as doing Palmer's dirty work.'

'So what's the plan?'

'I print the story about Palmerstown; after that we let things take their course.'

'We have to be careful, Charlie. That Farrington woman is a nasty piece of work. Imagine using that poor transsexual with the Zimmer to beat you up?'

'You're a very considerate soul, Jill Barker.'

He totally forgot himself and kissed her. She didn't resist. He tried for another, but this time she drew her head back.

'Two things,' she said earnestly. 'Firstly, remember I'm angry with you for getting me into this mess. Secondly, think of Barbara – she's the reason why you're doing all of this.'

'I'm sorry, you're right.'

They lay in silence, staring into each other's eyes, Charlie thinking how beautiful she looked, while she was probably wondering what to tell her mother. He was lying naked beside a gorgeous semi-naked woman, only natural that he should be aroused.

'Put him away, Charlie.'

'Sorry.'

Sleep was not easy. His whole body seemed to throb. He'd lost count of his injuries, but each time he tried to shift to a more comfortable position he got a painful reminder. Every ten minutes Jill awoke in a panic and struggled to break free. He had convinced himself it was better that her mother found them lying peacefully as Sheila had left them. But when dawn came Jill's panic increased, and her ideas for escape grew more bizarre.

'If you would just do as I ask, we could be out of this mess before I have to explain everything to my mother.'

'You've been wriggling all night, and it's got us nowhere.'

'I want to get a knife from the kitchen.'

'But we've already tried that. We nearly strangled each other when we stood up.'

'This time we do it lying down,' she said. 'If we roll off the sofa and across the floor, we can squeeze into the kitchen. Then you can reach the cutlery drawer.'

'Why can't we wait for your mother? She'll understand, once you explain.'

'It's what'll happen before I explain that worries me. Look at the state of the place. My TV has been smashed, our clothes are everywhere. The shock of seeing us together could kill her.'

'Thanks very much.'

'You know what I mean. Mummy has spent all her life in the WI, making scones and jam. A wild night out for her is an Aled Jones concert. She doesn't do sex. If I hadn't been married already she'd expect me still to be a virgin. Now will you please do as I say before she comes through that door?'

She thrust her body against Charlie's, and he rolled onto his back. The momentum pulled her on top of him; they ran out of sofa and dropped to the floor. Charlie yelped in pain, but it wasn't enough to deter Jill. Tumbling over each other, they moved towards the kitchen until they got jammed between an easy chair and the breakfast bar. At that moment Jill lay on top of Charlie. Also, at that moment, they heard a key slide into the lock of the front door.

Jill whimpered. Charlie tried to roll them back to the sofa, thinking they looked slightly more decent lying there. The living-room door swung open, and an elderly woman appeared. Jill's bum pointed skywards, her mouth tugging frantically at the cords between them. It resembled an out-take from *Sex and the City*.

'Oh my goodness.'

'It's all right, Mummy. It's not what you think.'

'Oh I feel faint. I must sit down. What's happened in here, Jill? Look at the television.'

'Hello, Mrs Em.' Charlie was stuck for the woman's name.

'My goodness, it's a man.'

She flopped on the sofa where Jill and Charlie had spent an uncomfortable night. Despite her confused state, she looked a gracious lady, well-dressed, tidy silver hair and a fresh face that belied her sixty-six years.

'Mummy, can you help us please?'

'Oh no, dear, I'm not one for interfering. If you want to do those Jackie Collins-type things that's your business. I only wish you'd given me warning.'

'Mummy, if you would just listen. I need a knife from the kitchen to cut these cords. I'll explain everything when I'm free and decent.'

Rising unsteadily from the sofa she padded to the kitchen, having to step over them to reach the cutlery drawer.

'Here you are, dear,' she said, handing Jill a bread knife, a hand over her eyes. 'I'll make some tea, and you can tell me when you've finished.'

When they were at last free, Jill bolted to her bedroom and, seconds later, reappeared in a dressing gown. Charlie gathered his clothes strewn around the room. Jill helped, without sparing him the time to button his shirt or zip his trousers. He had no chance of slipping on his shoes before she bundled him to the door.

'I'll see you on Monday,' she said. 'Stay out of trouble.' The door closed behind him.

Another day, another door. But he didn't ponder it for long. Rain lashed down, and he stood with shirt unbuttoned, holding his shoes, minus laces, in his one good hand.

'Thanks for having me,' he said to the door.

Chapter thirty-seven

'What the hell is he doing here?'

'You said I could invite a few mates, and Charlie is a mate,' said Trevor.

Joan scowled, first at her husband and then at Charlie. He didn't know how Trevor put up with her. She had all the charm of a booby-trapped bomb with a mercury tilt switch. It didn't take much to set her off. Charlie had known Joan longer than he'd known Trevor. In fact, with the exception of his parents, he'd known Joan longer than he'd known anyone. She had been raised beside him in Lothian Avenue, only a privet hedge between her house and his. Pity it hadn't been the Berlin Wall. They'd gone to the same primary school and shared a desk for the entire first year. She never liked him and frequently told him so.

'I hate you, Charles Geddis,' she used to boast, a depraved look in her eyes long before either of them knew the meaning of the word.

He wore it like a badge. If Joan hated your guts then you were quids-in with all your mates. Through her teenage years she developed an eternal look of disgust. He was never sure if it was solely for his benefit or for all mankind. It was a pity, because, in those days, she was good looking, with dark curly hair and a porcelain face.

Sadly, she had carried her manner but not the good looks into her thirties. Charlie didn't care, but it was a shame for Trevor who had to waken every morning beside her.

'Hello, Joan,' he said with a smirk, knowing full well his presence had curdled her Sunday afternoon. 'How's it going?'

Ignoring him completely, she laid into Trevor.

'I told you Barbara was coming. Why did you ask him? He'll only cause trouble. Look at the state of him.'

Trevor inspected Charlie's bruised face, fat lip and the clumsy bandage on his swollen hand.

'We're going to watch the race,' said Trevor, 'while you women have a chat in your new conservatory. Barbara and Charlie don't even have to speak if they don't want to.'

Now witness to a domestic, Charlie stood there, right hand in pocket, humming quietly while they fought for his virtue.

'That's not the point,' she said. Joan was fighting to hold back a tidal wave of anger. He could tell by the clenched teeth and controlled breathing through her nose. 'Barbara is bringing Malcolm. You can't expect that nice Mr Palmer to spend his afternoon with the likes of him.'

She nodded in Charlie's direction. He was chuffed. Surely there was hope in that?

With fateful, yet exquisite, timing the doorbell rang. They looked down the hall to see Barbara and Malcolm peering in. The art of fuming with a smile was well placed in Joan as she bounded to the door.

'Get him out of the way,' she said to Trevor. 'Hi, Barbara,' she beamed. 'And, Malcolm, I can't wait to show you my conservatory. Your people did a wonderful job.'

Trevor handed Charlie a Carlsberg. The two of them were reduced to casual bystanders as Joan launched into her overpowering hostess routine.

'Nice one, Trevor,' said Charlie.

'What do you mean?'

'I thought Palmer would be the last one you'd go to for a new conservatory.'

'Nothing to do with me. I only live here.'

'No doubt Joan got a bargain. Hasn't got anything to do with the article you were reading in *The Sun*? The one about the wife who will only have sex in her conservatory?'

'Don't talk rot.'

'Hello, Charlie,' said Barbara, without a smile or any interest in his injuries. His reply was lost in the chat as Malcolm greeted Trevor, and Joan led Barbara to join the other women in the conservatory.

Three others were already watching Trevor's new plasma-screen television, his treat to himself. Charlie recognised only one of them. Ed Curry, Trevor's lifelong friend, was a bachelor and proud of it. He was everything Trevor and Charlie, to their endless regret, had somehow managed to avoid. The two others Trevor introduced as Bobby and Colin, both neighbours, early forties, and very concerned about Hamilton's chances against Verstappen. They hardly noticed Charlie, gripped instead by Martin Brundle's preamble of the Monaco circuit.

Settling into an armchair, Charlie intended to ignore Palmer and enjoy the race, drinking as much beer as his stomach could hold. Palmer, however, couldn't keep his mouth shut.

'What do you think, chaps? Can Red Bull do it?'

'Let's hope so,' Trevor answered politely.

Charlie rolled his eyes and shook his head.

'What do you think, Charlie, can Verstappen win from pole position?'

He was amazed that Palmer could speak to him as if there were no issues between them.

'You're at the wrong house, Palmer. No Red Bull supporters here.'

Trevor cleared his throat, a reminder for Charlie to behave.

Verstappen was still leading by lap twenty-five, but everyone was agreed that Hamilton, in third place, was hanging in there. The same could not be said for Charlie as he fuelled up on Trevor's beer. His problems deepened when he challenged Palmer, firstly, on his knowledge of motor racing, and then his methods of conducting business.

'Verstappen is much too clever,' said Palmer. 'Hamilton might get to second, but I'll be damned if he can overtake Verstappen on this circuit.'

'Lewis will catch him easily,' said Charlie.

'But it's impossible to overtake at Monaco.'

The others muttered their agreement. Damned if Charlie would. Palmer was sticky, like toffee round your teeth. Takes a long time to get rid of it.

'Bollocks! You don't know what you're talking about, Palmer.'

'Charlie,' said Trevor intervening, but it was too late.

Some men with a feed of drink become teddy bears, while others fancy themselves as a bit of a stud. Charlie belonged to the pack known as debilitated antagonists. What he would like to do and what he was actually capable of doing, with a belly full of Carlsberg, were complete opposites. Probably the best lager in the world, but Charlie was probably not the best drunk.

'What the hell do you know, Palmer?' he said with a hick. 'Golf's your game. We don't give a toss about that, do we, lads?'

'Leave it out, Charlie,' said Trevor.

'What are you doing here, Palmer? Why aren't you out building more bloody houses? And *conversatories, conservativries*. Why don't you tell us what you're planning to do with Bally... hick... menace?'

'I'm sorry about this, Malcolm,' said Trevor.

'It's OK, Trevor; he's just had one over the eight. He doesn't mean any harm.'

'Go fluck yourself, Plamer!' He knew it was slurred, but it had the same effect.

'Charlie, that's enough.' Barbara stood by the door. Perfect timing. 'You apologise to Malcolm right now.'

Hamilton smashed into the barrier at Sainte Dévote, but no one in the room saw it. All eyes were on Charlie, tiny lasers tracking every move. He was trapped. What could he do? He needed the blazing speed of Max Verstappen to get him out of this one.

'I will not,' he said.

'It's all right, Barbara,' said Palmer. 'It's just the drink talking. Let's get back to the race.'

'Malcolm, he is not getting away with speaking to you like that. Charlie, you apologise right now.'

A hush fell over the room, even Martin Brundle was silenced. Everyone waited. Charlie stared at Barbara, though she was a bit blurry.

'Have you had your hair done?' he said.

Well, he had to say something.

'Is there any self-respect left in your twisted head?' she said.

He honestly thought the question was rhetorical and didn't reply. Barbara hurried away in tears.

'That was bang out of order,' said Trevor.

'What did I do?' Charlie looked at the others.

Ed, Bobby and Colin had returned to the race. Palmer, with a smug look on his glossy face, went after Barbara. Lewis Hamilton walked back to the pits.

Charlie sloped from the room and went in search of his wife. Unfortunately, he met Joan coming the other way, a perfect storm all over her face.

'I knew this would happen,' she said. 'Trevor!'

Obedient as ever, Trevor popped his head round the door.

'Get your so-called mate out of my house, right now.'

There was no contest; he had to go. Trevor had never won an argument with Joan. Since Charlie caused the dispute, he didn't stand a chance. He headed for the door.

'Get him out, Trevor,' Joan called from her kitchen. 'I'm about to serve the tea.'

'Careful your face doesn't sour the milk, Joan love.'

'Trevor, are you going to let him speak to me like that?'

Trevor opened the door, his eyes raised to the heavens, and Charlie stepped outside.

'Thanks, Charlie, I'll be sleeping in the spare room tonight.'

'Count your blessings, mate.'

The door closed, yet another door.

He sloshed along the rain-soaked avenue. His left shoe was taking on water, his jeans and polo shirt were soaked through, and the bandage on his hand was unravelling. It was not wise to drive after so much beer, but the truth was he'd forgotten all about the car when Trevor threw him out. Jill's flat was more than two miles away across town, the only place he wanted to be right now. Was he falling in love with her? And would she be pleased about that?

Chapter thirty-eight

'What do *you* want?'

'Hello, Charlie, how are you, would be nice.'

She glared at him through heavy eyes, the chain still on the door. He guessed she was feeling vulnerable after Friday night.

'I suppose you'd better come in; you're soaking wet. Where have you been?'

'Out for a walk.'

He dripped into the living room. She looked him up and down, while he stood like a schoolboy, hands and bandage dangling by his side, a vacant 'don't know what I'm doing' expression on his face. He sensed she wasn't overjoyed to see him.

'I assume from the state of you,' she said, stepping closer, 'and by the smell of drink, that you're in more trouble?'

'I didn't start it. Palmer got up my nose, then Barbara took his side, and Joan told Trevor to throw me out.'

'Charlie, I really don't want to hear this again. Not today. I'm sick and tired of Palmer and your problems. I have my own life to worry about. Besides, you never take my advice. You just stomp off and do the first thing that comes into your head.'

Now it was obvious. She wasn't too happy about him calling. She wore that peeved expression he'd been used to seeing at the office until recently when their friendship had blossomed. He felt lost, couldn't summon a word, never mind the right words for the moment. In slow rewind, he turned and dripped back to the door. He opened it and stepped outside. The rain was heavier than before, but he looked up at the grey sky and let the water peck at his face.

She called from the living room.

'Charlie, come back inside and stop being silly. I didn't mean to sound cross. I'm just tired. I didn't get much sleep on Friday night, remember?'

He remained on her doorstep catching the rain like a potted plant. He couldn't move. She had to pull him back indoors.

'I don't want to be alone anymore,' he said.

'Let's get those wet clothes off you first and then we can talk.'

* * *

He awoke to fluffy pillows and a teddy bear staring at him from across the bed. Jill's bed? His eyes widened. Yes, it was Jill's bed. He couldn't help the smirk spreading across his face. He didn't dare move in case he touched her. Couldn't bare it for long, though. He had to look, he had to reach for her, cuddle her, smother her with kisses, caress her, light her fire, tune her motor, stoke her boiler... He sat up, and the fantasy scarpered. Gone like every other dream he'd ever cherished. When finally he dragged himself from the bed and wandered into the living room, he found a note on the coffee table.

> *Get a move on or you'll be late for work
> again. And take that stupid smirk off your
> face; we didn't sleep in the same bed.
> Love, Jill.*

'Love, Jill' sent a nice warm sensation floating round his head. It collided with all the hair-brained ideas and warped emotions charging about with no purpose. That was his

life, totally, bang up to date. No particular place to go and
no plans on how to get there. 'Love, Jill,' was the most
promising start to a day he was ever likely to get.

He dressed, made some coffee and sat in the quiet of
her living room, talking to himself, trying hard to think in
a straight line.

'If she is serious, I suppose I could put all this crap
behind me? That means losing Barbara. But do I love
her? Hell's bells, I don't know. I want to sleep with her; I
know that much. Jill, I mean. I want to sleep with Jill. I
want to sleep with Barbara, too. I want to cause Palmer
some permanent damage, just for the hell of it. I want
him to be lumbered with someone like Joan for the rest
of his days. Joan having Palmer's love child and then
Trevor beating him senseless. Yeah, that would be great.
Just one day without thinking of anyone. Even better.'

* * *

Hardly a conscious decision to leave her flat but by
eleven he'd made it to the office. Between waking in Jill's
bed and settling down to a computer screen, he'd
somehow cleared his mind of all but one intention. For
the next five hours he typed, one-handed, scribbled little
notes, and several times disappeared from the office only
to dash back within the hour. He tapped furiously at the
keyboard and spoke to no one, not even Jill. At ten to
four he pushed his chair back from the desk and cupped
his good hand behind his head.

Madness or genius, he couldn't care less. Trevor
sauntered into the office, his timing absolutely spot on.
He spoke to Carol, but Charlie seized his chance.

'Hah!' he said.

Trevor glanced in his direction.

'Is that a happy sound I hear from Charlie?'

'Just finished my story, that's all.'

'Must be a good one.'

'I think so.'

When Trevor came over to have a look, Charlie clicked the mouse. The screen blinked to reveal a headline.

BIG PLANS FOR BALLYMENACE

'Are you going to show me,' said Trevor, 'or do I have to buy a copy of my own newspaper?'

Charlie scrolled down to let him read the text.

'That's more like it,' said Trevor, scanning a story that described the plans for Ballymenace Cricket Club's proposed new pavilion. Included were interviews with the club president, captain of the firsts, and Archie Mildew, head groundsman of thirty years standing.

'Great,' Trevor said, 'but I wouldn't get too carried away on a romantic description of the place. It's only a sports ground.'

'It's passion for the game,' said Charlie. 'Passion and ninety-eight years of tradition. Just think of all the fascinating people who have graced that turf over the years. It's a piece of history.'

'Jeez, Charlie, who's tweaked your G-spot? It's fine but keep it coming. One swallow doesn't make a newspaper.'

Trevor left the room, and Charlie hit the save icon on his screen.

'Hah!'

Chapter thirty-nine

'What the fuck is this?'

Trevor was already hoarse. Or somebody had him by the balls, twisting hard to get the highest notes. A bit more practice and he could do *Stayin' Alive* by the Bee Gees at a karaoke. So Charlie thought, standing at the open door of the editor's office. Purple-faced, Trevor stamped his feet, thumped his desk and waved the latest edition of *The Explorer* in the blue air.

'You're a sneaky bastard, Geddis.'

Trevor's wailing sent shock waves throughout the building, but Charlie had spent the past two days rehearsing his calm demeanour. He was the picture of self-control.

'I had to do it, Trevor. I can't let Palmer get away with it. The public has a right to know.'

'Bull – bloody – shit! The public isn't the least bit interested. They only care if it's taking pennies from their pockets. It's all about you, Charlie. You brought your personal troubles to bear on this paper. Didn't you realise what could happen? I've had the mayor, Councillor Farrington, the rest of the council planning committee, Palmer and his brief all yelling down the phone. They're going to sue the arse off me and this paper.'

Trevor stared at the story that metaphorically speaking was the hand twisting his balls. The headline 'BIG PLANS FOR BALLYMENACE' sat above three columns of text, none of it referring to Ballymenace Cricket Club. Instead there was an exposé on the building of a new town, a town that would 'engulf, digest and render extinct' the ancient Borough of Ballymenace.

Realising this news alone would not inflame the jowls of the Ballymenace public, Charlie had slighted Malcolm Palmer and every elected official in the Borough. He hinted at Palmer's private affairs and drew attention to planning applications, past and present, with little pointers given to councillors' penchant for new conservatories, Caribbean cruises and timeshares in Spain. He was deliberately vague, referring to Sheila, unnamed, as the hired help and the 'mystery' woman who'd had him beaten up. If challenged he had little proof, but the outline would allow any randomer on the street to colour in the pictures for themselves.

'You're sacked, Charlie. You've gone too far this time.'

'You don't mean it, Trevor,' said Charlie.

A firm hand was now yanking his balls. He hadn't seen this one coming. Trevor was his mate, for goodness sake. A mate first, and then a boss. Mates don't sack mates.

'You're just a bit angry,' he said.

Trevor turned a deeper shade of purple, his eyes about to pop their sockets.

'I mean every bloody word. By tonight the rest of us could be joining you. You keep forgetting that Mr Palmer has big connections. I'll call him Mr for practice, because this afternoon I've got to ass-lick on a cosmic scale when he comes to see me. Funny you didn't mention anything in your story about Mr Palmer and one of his best friends, Jack Kelly. You know who Jack Kelly is, don't you, Charlie?'

Charlie was overcome with exhilaration, like a racing driver who's braked too late for the hairpin and is about to trash a million quid's worth of car into a crash barrier.

'He owns half a dozen rural papers, including *The Explorer*,' said Trevor. 'By this afternoon I could be looking for a job in the classifieds, instead of writing them. So clear your desk, Charlie, and get your sad ass out of here.'

'Jack Kelly, eh? Palmer does have his fingers in a lot of pies.'

He pondered this new information. Trevor stood by the window, watching the girl across the street.

'Just clear off, Charlie. I'm not interested in your squabbles with Palmer.'

Despite the shouting, it was the phrase and its tone that finally convinced him that Trevor was serious. He *had* gone too far this time. His job as a journalist was the only weapon he had to fight Palmer, and now it was gone.

'One thing you might like to know, Trevor. It might come in useful.'

'What?'

'The girl you're gawking at, her name is Shirley. She's a real honey.'

'So what?'

'Might be worth a try if you ever get tired of Joan.'

It seemed to Charlie that Trevor's deep sigh was one of agreement, or a forlorn hope. He backed from the room leaving his former boss to a wistful dream. Might be just the thing to cool his temper and change his mind.

'Yep, Shirley Wallace is a real looker,' he called from the stairs. 'It's a pity though.'

'What is?'

'Her boyfriend.'

'Boyfriend?' Trevor sounded crestfallen.

'Boner McCluskey. Got out of prison last month. Used to play in the front row for Ballymenace Rugby Club? Caught some poor bloke chatting up Shirley, squeezed his privates through a garlic press. Pity about that, Trevor, if it hadn't been for Boner you might have had a chance with young Shirley. See ya, mate.'

* * *

Jill sobbed. Carol looked bewildered as Charlie tipped the contents of a drawer onto his desk: a couple of notebooks; last Thursday's chicken-tikka sandwich – unopened, blue and furry; a shrivelled mandarin orange; three pencils – leads broken; a tie – lime green with coffee stain; a half-eaten Rich Tea; a five-pack of Mates (ribbed) – unopened, and a letter from Barbara's solicitor – unopened. He held the bin to the edge of the desk, swept it all away and started on the next drawer. News clippings, mostly regarding Palmer. He stuffed them in a Tesco's bag and set them to one side.

Third and final drawer: his literary epic, dog-eared pages in no certain order. A thrilling account of a top reporter's struggle to flee a country in the grip of a military dictatorship. He couldn't even manage to flee Ballymenace. Another Tesco's bag filled and he was ready to go.

He looked at Carol who glanced away and pretended not to notice. Jill dabbed her eyes with a tissue. He would miss her; they were good together these past few weeks.

'Will you be all right?' she asked.

He shrugged.

'Come over tonight, have dinner with me?' she said, blinking away more tears.

'Excuse me?' said a squeaky voice. 'Can you tell me where I might find Mr Geddis?'

Feeling anything but polite, Charlie spun round to put a face to the voice.

'You're looking at him.'

His mouth dropped open. It was the ketchup bomber, as he had labelled her after the disrupted meeting about the old mill. He sensed she wasn't impressed. Her pale cheeks, penny glasses, small mouth and tight lips: nothing flinched. He suspected that underneath the cold exterior lurked a little tiger.

'My name is Jemima Pinkerton. I wonder if I might have a word? In private,' she said, glancing around the office.

'Sure thing, love. I've all the time in the world, now that I no longer work here.'

'Oh, I see.' She sounded disappointed.

'You're that girl, aren't you?' said Jill, pointing a finger. 'The one at the meeting. You were throwing bombs at the speakers.'

'We read your article, Mr Geddis,' she said, ignoring Jill's accusing finger.

'Who's we?'

'I'll explain over coffee; there's a shop on the corner.'

'Could do with a few stiff ones right now,' he mumbled.

'Pardon?'

'Lead on, I'm all ears.'

He gathered the remnants of his journalistic career, shrugged at Jill, and followed the girl out of the office.

Chapter forty

She made a beeline for a table in a corner of McBride's Coffee Shop. It was an austere place with dark-wood tables, chairs and panelled walls. Three wooden-faced, middle-aged ladies tended to the eight or so customers. It was another of Ballymenace's traditional establishments, steadfastly resisting entry to the twenty-first century.

The instant they sat, the little tiger sprang forth from her guise as the phantom ketchup bomber.

'You stupid man,' she said in a harsh whisper. Her eyes looked much bigger now behind the glasses, certainly keener. The tiny mouth suddenly took the form of a man-eating shark, or tiger. 'Two and a half years we've been watching him, TWO AND A HALF YEARS.'

'Easy on, love. What are you talking about? Two and a half years for what?' She may have been pint-sized but he was getting frightened.

'Then you come along with your cheap, irresponsible, inaccurate story and ruin everything.'

'Whaddya mean inaccurate?'

Jemima ordered two cappuccinos and one slice of lemon torte with fresh cream. She waited for the waitress to leave and then still in a whisper and leaning over the table, she continued. Charlie sat forward to catch what she said.

'We in CAKE are alarmed, disgusted and angry that you could be so foolish. Have you any idea of the trouble you've caused?'

'Cake?'

'Shush! Please, keep your voice down. Walls have ears, you know?'

Her eyes flitted round the shop. Charlie felt obliged to follow suit, but he didn't know what to look for: the Third Man, the CIA, Gestapo, or Social Services? He was in no mood for theatrics. Jemima Pinkerton seemed astonished that he'd never heard of CAKE.

'Citizens Against Killing the Environment,' she whispered.

'Oh, right,' he said, suppressing a smirk.

'It is no laughing matter, Mr Geddis.'

'What does CAKE want with me?'

'We need your assurance there will be no further vague stories and futile allegations made against Malcolm Palmer.'

'Wait a minute, whose side are you on?'

'We're out to get Palmer all right. We just don't need overanxious reporters stirring things up before we have the chance to strike. We want to rid society of bloodsuckers like him. The people have a right to know what his plans mean for the countryside and how we all suffer for the sake of his profits. But not yet. Not until we are ready. Developers are spoiling the land with ugly houses, built for profit not beauty. He will be stopped.'

Her face glowed, a woman passionate for her cause.

'That's all very well,' said Charlie, 'but chucking a drop of Heinz sauce over a few of his gofers won't stop a man like Palmer.'

The refreshments arrived. Charlie sipped foam from a cup, while Jemima set about the lemon torte. She didn't speak until she'd finished.

'Mr Geddis.'

He was getting used to this 'Mr Geddis' business; he'd never been called Mr so many times in one day.

'You underestimate the strength of our organisation.'

'Well yes, you see, I've never heard of you. Seems like a one-man show, or a one-woman show.'

'Mr Geddis, thanks to your story we have had to change our plans. Plans that have taken two and a half years to put in place. As we speak dozens of my comrades are working to repair the damage you've caused.'

'Damage? I've done this town a favour telling them about Palmer. What exactly is wrong with my story?'

She pulled the latest edition of *The Explorer* from her satchel.

'Listen to this,' she said, and quoted from his story. 'Palmer Developments intends to build some fifteen hundred homes on the land that lies between Ballymenace and the town bypass. Not true. The figure is three and a half thousand homes.'

'So, the numbers are a little out. People will get the idea.'

She continued to read.

'Palmer Developments have acquired the land necessary to complete the project, but it appears the assistance of local councillors is required, in order for building to proceed. Maybe Palmer Conservatories or Palmer Timeshare can persuade the local planning committee that Palmerstown will be of benefit to the Borough. Have you any idea what you're saying, Mr Geddis?'

'Don't tell me that CAKE doesn't know Malcolm bribes councillors to get his plans approved?'

Now she was laughing at him. He hadn't thought her capable of laughter.

'Have I said something funny?'

'Mr Geddis, is that it? Is that the sum total of your knowledge of Malcolm Palmer?'

'No. He's also trying to buy my family home so he can build a road through it and, just for your information, he's shagging my wife. I suppose you're going to tell me I've got that wrong too?'

'Mr Geddis, there is no need to be crude. It appears you lack considerable information regarding our friend.'

'But I've exposed him as a crook!'

Jemima shook her head in frustration, or disgust at his ignorance, or both.

'You're missing the point,' she said.

Charlie was blank.

'Why do you think we have been watching Palmer for so long?' she said. 'Why do you think we are prepared to let him have his way a little with this Palmerstown project? If we really had him and his cohorts in the bag, don't you think we'd have acted by now?'

'Well yes, I suppose you want to get everyone from bottom to top?'

'Correct. And that is why your story was so unhelpful. It's put Malcolm Palmer and his partners on their guard.'

'Then how do you intend to get him?'

She glanced about the shop. Everyone seemed occupied with cups of foam. She slipped a large piece of paper from her satchel, unfolded it and spread it over the table. His eyes widened in surprise and, he had to admit, admiration. Here lay a copy of the plans for Palmerstown. He'd glimpsed the same in Palmer's office.

'How did you get this?'

'We have our contacts, Mr Geddis. See here?' she said, placing her forefinger near the centre of the chart. 'This forest-'

'Ballymenace Glen, yes I know it well,' he said eagerly. 'And this is my house, and this is where the road will go through.'

'Yes, yes, we'll discuss that later. Look at the glen for now.'

Her finger traced slowly round the edge of the entire forest, from the narrow section above Herbie's farm to the widest point with the pond and the public right of way alongside.

'These trees,' she continued. 'Thousands of them, countless oak, sycamore, beech, lime, birch and chestnut. Beautiful. Some are hundreds of years old. The whole forest, the valley, it's virtually unchanged since Norman times.'

He wanted to tell her that Palmer had murdered someone at the very spot where her finger now rested, but he didn't think she would buy the disappearing corpse thing, not from a journalist. He wished she'd hurry up and get to the point.

'That's council-owned land,' he said.

'It is land for which the council is responsible. I wouldn't go so far as to say the council owns it. The forest belongs to the people, to nature itself. The golf club has no right to it and neither do the farmers in the area. No one has the right to interfere with it. There is a footpath, for public use, that is all. This is the place that needs protecting from Palmer. He may find, however, that this wonderful forest will be his downfall.'

'He's bought nearly all of the surrounding land,' said Charlie, 'Most of the farms and even the golf club. Won't be long till he gets his hands on the glen.'

'Here, Mr Geddis, is where we stop him dead in his tracks.'

'I don't see how. What's to stop him going ahead with the clearance, building his houses and then taking on the planning laws?'

'As far as the farmland is concerned he probably can do exactly that, but there's a bigger hurdle to clear before he gets his hands on Ballymenace Glen.'

'You mean Herbie Smyth's farm? I happen to know that he has refused to sell.'

Charlie was chuffed he'd been able to add something to Jemima's bank of knowledge. She, however, looked thoroughly disgusted and began folding the map.

'It is quite clear, Mr Geddis, you still have not grasped the fundamentals of our campaign. Quite frankly, I'm wasting my time here. Please do not spoil it for us by writing any more tittle-tattle on the subject.'

She packed the papers in her satchel and rose to leave. Charlie tugged her sleeve.

'I'm sorry, did I say something wrong? Why isn't Herbie Smyth the stumbling block for Palmer?'

Either she'd taken pity on a severe case of brain fade, a bruised face and bandaged hand, or she still had a use for him. Whatever the reason, she resumed her seat and again scanned the room.

'The building of Palmerstown does not hinge upon the acquisition of Herbie Smyth's farm. Palmer can simply build around it. One day perhaps, when Mr Smyth finds himself surrounded by suburbia, he will decide to sell up. Palmer can wait.'

'Then what *is* the stumbling block?'

'The *trees*, Mr Geddis, the *trees*.'

'The trees?'

'He can't lay a finger on them, not without getting the preservation order revoked.'

'Preservation order?'

That look of disgust again.

'Tree preservation order, Mr Geddis. Surely you know about that?'

Blank face.

'Perhaps not,' she sighed. 'Take it from me that Malcolm Palmer cannot remove one tree from Ballymenace Glen without having the preservation order revoked.'

'And how does he do that?'

'He needs the Minister for the Environment to revoke the order and the local council to relinquish the public right of way that runs through the glen. Councillor Farrington has to buy off a majority of the planning committee to make sure the plans go through without a fuss. And someone has to sweet-talk the minister.'

'Why doesn't Palmer build around the glen?' Charlie thought he'd asked another dumb question, but by now Jemima seemed used to it.

'He needs the glen more than any area in the entire project. The river valley provides him with convenient channels for sewage removal. It is also the obvious place for the main road system to pass through from Ballymenace, over the hills, to the bypass. The road that will destroy your family home.'

'So we just wait until the minister and the council make their move?'

'Too late for that, thanks to your story. As soon as *The Explorer* hit the streets this morning you can bet Palmer was on to his friends, trying to hurry things along. The Minister for the Environment is currently on holiday in the Caribbean, we believe at Palmer's expense. It's only a matter of time before he revokes the preservation order. We've had to act quickly. By midnight tonight, two hundred people will be camped in the glen. By tomorrow morning it will be secured, and soon the world will know that CAKE exists to fight tyranny and corruption. Malcolm Palmer will regret setting foot on this beautiful earth. Are you with us, Mr Geddis?'

'What can I do?'

'You're a reporter.'

'An out-of-work reporter.'

'Help us, Mr Geddis. Clearly you have a great concern for what Palmer is doing to this land. Given the correct information you can help us tell the world.'

'Easy on, love, I'm no freedom fighter. I just want my wife back.'

'Together we can be rid of Palmer forever.'

'Whatever you say.'

He didn't think it wise to argue; he couldn't afford another enemy. If this lot were about to destroy Palmer, fair enough, it would save him the trouble.

'I must go now,' she said. 'There is much to be done. Take heart, Mr Geddis. Despite your shortcomings, which are many, you have helped set the wheels in motion.'

Another wary glance about the room and she rose to leave. Charlie wasn't sure about going with her or, in true espionage style, allow her to slip out quietly. In the end he didn't have a chance to move. As Jemima closed the door behind her the waitress set the bill on the table.

'Very bloody clever,' he mumbled.

'I beg your pardon?' said the waitress.

'Nothing.' He handed her five pounds. 'Keep the change, love.' She rolled her eyes in disgust, two pence richer.

Chapter forty-one

She wore a cheery smile and a long purple dress with a low front and a deep cut at the back, held together by a tempting string, a lot less complicated than her bustier. A table of china and crystal was set for dinner. She'd gone to a lot of trouble.

'I just want you to feel valued,' she said, placing her hand on his arm. 'I care about what happens to you.'

'Pity I'm not worth it.'

'Oh, Charlie, you mustn't think like that. I believe in you. You've just had a bad press, as they say.' She gave his arm a little squeeze. He made to kiss her, more of a snog really, and for a moment he succeeded, but in a flash she pulled away. 'Any more of that and dinner will be ruined.'

He knew she was right to cool it, but tonight insatiable lust was up there holding sway over respect and gratitude. As common sense would have it he poured the wine, while she served the dinner, fillet steaks and black pepper sauce. Lately, the only time he seemed to eat a decent meal was in Jill's company. His jowls tingled. He'd been here before and couldn't help wondering about dessert.

'I hope you like it.'

'It's lovely,' he said with a mouth full. She smiled and began to eat.

He watched her in the candlelight, her prim face with the hint of a smile, a look of comfort, of being at ease. Their eyes met briefly; she looked embarrassed, her cheeks glowing in the dim light. He was useless at tender moments, but he felt a change within, and, for once, it wasn't crude. Something would be different after tonight, but he didn't know what that something would be. He continued to watch her, while eating slowly, forgetting he still had the ability to speak.

'You've gone quiet.'

'Enjoying my food and the company.'

'In return for dinner,' she said, 'you can tell me how things went with the ketchup bomber.'

'She's loopy. Sees herself as some kind of environmental revolutionary, going to save the world by chucking sauce at anyone who gets in her way.' He told her about CAKE and their two and half years of stalking Palmer. 'It seems they have hundreds of members all ready to put the boot into old Malcolm. They're going to squat in Ballymenace Glen to stop him cutting down the trees. Apparently, their main line of business is tree protection.'

'Good for them.'

'Can you picture it? Dozens of Jemima Pinkerton clones lying in the road, with a JCB about to blitz its way through. What are they going to do when Palmer sends in his heavies? Swat them with handbags? At most they'll last for a few days. It'll fizzle out by the weekend, and Palmer will have free publicity for his new town. Why can't people see through him?'

'Calm down, Charlie. Have another drink.' She refilled his glass with red wine. 'Here's something that'll make you feel better,' she said. 'Trevor went home at lunchtime with a migraine, brought on by stress, he claimed.'

'The suffering will do him good.'

'Glad to see you're not bitter.'

After dinner they got drunk, very drunk. He could remember taking the last of five bottles from her wine rack in the kitchen. He also remembered drinking it and rolling about on the floor in hysterics at Jill, who collapsed in a fit of giggles at something he did with a profiterole. The last drops of Oxford Landing dribbled over them; they removed their clothes and somehow touched each other in all the right places. He had faint recollections, although he may have been reliving another hallucination, of some rather speedy sex taking place, when they kissed each other goodnight. He was fairly certain Jill closed her bedroom door behind her, leaving him on the sofa nursing an empty bottle.

'Charlie, wake up! It's on the news.'

His brain flickered, trying to open for business. His eyes didn't. Somebody was yelling, and he was dreaming of toast and percolating coffee. He cuddled the bottle and turned on his side. Somebody stabbed him in the neck. His eyes opened. She, whoever *she* might be, was flitting about the room in a bit of a haze. Maybe she had stabbed him? He gripped the bottle tighter as the figure approached.

'Quickly, Charlie. Listen to this,' the body said. He jumped up, arms flailing ready to deal with his attacker, who smelt of coffee and toast. 'It's been on the local news all morning,' she said.

'What has?' He dropped the bottle and rubbed his face. There was Jill, smirking at him. He was naked again; she didn't seem bothered.

'Those people you were talking about. CAKE, they've taken over Ballymenace Glen. Hundreds of them. Hurry up; drink this.' She handed him a mug of coffee. 'You need to get down there.'

'Me? Why?'

'You started it, Charlie. You have to be there for the finish.'

He tried a few sips of coffee, enough to shake him down a little.

'I'm not getting involved in all that protest shit.'

'Yes you are.' She turned up the sound on the television.

'...The protesters allege the development will mean the destruction of thousands of trees in Ballymenace Glen,' the newsreader said. 'They have also expressed concern over the proposed closure of the public right of way through the park and the intention to culvert the Ballymenace River. In a lengthy statement the protesters, known as Citizens Against Killing the Environment, or CAKE, have drawn attention to the activities of Palmer Developments and its relationship with members of the local council and the Minister for the Environment, Mr John Fielding. Most of these allegations were published recently by a local newspaper, *The Ballymenace Explorer*. It seems the protesters have acted on this information. A spokesperson for Palmer Developments refused to confirm that preliminary site clearance work was due to commence on Monday. This protest now makes that seem unlikely...'

'You see; it's working,' said Jill. 'People *are* taking notice. Now you can stop him, and it won't just be your fight. Hurry up and get dressed.'

He had little choice but to do as he was told.

Chapter forty-two

When Jill and Charlie reached the side road that led to the entrance of Ballymenace Glen, several police officers blocked their path. Charlie presented his press card to a constable, who was doing a fine job of guarding a metal barrier.

'*Ballymenace Explorer*,' he said. The policeman had a cursory look at the plastic card.

'I can let you through here,' he said, 'but you won't get beyond the entrance gate to the glen.'

The policeman dragged the barrier from the centre of the road allowing them to drive through. Half a mile further on, they encountered a huge gathering of police, civilians and their vehicles. Charlie parked the car behind a BBC van, and they walked the two hundred yards to the entrance of the glen.

Television cameras were already perched on a gantry, and news reporters delivered spiels about environmental protesters seizing land from under the noses of developers. A banner, with red lettering on a white background, hung across the lane leading into the woods.

'LAND NOT FOR SALE', it read.

Several placards had been nailed to the entrance gate: 'NO ENTRY – TREE LOVERS ONLY'. Another one read, 'LAND ABUSERS SOD OFF!'

They headed for the lane into the forest, but a burly policeman, who had no metal barrier to look after, caught Charlie by the arm.

'Ah no you don't, sir,' he said. 'Can't let you do that, I'm afraid.'

'We're press,' Charlie replied, still held firmly by the policeman.

'For your own safety I can't let you into the glen. We're not sure how peaceful this protest is going to be. Stand over there with the rest of the media people, and we'll keep you posted as best we can.'

He let go of Charlie's arm in a way that propelled him towards the other reporters. Jill had already obeyed the policeman's order and was there to welcome him.

'I'm not hanging round all day with these clowns,' he said.

'Isn't it exciting?' said Jill. 'All these cameras in Ballymenace and all because of you, Charlie.'

'Thanks for reminding me. Don't forget, you played your part too. When they start dishing out blame for causing this disruption, just remember what you got up to in Palmer's office. Come on, I have an idea.'

She looked doubtful, so he took her by the hand and led her along the road away from the crowd. A hundred yards on they rounded a bend, and he swung open a gate into a lane enclosed on both sides by a hedgerow of hawthorn. Now, a field away from the glen, they trekked uphill towards Herbie Smyth's farm. Gaining height, they could see most of the lower glen and the golf course beyond. There was no sign of any protesters. Veering downhill into the valley that held the river and the precious trees, they saw the huddle of farm buildings ahead.

Charlie still had a hold of Jill's hand, scarcely giving her time to put one foot in front of the other. She was dressed for work: high heels, sheer tights and clinging skirt, not the most practical for marching in the highlands.

'Slow down, please. I can't walk fast in these heels. And you still haven't told me where we are going?'

'To see if Herbie knows what's happening.'

He released his grip and bounded on a few paces, while Jill tiptoed through a muddy patch.

'Halt!'

Jill yelped as a figure jumped out of the hedge. She was beside Charlie in a flash, clutching his arm.

A grubby youth stood before them in khaki jeans, shirt, and a pair of Moses sandals. Unkempt hair and wielding a long wooden staff, he didn't look friendly. He didn't speak but a voice came from within the bushes.

'Who are you?' the voice said.

'Who are you?' Charlie replied.

'I asked first,' said the voice, sounding put out at having to debate the point.

'We come in peace,' said Jill.

'And just where do you think we are?' said Charlie, 'Up the Amazon?'

Jill shrugged.

The silent youth stared them up and down and from one to the other, looking less intelligent than a baboon picking fleas from its belly.

'Did Palmer send you?' said the voice.

'No. Palmer didn't send me,' replied Charlie.

'Are you peelers?'

'No, I'm a reporter. Now show your face before Little John here fancies his chances.'

After some rustling in the bushes a figure appeared on the bank overlooking the path. Peering down at them he, too, held a wooden staff but in a way that showed authority, at least, over the likes of his vacant companion. He held the pose for a time then picked his way down the grassy slope and resumed his stance before them.

'Will Scarlet, I presume?' said Charlie. He was wholly unimpressed by the wimpish figure standing proud, with a full quota of self-belief. 'I'm Robin Hood and this is Maid Marion.'

'Ha ha, very funny,' he said in a tone matching his dismal appearance.

He'd probably heard all the smart comments before. Straggly hair and beard – although better kept than his friend – he, also, wore khaki jeans, a combat shirt and Moses sandals. Charlie wondered if this CAKE lot were some kind of religious cult, their ultimate plan to build a commune in Ballymenace Glen, maybe sacrifice a few virgins, or to roast Palmer in a ritual burning. Or maybe they were extras in *Game of Thrones*. In any case, he wasn't prepared to stand all day while this vagrant looked them up and down with no idea what to do next.

'Take... me... to... your... leader,' said Charlie.

'Only doing what I'm told, you know. No need for the sarcasm. It's not like I get paid...'

Looking peeved, and continuing to bemoan his lot, the eco-warrior turned around and led them across a field and down a winding trail into the woods. The youth stayed behind, no doubt awaiting the next trespasser.

Soon the trail joined the main footpath that ran beside the river through the glen. Charlie's attention was drawn to a group of people, high in the trees, calling out to each other. He saw ropes and ladders, and bodies dangling from branches. He felt as though they were being led to the secret hideout of a notorious outlaw. They might even have to wear blindfolds as they got closer to the den. Maybe Robin Hood in Sherwood Forest wasn't so far off the mark.

Jill had come over all petrified and still had a firm grip of Charlie's arm. They came into a familiar clearing, the place where he'd fallen from the bridge, where all his recent troubles had begun. They were now adjacent to Herbie's eleven-acre field, and the number of people and level of activity was greatly increased. Orders were shouted, hammers hammered, and Fat Boy Slim boomed from a sound rig. There were tents and campfires, crates and boxes, and people working like beavers. Amidst it all stood Jemima Pinkerton, clipboard in hand, Moses sandals on feet, counting a row of cardboard boxes laid out on the path.

'Mr Geddis,' she called, 'I'm so glad you could make it.'

'How's it going, love?'

As soon as Will Scarlet realised they knew Jemima he left them and headed back the way he'd come.

'And what do you think of our little protest?' she asked proudly.

'Don't know yet.' His eyes ran down the khaki jeans and Moses sandals. 'Interesting uniform. Are you sure this isn't a weirdo cult setting up shop?'

'We have our ways, Mr Geddis. As I said yesterday, do not underestimate us. Mr Palmer will rue the day he ignored our pleas to save this forest.'

Suddenly from the far side of the woods he heard people cheering and horns blaring. They hurried down to the pond, over the bridge and through the trees. The narrow trail joined a laneway that served as a minor exit road from Ballymenace Golf Club. About thirty protesters, in the combat gear and Moses sandals of the CAKE organisation, were face to bonnet with the Aston Martin of Malcolm Palmer. The demure Michelle Eastman, marketing and PR executive of Palmer Developments, looked fraught behind the wheel. Palmer was beside her, seemingly ice-cool amid threats of disembowelling.

'Destroyer! Destroyer!' the crowd chanted as one of them stuck a leaflet under the wiper blade of the car.

Michelle tried edging forward, but the people were not for moving. Two warriors sat down on the lane, and immediately the entire gathering followed suit. Jemima had a devilish smirk on her pale face. Charlie saw her now in yet a different guise: calm, controlled and powerful. He wondered if Michelle had recognised the tiny woman who had doused her in tomato ketchup.

'Destroyer!'

'Vandal!'

'Abuser!'

Palmer lowered his window and dared to pop his head out.

'OK,' he called, quite good-naturedly, Charlie thought. 'You've had your fun. Now please allow us to pass.'

The crowd were not impressed.

'This is not *fun*,' said a long-haired waif of a girl, who had approached the window of the car. 'We are exercising our legitimate right to protest against your intended action. Your development will bring to an end thousands of years of natural growth in this forest.' The crowd cheered and the girl continued, waving her arms like a fairy casting a spell. 'You must not be allowed to rob this forest of its beauty.'

'Yes, dear. That's all very well. But this is progress, times are changing; people want houses, not a clump of old trees. Besides, I have a business to run. We will consider your opposition to this project. Now kindly move off the lane and allow us to pass.'

'Piss off, you old fart,' said the girl.

Charlie joined in the laughter until Palmer spotted him.

'Well if it isn't Charlie Geddis. I might have known you were behind this.'

'Nothing to do with me,' said Charlie. 'Voice of the people, old chap.'

Palmer's face reddened. At last, Charlie had touched a nerve.

'You want to fight, Charlie? You've picked the wrong man. I've been too patient with you. Barbara was right, you *are* good for nothing.' He called out to the others. 'I hope you're not relying on this man to lead you? I have it on good authority that he is the most unreliable soul ever to befall this town. His wife said so, and she should know. Right, Charlie?'

The words stung. Did Barbara really believe that? He could feel every head, every pair of eyes awaiting his response.

'Let them go,' he said. Jemima nodded at the crowd, and one-by-one they made way. Wheels spun on the gravel, and the car roared off. Charlie headed back to the sanctuary of the trees.

'Don't let him get to you,' said Jill, trying to keep up in her heels. 'Not when so many people are fighting your corner. Palmer is a pompous man, and he'll get his comeuppance.'

'This lot are only playing games,' said Charlie. 'He's just letting them have their fun. When he's good and ready he'll move in and crush the lot.'

Jill gave him a hug; it was just what he needed.

'Come on, let's get out of here,' he said.

'No. You can't leave,' said Jemima, catching up. 'Please stay, Mr Geddis. You're a journalist; tell the world our side of the story.'

'It's great that you're taking on Palmer, but you won't win. I've already lost. I've no wife. No job. I haven't even signed on the dole so there won't be a cheque in the post that I can use to feed the drinking habit I'm about to resume.'

'Then you have no reason to go and every reason to stay,' she said.

Strong words. Jill was smiling, and even Jemima appeared human.

'Besides,' she said, 'you might have some difficulty leaving now. The lower glen is barricaded.'

'That's just great,' said Charlie.

Chapter forty-three

In the calm of evening, the protesters relaxed after a hard day's work. About forty of them were dotted around the woods, some guarding the gates to the glen and some hiding in the trees keeping watch. That left about two hundred to enjoy the evening camped by the river.

Jill and Charlie sat on fold-up chairs soaking up the last of the warm sun, digesting their dinner of burgers and chips. A fleet of mobile caterers had parked in Herbie's field adjacent to the glen. Someone provided a television, running off a car battery, and several of the troop gathered round it to see if they had made the national news.

CAKE was a strange bunch, not too many locally bred, but mostly Irish, English and Scots, seemingly happy to be there. Charlie supposed their love of trees transcended national boundaries.

Considering her immediate future had been decided for her, Jill seemed relaxed. Sipping from a can of Foster's, she looked out of place in her business suit. Charlie couldn't help feeling responsible for her and hoped that she viewed the situation as the big adventure she'd longed for.

Laughter and cheering broke the peace and quiet, as a band of people emerged from the dimness of the woods. Jemima led the way giggling on the arm of a tall, dark and smiling man. He looked about forty, swarthy with stubble. Neat denim jeans and shirt, broad shoulders, strong walking shoes rather than sandals, he looked a cross between James Bond and Indiana Jones. Jemima seemed taken by him, as were several other girls and one or two guys. They laughed and giggled at his every word.

'Oh, Charlie,' Jemima said in chirpy spirit. It was the first time she'd dropped the Mr Geddis and called him by his first name. He wasn't sure if that was a good sign. 'There's someone I'd like you to meet,' she said.

Charlie remained seated as the man towered over him. When he got to his feet, the man still towered over him.

'Charlie,' said Jemima, looking as though she were about to curtsey. 'This is Stuff, our wonderful leader.'

'Stuff?' Charlie doubted his hearing.

'Good evening, Charlie,' said the man in a sanguine voice, his hand outstretched.

'Hi, there,' Charlie replied – no reference to his height intended.

Jill coughed, deliberately so. Jemima ignored her, but Charlie took the hint.

'This is my colleague, Jill Barker.'

'How do you do, Jill? Delighted you could join our little troop.'

Taking her hand, he bowed slightly. Their eyes locked. She made no effort to pull away. For a second, all movement was frozen as if no one else were present. It was *Brief Encounter, Notting Hill, Sleepless in Seattle,* all of the above.

'Stuff is a vet,' said Jemima, obviously her attempt to break the spell.

'Oh right,' said Charlie, wondering why a propensity for sticking one's arm up a cow's bum was relevant to saving a forest from destruction. Jemima clocked him.

'No, Charlie, he's a veteran: Newbury Bypass? Manchester Airport? Fairmile? Drax Power Station?

Terminal Five? There hasn't been a major campaign in this country without Stuff. He's wonderful.'

Her eyes flickered, vying for his attention. But Stuff and Jill remained locked in transcendental fornication.

'Not such a high success rate,' said Charlie, the pragmatist.

'It's up to us to make this one different,' Jemima replied. 'Isn't that right, Stuff?'

Stuff was oblivious to their discussion. He had yet to release Jill's hand.

'I was just saying how we all need to pull together for the good of the campaign?' said Jemima, trying again.

'Quite,' he said at last.

Two gallant eco-warriors set light to a campfire, and the jovial party gathered around. A guitar appeared, complete with a Bob Dylan wannabe, bottles of wine and one or two aromatic herbs. Charlie supped a can of beer, trying to get his head round these latest circumstances. He'd spent years fighting his way out of Ballymenace and now, it seemed, he was signed up to battle for its survival.

He watched Mr Stuff, who continued to woo an acquiescent Jill. Something was missing from Charlie's brief knowledge of the man. Stuff was just about everything he was not: good-looking, strong, refined, and possessing a confident charm. Charlie had gleaned little from their introduction except that he was a superhero to the protest world. But this man, he thought, had more to tell. For one thing, he appeared too full of the good life. The upper-crust accent, well-educated at least, didn't fit with his present company. His blue denim, down-to-earth look didn't ring true. More like a Royal displaying his common touch at an outward-bound scheme for young offenders. Charlie wondered how Stuff's presence would influence matters in this corner of darkest monotony. So far, on this sultry evening, his attention was centred entirely on Jill, who didn't seem to mind at all.

* * *

The birds sang in the trees; the river trickled by; the sky was blue and loaded with fluffy clouds. Someone had put him in a sleeping bag, and he lay in a T-shirt, which was strange because he hadn't arrived in one. Whatever he'd drunk, smoked or snorted he couldn't remember, but hey, the music was cool, the stars were far out and the sex?

'Morning, Charlie,' said a young girl with flowing blonde locks, wearing a long white flowing dress, the morning sun flowing right through it. Go with the flow, he thought.

'What's happening?' he said, wondering if he'd just suffered another out-of-body, near-death experience. She crouched beside him, stroking his tortured head.

'Precious, Charlie,' she said smiling, her voice childlike, a gentle tone of Middle England. 'You were wonderful last night.'

'Wonderful?'

'Stop teasing. You know what I mean.' She gave him a squeezy hug, her skin soft against his bristled face. 'You were such fun singing.'

'Singing? Me?'

'Dancing, and telling stories, wonderful stories. Tell me one now, please?'

In a fluster he scraped her off his shoulder, struggled out of the sleeping bag and got to his feet. She giggled.

'Ooh, Charlie.' He pulled down the T-shirt.

'My trousers?'

She crawled into a nearby tent and returned seconds later with his shirt and trousers.

'Breakfast is ready. I hope you like porridge.'

'No thanks, love. It's time I wasn't here, wherever here is?'

'Why don't you relax, chill out. The world's not going anywhere.'

'Yours maybe, but mine's headed for the toilet.'

He looked round what he now recalled was the protest site. Scrambling into his trousers, he couldn't fend her off as she threw her arms round his neck and pouted, waiting for a kiss. Under duress he would admit to being tempted and, for a moment, he wasn't sure if he was putting his trousers on or taking them off. She had simple, natural beauty, milky-blue eyes, long lashes, a wide mouth, full lips and a sprinkling of freckles on the bridge of her nose. And a killer of a smile. Suddenly he realised just how young she looked. A young-looking eighteen or an old-looking fifteen? Oh shit. He had more than enough women to worry about.

'Shouldn't you be at school?' he said, unclasping her arms.

'Why are you so cross with me? You're a big grumpy Charlie this morning. Don't you want me anymore? Didn't we have a lovely time last night?'

'Listen, love, I don't know who I am anymore, never mind who you are, or what we've done.'

The sound of engines, lots of engines and calls of 'they're here!' bounced round the trees and through the camp. The perforating sound of an air horn filled his ears. He would have loved to strangle the git who thought air horns were a clever invention.

'Come on, let's go see,' said the girl.

She tugged his hand, and reluctantly he followed. This protest business can wear you out, he thought. They took the path to the fields on Herbie's side of the glen. Climbing over a wire fence, they dropped into his eleven-acre field where, only yesterday, a herd of Friesians had been munching the lush grass. Charlie expected to witness a heated confrontation between protesters and Palmer's men, but he could scarcely take in what lay before him. Lorries everywhere, people carrying, hauling and erecting. A large stage was under construction at the lower end of the field. Talking of construction, Palmer's men were strangely absent. A couple of big yellow earth-movers lay idle in the golf course across the glen, but there was no one around to suggest an imminent invasion of the forest. Four policemen stood at the open gate to Herbie's eleven-acre, content to watch. One of them, guarding a metal barrier, directed the lorries to the appropriate area of the field: those vehicles carrying staging to the bottom, the burger vans and market traders to the top.

In the midst of it all was Jemima, attached to her clipboard. She waddled from one nest of activity to another, scribbling furiously. Charlie wondered if anything useful was noted, or was it part of the duties of chief organiser to merely write everything down?

'Morning, Jemima,' he called, but she was far too busy for the likes of him.

'Morning, Destiny,' said a lanky eco-warrior striding by, loaded with climbing tackle: harnesses, clips, loops and karabiners.

'Good morning, Zoot,' Destiny replied.

Now, at least, Charlie knew the girl's name. Next task was to get rid of her. He found her unnerving, heart-warmingly beautiful but unnerving. She held onto his arm as if they were never to part, that breaking contact would condemn them to a pit of everlasting fire. Right now, it had a certain attraction. He didn't think he could stomach much more of this crusade. He wasn't cut out for noble causes.

Meandering across the field to a cluster of market stalls, already open for business, he struggled to see where all of this organisation would lead them. The issue now was much bigger than his dispute with Palmer. It was beyond his control and, judging by the media setting up camp, the whole thing was positively global. What was Barbara thinking now? Surely, she wouldn't believe this protest was down to him? And what about the Shroud of Old Trafford? What if it made another appearance? Would the police finally put all the evidence together, jump to the wrong conclusion and arrest him anyway for stirring up trouble? He should've gone for trauma counselling after witnessing the murder at the duck pond. He'd heard stories about people who suffered recurring hallucinations after heavy boozing. But he felt certain the dead body really did show up in his flat. After all, he'd lost his duvet, hadn't he?

They found Jill, hanging on the arm of Stuff in the same manner as Destiny was attached to Charlie. Maybe it was a CAKE thing. He noticed also that she wore only a man's white shirt and a pair of those Moses sandals. Oh, and a beauty of a smile. It should have been clear how it got there, but Charlie was not too quick at jumping to romantic conclusions.

'Good morning, Charlie,' said Stuff, more a proclamation than a greeting. He, too, was beset, and smiled broadly. 'I'm delighted you have decided to stay with us.'

'Yeah, well,' Charlie said, clearing his throat.

'How's the head this morning?' Jill asked.

'Could be better.'

'You were wild last night,' she said.

'So everyone tells me. You can fill me in later.'

Jemima trundled over to join them. Her face plumbed the depths of pale when she noticed Jill, arm in arm with Stuff.

'Two more deliveries to come,' she said. 'Food supplies and more rope for the tree people.'

Stuff didn't seem that interested. Jemima fired daggers at Jill.

'So, Charlie,' said Stuff. 'What do you think of our plans?'

'To tell you the truth, Stuff old boy, I can't quite see what your plans are.' Mimicking Stuff's accent was not intentional; it just came out that way, his inferiority complex kicking in. He hoped the man wasn't offended.

'I don't think Palmer will be too worried by what he sees here.'

'That will be to his cost,' said Stuff. 'He has never encountered people like us. Always had things a trifle easy. But he will lose this battle, and our victory will come swiftly if he underestimates our strength.'

'Spoken like a true general, but how come I've never heard of CAKE?'

'When this campaign is over, Charlie, you will never be able to say that again.'

A wonderfully evasive answer. Charlie had still to make up his mind about Stuff or any of this CAKE lot, but he supposed if they could put one over on Palmer then he would be happy.

'So what are the plans for today?' he asked, picturing military manoeuvres, stand-offs and pitched battles.

'We'll let these good people continue with their work, I think.' Stuff turned to Jill. 'Fancy a spot of bungee jumping? How about you, Charlie, are you game?'

'No thanks, mate.'

'Oh don't be a spoilsport,' said Destiny, jumping up and down with excitement.

Stuff and Jill were already strolling towards a huge crane sitting at the edge of the field, beside the duck pond.

'Come on, Charlie,' Jill called back. 'Where's your sense of adventure gone?'

'My life is wild enough, thank you very much. Besides, I've been in that water already.'

Looking dejected, Jemima returned to her clipboard and her organising.

'Please come,' said Destiny.

'No thanks, love. I've got something to do. You go and have some fun.'

'I will see you later, won't I?' Reluctantly she released his arm and went skipping down the hill like Julie Andrews.

Chapter forty-four

'Hello there, young fella,' said Herbie, climbing down from his tractor, the big John Deere one. He'd been working in the field next to all the activity, and had spied Charlie leaning on the gate. 'I thought you might be in the middle of all this.'

He nodded at the pond, where a series of high-pitched screams accompanied a figure diving from a high platform. There was a brief splash, and the body flew into the air again then disappeared behind the trees.

'They're having fun,' he said.

'Don't you mind all these people camping on your land?'

'They're a fine bunch. They mean well.'

'I'm not sure what they mean. They seem to have appeared from nowhere.'

He couldn't help searching the old man's face and, not for the first time, thought he saw a glint in his eye.

'As long as they rid the place of Mr Palmer, will you not be a happy man?' said Herbie.

'I just can't see that happening. Palmer's too slippery to let a bunch of tree huggers stand in his way. He has too many friends in high places.'

'I wouldn't be so sure. I think he's a worried man.'

'Why do you say that?'

'He came to see me yesterday, offered more money for me to sell up. Darn near doubled the price.'

'I suppose if he owned the land he could throw these people off it. What did you tell him?'

'I told him I wasn't for buyin' or sellin'. Says he, "You might reconsider when you have a new town on your doorstep." Says I to him, "I don't see that comin' to be." His face went as red as a rooster's wattle. Says he, "Next time, Mr Smyth, I may not be so generous." Says I, "Next time, Mr Palmer, you might not be in a position to be so generous." Didn't like that one bit. Turned on his heels, took his cheque and his young woman friend with him. A fine pair of legs she had, I must say.'

Another round of screaming burst over the woods as Jill dangled from the bungee cord. She and Charlie hadn't spoken privately since their arrival in the camp. How much did she remember from their last evening at her flat, he wondered. Had it meant anything to her? Was his heart telling him to move on, that Barbara was a lost cause? Jill and Stuff, surely that was nothing serious? She knew nothing about the man. Still, he couldn't understand his sudden feeling of emptiness.

'I think it's about time I cleared off,' he said to Herbie. 'I need to find another job.'

'There's time enough for that. Why don't you stay here and see how things turn out?'

'Palmer will laugh his head off at this lot.'

'Don't be so sure, young fella. Give these folk a chance to show what they can do.'

* * *

Later on that day, having been talked into staying, first by Herbie, then Jill and finally Jemima, Charlie got a better idea of how CAKE might perform in the developing protest. Palmer and Michelle Eastman arrived with an entourage of surveyors, engineers, architects, and the dapper Jeremy Bolton with laptop, escorted by police.

Immediately a crowd gathered round the fleet of cars. Palmer got out, followed by Miss Eastman, who seemed more assured behind a pair of sunglasses. Jeremy Bolton had a close encounter straight away with a cowpat and tried in vain to wipe his shoe in some long grass. As Charlie had come to expect, Palmer spoke in a calm and dignified manner.

'Who is in charge here?' he asked, panning his voice round the masses of CAKE volunteers.

Rapturous cheers and whistles greeted Stuff as he stepped from the hoards. Throw in a few kilts, blue face paint, a Scottish-Australian-American accent and Braveheart was about to address King Edward.

'Good day, Mr Palmer, how may I help you?' said Stuff.

'And you are?'

'I am what?'

'Your name, what is your name?'

'My friends call me Stuff.' There was a volley of raucous cheering.

'And why do they call you that?'

'Because he don't like *stuff*.' Someone shouted from the ranks. It was followed by more cheering.

Stuff silenced them with a calming gesture of his hand. Palmer appeared to study the man who demonstrated such control. He looked confused.

'Forgive me, Mr Stuff, but haven't we met before?'

'Perhaps.'

'Your accent, not one I would associate with this area or this sort of activity.'

'And what activity might that be, Mr Palmer?'

'Preventing my employees from clearing this land for development.'

'Development or destruction?' said Stuff.

'It's progress. I'm improving this area.'

'I believe these fields are the property of Mr Herbert Smyth and his family, and have been for a hundred years.'

'I'm speaking of the glen,' said Palmer. 'It is scheduled for clearance.'

'Ballymenace Glen is public land, the responsibility of the local council, is it not?'

Charlie squeezed his way to the front of the crowd. If he was going to write the story of how the woods were won, he'd better start now. Palmer spotted him and didn't seem pleased.

'It *is* council land,' said Charlie. 'But Malcolm has bought most of the councillors. Isn't that right, old chap?'

'I could sue you for slander, Geddis, but I already have everything of yours that's worth having.'

'Ooh!' The crowd drew breath. Charlie was defeated again.

'Are you going to end this nonsense, Mr Stuff, and allow me to continue with my business?'

'You are free to do whatever you please on the land you have acquired. That does not include this field or Ballymenace Glen, which you agree is in the charge of the council. We shall not interfere in any of your legitimate operations.'

'Then why on earth are you here at all?'

'We were invited by Mr Smyth. We are simply making preparations for a grand party.' Stuff swept his arm around the field. 'You are welcome to join us.'

The crowd erupted. Palmer stood fuming; Charlie stood smirking, it was a relationship of contrasts.

'I might have known that old man was behind this fiasco,' said Palmer. 'He'll regret the day he refused my offer. When I'm finished his farm won't be worth a tuppenny dam.'

'Sounds like a malicious threat, Mr Palmer,' Stuff said.

'I'm warning you, sir. Don't cross me.' Palmer stomped to his car, his loyal aides tagging along like baby ducklings. 'I'll be back,' he shouted. The crowd cheered.

'One-nil to us, I believe,' Stuff said to Jemima, who had come to his side. 'I think it is time to implement our plans in full.'

'Yes, Stuff, everything will be ready.' She waddled off, scribbling obsessively on her clipboard.

Stuff turned to Jill, bedraggled after her dipping experience on the end of a bungee rope. Hair matted to her head, her shirt was translucent and dripping water. He kissed her on the forehead, sliding his arm around her shoulders. Charlie gaped, mouth open. Couldn't take his eyes off her, and yet it seemed he'd lost her to a tall man named Stuff.

'The battle lines are drawn, Charlie,' Stuff said. 'Are you up for it?'

'Er yes,' Charlie replied vacuously.

'Tell me,' Stuff continued. 'What has been the greatest success of the modern age?'

'I have no idea.'

'Is it the computer?' said Jill as if it were a table quiz.

'Cancer.'

Such a nasty answer.

'Cancer is the most successful thing known to man. But we have to match it. Unless we put up a fight it just keeps growing, multiplying, dividing. Palmer is a cancer.'

'He's certainly a bit of a pain,' said Charlie.

'His type is gnawing away at the beauty of our world for mere profit. If we don't fight, soon there will be nothing worth fighting for. Believe me, I have learnt from previous mistakes.'

With that harrowing thought Stuff guided Jill away, and the crowd parted to let them through. There were no signs of loaves and fishes, but the speech, Charlie thought, had that epoch-like ring to it.

Chapter forty-five

Six days of intense preparation took place at Ballymenace Glen. On the seventh day they rested.

Palmer installed plant machinery, portable buildings and construction materials on the fifteenth fairway at Ballymenace Golf Club. From there he could look over the glen to Herbie's eleven-acre field, where the stoic members of CAKE applied themselves to preparations for their grand party.

The narrow roads and lanes around the site became the scene of traffic chaos, while thousands of onlookers, well-wishers and the media descended on Ballymenace town centre, that is, once they'd managed to find it using satnav or the AA Roadmap of Ireland. News teams besieged The Ballymenace Arms, the town's only hotel, though it was little more than a guesthouse with ambition. With four to a room, they had to be colleagues who got along. St. Matthew's Parish Hall opened its doors for a modest donation to the church restoration fund. The scout troop hired out their tents to a party from CNN, thereby financing their summer camp to Scotland. The Livelife Nursing Home locked its doors to a group of Japanese journalists who didn't quite understand the purpose of the establishment.

With so many people laying siege to the town and countryside, local entrepreneurs saw it as their best chance in years to earn a few quid. Market stalls sprang up in the fields around the glen and on the fairways of the golf club. Everything imaginable was for sale: food, drink, pots, pans, clothes, blankets and camping equipment. T-shirts with slogans 'Born to save Ballymenace Glen' and 'Tree lovers – branching out' were printed for the protesters, and 'Bulldozers make the earth move' for the builders. Souvenir maps with details of the contentious site, mugs, plates, keyrings, towels, balloons, pencils, and chocolate boxes all were marked, 'Siege of Ballymenace Glen'. Packs of condoms were labelled, 'A present from Ballymenace' and 'A Chip off the Old Block'. For a modest fifteen quid, photographers ran a portrait service where mothers could have their bouncing babies pictured beside a JCB or clinging to a young oak tree.

Confused by day, in the evenings blind drunk and occasionally stoned, Charlie was resigned to staying around this band of brothers for the duration. But, strangely, he felt relaxed for the first time in years. He slept well (the drink again); he was eating well too, and Destiny poured all of her affection on him. Having discovered she was twenty-two, he no longer felt the same compunction to resist her. The weather was fine and dry, and life was fun. In fact, he ceased pondering his future altogether. Live for the day, that's what Jemima told him. A paid-up member of the rat race might not readily take advice from a capricious environmentalist in Moses sandals, but Charlie was a much-improved listener. If he weren't so brain-soaked he'd swear he was brainwashed.

Local television and newspapers reported every development. The main players of the protest were the latest thing in reality TV. Telephone polls put the protesters well ahead of the builders in public support. There were special features on news programmes. Alan Titchmarsh did a special on *Trees of Britain* and Jeremy Clarkson wrote off a JCB, just for the hell of it. Every day, as their fame increased, Charlie was faced with a string of visitors to the site. First up was Trevor.

'Charlie!'

His shouts came from the far side of the eleven-acre field beside the marquee which housed the media communications centre.

'It's me, Trevor.'

Charlie hid behind a French cheese stall and then tried to mingle with a party of American tourists, who'd strayed from their traditional excursion through Stormont, the Titanic Quarter and the Giant's Causeway. Still the voice came. Destiny, clinging to his arm, stated the obvious.

'I think someone wants to speak with you.'

'Do you think so?' She nodded and smiled innocently; his sarcasm lost on her.

'Charlie,' said Trevor, his legs wobbling from trekking over fields. 'I've been trying to find you. I never thought this place was so big.'

'It's big all right,' said Charlie. 'And now you've found me.'

'Well, how are you?'

'Never been better.' He gave Destiny a long, passionate kiss just for effect. He sensed Trevor was drooling. One thing about Destiny, her beauty would reduce the most celibate of males to puddles on the floor. Charlie was dead lucky, and Trevor couldn't take his eyes off her.

'What do you want, Trevor?'

Trevor wiped saliva from his mouth.

'I was just wondering how the story was going?'

'What story?'

'The coverage of the protest. I can't wait to get an insight into this lot. I've planned a big spread.'

'Hold on a minute,' said Charlie. 'I don't work for you anymore. You sacked me, remember?'

'That's a bit harsh. I wouldn't exactly call it sacking.'

'And what would you call it?' Charlie asked.

His former boss squirmed. Not one to let such an opportunity slip by, Charlie kissed Destiny once more then listened to Trevor grovelling.

'It was more of a reprimand. I was angry, Charlie. I'd had a bad morning. I shouldn't have taken it out on you.'

Charlie smiled, and Trevor seemed to take it as an absolution.

'Have you been working on a story?' he asked, as if all bridges were mended.

'I have.'

'Great, when can I read it?'

'Buy *The Sun*. It's an exclusive.'

'But what about *The Explorer*? Don't we get a scoop?'

'Not from me. I don't work for you anymore.'

'But I've apologised for sacking you. I didn't mean what I said.'

'I quit anyway. Go write the story yourself. Here's a pencil; sharpen your own lead.'

He pictured Trevor's day after he left the field, with a cheeseburger and a blunt pencil. He would drive back to the office and swear at Carol, who would swear back. He'd tell Billy to get his fat arse out of his seat, get down to the glen and find a story. With a headache coming on, he'd take two Disprin, go home early, and compound his bad day by telling Joan all about it.

Chapter forty-six

The following day Charlie watched Joan tiptoe around the field, no doubt looking for him. It was a blazing hot day, but she wore an overcoat and carried a folded umbrella. She always liked to think she was in control, even of the weather. If Carol Kirkwood hinted that a cloud was expected over Ulster by noon, then Joan would be prepared for a hurricane. For once, Charlie made things easy for her. He felt so laid back, he was confident of tackling anyone or anything.

'Hi, Joan. Looking for me?'

'Hi, Joan,' said Destiny, mounted on Charlie's back. Joan looked on the point of collapse. Her mouth dropped open; her heels sank in the ground.

'I want a word with you, Charlie Geddis.'

'I'm all ears, Joanie baby.' He knew how to rile her.

'In private.'

Charlie glanced around the field. There was no one close except for Destiny.

'Go ahead.'

Joan cleared her throat.

'Don't mind Destiny,' he said. 'We have no secrets.'

He knew that would sting, but this was fun. This was revenge for years of acid remarks. For years of interference in his marriage, telling Barbara what she would do if Charlie was her husband. What she would do if he came home late. That Barbara was a saint for putting up with him. That she would never allow Trevor to behave that way. It was revenge for telling Miss Taylor, in primary school, that he had written Miss Piggy in her English homework book. For telling Mrs Woodcock that he'd told her what cock meant. For telling Mrs Biggins, the headmistress, that he'd shared the contents of her lunchbox with his mates. This was retribution time for Joanie.

She began at quite a pace.

'You should be ashamed of yourself, Charlie Geddis. My Trevor gave you back your job. He didn't have to, you know? He was doing you a favour, and you threw it in his face. Too damn soft, that's his trouble. He was very upset by what you said. And what about poor Barbara? What do you think it's doing to her? And here's you not giving a damn. Now you've met some floozy. You're old enough to be her father. Behaving like a teenager. Displaying your lust in front of my Trevor. My Trevor doesn't go in for such things. It's not decent. Does your mother know what you get up to, love?' she said to Destiny. 'If I was her I'd ground you for life. Look at the pair of you. Hardly wearing a stitch between you. Is this a commune, one of them funny religions? What are you going to do when all this blows over? You needn't think for one minute, Charlie Geddis, that my Trevor's keeping a job for you. Not after the way you've treated him. If you ask me, you're scared of a hard day's work. Life's not all fun and games, you know?'

'It's been nice talking to you, Joanie,' said Charlie, 'but we'll have to push on. We're going to pick some wildflowers.'

'You can come if you like?' said Destiny, as only a sweet thing might do.

Joan's puffed face was ample reply.

'Come, is not a word that's familiar to our Joan,' said Charlie.

Destiny laughed, although it was obvious she didn't get the double entendre. Joan gasped, a wonderful act of being affronted.

'Barbara is well rid of you, Charlie Geddis.'

She stormed off. Just like the good old days, when she ran to tell her mother about that awful Charlie Geddis trying to peek at her knickers.

* * *

It may have been coincidence, but the day after Joan's visit there was an upturn in the level of security around the site. Palmer, apparently, had demanded the council and the police take firm action. As a result Ballymenace Glen was sealed off completely, to all but the protesters. Those eager to observe had to do so from behind a police cordon. CAKE felt a greater threat that soon, and without warning, the police would barge into the glen and evict its caring residents. Herbie's field was a different matter. Hordes of traders, protesters and well-wishers came and went under the noses of the few police assigned to guard the metal barriers at the farm entrance. Stuff ordered that CAKE warriors should remain as close as possible to the glen in order to guard its precious trees.

Tension heightened after another familiar face appeared on site. Councillor Jim Farrington of Ballymenace Council strode into the field demanding to speak with the 'leader of the gang'. When Stuff's presence was called for, Charlie was also invited as honorary scribe of the CAKE organisation.

A haggard-looking Farrington stood in the centre of the field. He had a briefcase at his feet and a police constable by his side.

'Jim Farrington. Ballymenace Council.' Ignoring Charlie, he offered his hand to Stuff.

'Good day, Mr Farrington. My friends call me Stuff. What can I do for you?'

Farrington seemed ruffled by the strange name. He glanced at Charlie, who saw it as a cue to introduce himself.

'Charlie Geddis.' The mention of a proper name was met with a higher degree of respect until Charlie muddied the water. 'You may remember me; I'm a reporter. I'll be taking a few notes, for the record.'

Farrington glared at them both for a moment and seemed nervous about continuing.

'Mr Stuff, I'm here as an elected representative with a message from the council for you and your companions.' He read from a sheet of paper. '*The council wish to make clear they have not granted permission for you to take up residence on council property namely, Ballymenace Glen. We trust that now you have expressed your views to the media, you will vacate this area at the earliest possible time. The council does not believe your presence here is helpful, moreover, it is disrupting normal community life.'*

Stuff made no reply. Farrington plugged the gap.

'Of course, it goes without saying that if your people leave forthwith, no action will be taken against them and the matter can be laid to rest.'

'Is that so?' Stuff said pensively. 'If we were to leave forthwith, as you say, will the prospective developers of this land also leave?'

'That is a matter for them to consider. They have not broken any of the council by-laws. They are fully entitled to be here. You, on the other hand, are not.'

'Is it the council's intention to allow the clearance of trees for the building of houses?'

'All decisions will be taken in accordance with legislation.'

'Has the council granted planning permission for work to proceed?'

Farrington was sweating. He adjusted the knot in his tie and lifted his briefcase ready to escape.

'Information on planning is available from the council planning office. I am simply here to inform you that if you continue with this protest the council will take steps to have you evicted. By force, if necessary.'

'Thank you for stating your case in such clear terms, Mr Farrington. My colleagues and I will give due consideration to your warning.'

'I'll be off then. Don't take too long over it. The council has more important matters to deal with. We need this mess cleared up as soon as possible.' He turned to walk away.

'One question, Mr Farrington, for you and your council?'

'Yes, what is it?'

'Are you aware of the tree preservation order in relation to this glen, that no one can remove one tree from this place without the order being rescinded?'

'Yes, yes. The council is fully aware of the situation regarding the trees.'

'Then perhaps you might inform Mr Palmer of the situation.'

Farrington glared angrily at Stuff, who met his stare with a placid smile.

'Hey, Jim,' said Charlie. 'How's the missus? Lovely woman.'

Farrington, looking bewildered, marched off the field.

Chapter forty-seven

He'd been up and around for more than an hour when Jemima appeared, looking less than happy. Destiny bid her a cheery good morning but was blanked completely. Instead, Jemima made straight for Charlie.

'They're holding a press conference at nine,' she said brusquely. 'Stuff would like you to represent us.'

'Me?'

'I know. I wouldn't choose you either, but for some reason he thinks it's wise that you put our case.'

Charlie looked as rough as he felt. Unshaven, unwashed and unable to see sense in what Jemima said.

'Why can't Stuff do it?'

She didn't look too pleased at having to explain everything in simple terms. He wondered also if she was disappointed at not being chosen for the task.

'Stuff prefers to keep a low profile when dealing with the media.'

'A bit shy is he?'

She frowned behind her glasses then pulled a note from her satchel.

'Here is the statement you are to read. You don't have to add anything. If someone asks you a question, simply refer to the statement. Is that clear?'

'Perfectly.'

'Don't mess it up. It's your glen we're trying to save.' She bounded off in busybody manner.

'Where do I go?' he called after her.

'The entrance gate,' she said without turning around.

'The entrance gate,' he mimicked. 'Don't mess this up, you silly sod or you'll suffer death by ketchup, and by the way can you read?'

When he reached the main gate he found a Portakabin installed at the lay-by, surrounded by reporters, photographers and TV cameras. A policeman allowed him through the gates, padlocked since Farrington's visit. It appeared everyone had been waiting for him, because a rather vexed-looking girl in jeans and T-shirt, holding a BBC clipboard, took him by the arm and bundled him through the door of the Portakabin. He was seated behind a table before anyone bothered to ask his name.

'You're from CAKE, right?' said the girl.

'Yes,' he replied, glancing at the people gathered around him.

Michelle Eastman sat to his right and beside her a simmering Malcolm Palmer. To his left, Jim Farrington leafed through a set of papers. None of them acknowledged his presence with anything more than a sniff. He'd managed to wash but not shave, to brush his teeth but not his hair. His clothes, after about two weeks of pottering about in a forest and sleeping in a tent, weren't exactly dapper.

'One minute, yeah?' said the girl jumping outside as a dozen reporters, photographers, a cameraman and soundman squeezed in. Charlie felt the wooden floor sagging under the weight as they jostled for the best position in the room. They stared at each other across the table. He gazed at his alarmingly brief prepared statement.

'Right!' the girl called, stranded on the outside. 'Let's have the builder bloke first.'

Palmer didn't appear to enjoy being called a builder bloke. He nodded to Michelle Eastman, and she straightened in her seat and cleared her throat.

'I should firstly like to thank you for this opportunity to explain our position in this current situation,' she said confidently.

Squeaky bloody clean, thought Charlie.

'What's your name, love?' a reporter called out.

'Michelle Eastman. I represent Palmer Developments.'

There was a flurry of writing, while others thrust microphones closer to the table. Miss Eastman refocused on the notes in front of her.

'I want to outline our intentions regarding the development of this area.'

She produced a large piece of card from behind her seat and propped it on the table in front of Charlie, who then was cut off from the eyes down. Cameras clicked, and the pack shuffled closer to study the details of a map printed on the card.

'This is a plan of the immediate area,' she said, pointing out several features on the map. 'I've marked the points of interest... The town centre of Ballymenace, the golf club, the bypass road to Belfast, and the most contentious area, Ballymenace Glen...'

'Show them my house,' said Charlie, jumping to his feet.

'Be quiet,' said Palmer.

'It's only fair you point out where my house lies in your grand scheme.'

'Sit down,' said Farrington. 'It's not your turn to speak.'

Charlie blanked the remainder of Michelle Eastman's presentation, although he was vaguely aware of the questions from journalists regarding trivial details: house prices, civic amenities and incentives for people to relocate from the city to rural Palmerstown. There were no challenging questions from the press. Charlie didn't care, wasn't interested.

'Councillor Farrington next,' said the BBC girl, having gained a place by the door.

Farrington straightened his tie, adjusted his glasses and lifted a sheet of paper from the table. He began to read, 'At an extraordinary session of Ballymenace Council and preceded by an emergency meeting of the council's planning committee, it was decided the aforementioned council do endorse the intention to proceed with the development of the former agricultural land acquired by Palmer Developments over the previous two-year period. Furthermore, the council has no objection to the development of the former Ballymenace Golf Club as applied for, under Planning Order number...'

Charlie felt as though someone was talking in his sleep. Farrington droned on for ten minutes, listing each planning application separately in its entirety. Charlie used the time to prepare for his statement of CAKE's position.

When he'd finished, Farrington waited for questions. No one could be bothered.

'Protesters next,' the girl said.

'Em, right,' said Charlie. 'This is em, a statement, er, from...'

'Get on with it,' said a voice from the pack.

'Your name first,' said another.

'Charlie Geddis.' Never thought he'd feel so nervous, mouth drying up, hands trembling and seeping sweat.

'One d or two?'

'Two.'

His tongue was about to seal his throat closed. There was a jug of water and four glasses on the table beside Farrington, but he was too embarrassed to reach across. Palmer watched him, smug as a bookie who has just seen the favourite fall at the last fence.

'We, the Citizens Against Killing the Environment, welcome the opportunity to put our case this morning.'

'That's CAKE, right?'

'Spongers, if you ask me,' said Farrington, allowing himself a little titter.

'Our objective is to alert the people of Ballymenace to the grave disservice their council is doing to their community.'

He sounded just like Farrington, droning along in monotones. Whoever prepared the statement, Stuff or perhaps Jemima, was well practised in long-winded delivery. Getting to the point was not a major feature, but he listed the grievances and handed out warnings of the consequences for abusing the countryside. Charlie was disheartened to see Palmer smiling when he reached the end.

'Any questions?' said the girl from the Beeb.

'Mr Palmer,' said one reporter, hidden behind several others. 'How much will you make from this project?'

Palmer said nothing but turned to Michelle.

'We have already invested considerable time, effort and capital in this venture,' she said. 'Obviously we expect a reasonable return on our investment.'

The same reporter, big voice, small in stature, slipped to the front of the pack. Mid-thirties, round face and a number two haircut, he smiled weakly at Charlie.

'Jamie Collins, *The Sun*,' he said. 'Charlie, you're a journalist, isn't that correct?'

'Yes.'

'You wrote an article in the local paper which sparked off this protest?' There was a flurry of clicking, flashing and anxious microphones.

'I drew attention to the problem, if that's what you mean?'

'Don't you have a personal involvement in this dispute with Palmer Developments?'

Charlie felt himself glow. How did he answer that? He couldn't refer to the statement as Jemima had instructed. This guy had sniffed around, dug in the dirt. It wasn't fair. He should be in that pack of reporters, asking the questions. He should be on the phone to his editor with a scoop. He should be Jamie Collins. Now, when it really mattered, he was on the wrong side of the table. While everyone waited for the answer, Charlie wondered how much Collins knew already.

'Palmer Developments tried to buy my house,' he said. 'It lies in the way of the main road that will pass through this new town.'

'You're also well acquainted with Malcolm Palmer, isn't that right?' said Collins.

'I know him, yes.' Why did he ever think he could do this? Jamie Collins was hanging him out to dry.

'But your wife knows him a lot better?'

There was a splurge of excitement as everyone moved in for a bite of this tasty cake.

'What's her name?'

'Did you know about this, Charlie?'

'How long have you been married?'

'Malcolm, what's your relationship with Mrs Geddis?'

Palmer shrugged but said nothing.

All Charlie could do was to sit and watch as they tore him limb from limb. The girl from the Beeb seemed to realise they would get no further information until the room settled. Jamie Collins accepted the role of question master.

'Charlie, you wrote an article a while back about a murder in Ballymenace Glen.'

A hush descended on the box room. He could feel the pulse in his temples; Charlie knew what Collins was about to suggest.

'Is there a connection between the killing and the development of Palmerstown?'

'Preposterous,' said Palmer.

This guy must have read everything he had written in the last five weeks, thought Charlie, and put the proverbial twos together. He had to fend him off or the entire protest would be a farce, and Stuff would have him for firewood. There was no way he could point the finger at Palmer without proof. He'd suggested in *The Explorer* a connection between the murder at the duck pond and a local businessman, but he had to stop short of naming him. Now he would have to deny what he believed was true.

'The stories are not linked,' he said.

'How can you be so sure?' said Collins.

'The police didn't find a body. Without it we have no proof.'

'Yes, of course,' said Collins. The two men stared at each other. It was clear to Charlie that Collins did not believe him. At least someone had read his stories and had taken notice. Collins ended their engagement with a wry smile.

'Final comments from the table please?' The girl said above the din.

Farrington repeated the council's intention to have the protesters removed from Ballymenace Glen. Michelle Eastman added a touch of loving colour to her description of Palmerstown and expressed hope that the protest would end soon for the benefit of all. Charlie could only manage a return to the safety of his prepared statement.

'CAKE wishes to invite all the residents of Ballymenace to a grand party on Saturday evening, at seven o'clock, on Herbie Smyth's farm.'

'Thank you, ladies and gentlemen,' said the girl. But Jamie Collins had more to say.

'Councillor Farrington?' He had already left the table. 'Is there any truth in the allegations that council officials have accepted gifts and hospitality from Mr Palmer?'

'None whatsoever.'

'So it's never been a case of, I'll scratch your back if you scratch mine?'

'Absolutely not.'

That was a good question, thought Charlie, despite the cliché. He had used it on Farrington after the meeting about the old mill. Maybe he wasn't such a poor journalist after all. Jamie Collins still had not finished.

'Mr Palmer?' he said. 'Is your relationship with Mrs Geddis founded on your need to acquire the Geddis family home?'

'Oohs' rose from the pack. Michelle Eastman didn't seem prepared to answer that particular question on Palmer's behalf. It wasn't in her remit.

'Your suggestion that Palmer Developments *needs* to acquire the house owned by Mr Geddis is inaccurate,' said Palmer. 'The success of Palmerstown does not depend on the location of just one house. The acquisition of the Geddis home is neither here nor there.'

Another barrage of questions followed as everyone who'd been at the table tried to leave the Portakabin.

'Why'd you call the place Palmerstown?' asked one reporter. Palmer grinned broadly.

'Easier to say than West Ballymenace,' Michelle replied.

'You sleeping with Mrs Geddis, Malcolm?'

'Are you living together?'

'What's your wife's name, Charlie?'

'Is your marriage over?'

'How big is her chest?'

'Any boyfriend, Miss Eastman?'

Frankly, he couldn't wait to get out and breathe fresh air. What was Stuff going to say? The meeting had descended to a symposium on his marriage. Hardly a mention of the protest. And what about the trees? He had to say something, quickly.

'Tell them about the trees, Councillor?' Charlie called out. Farrington was trying his best to escape. 'Tell them about the tree preservation order.'

Reporters chased after the councillor, Palmer and Michelle Eastman. When Charlie reached the door he tried again.

'What about the trees, Palmer?'

A microphone was thrust under Palmer's chin.

'The tree preservation order is a matter for the Department for the Environment,' he said.

'How many trees will be left? Answer that, Palmer,' said Charlie. 'You're going to kill all of them, aren't you? And the minister is going to let you do it.'

'Where is the minister?' a member of the pack shouted. 'Why isn't he here?'

'The minister is currently out of the country,' said Farrington.

'He's on holiday in the Caribbean,' shouted Charlie. 'Wouldn't you like to know who's paying for it?'

Michelle Eastman stepped in front of the microphone.

'Palmer Developments is taking all possible steps to ensure only the minimum number of trees will be removed from Ballymenace Glen.'

Charlie barged over and, with the jostling of the crowd, was pressed close to Miss Eastman.

'What do you call a minimum number?' he shouted into the microphone.

Miss Eastman took a step backwards to avoid the crush. She stumbled on the kerbstone, fell over and Charlie landed on top of her. Palmer and Farrington, coming to her rescue, lunged at Charlie, and the three of them wrestled on the ground. Cameras whirred, while reporters jockeyed for the best view.

'Get off me,' said Charlie. 'I only asked a question.'

'I've had just about enough of you,' said Palmer.

Farrington didn't look as if he could take the strain as Michelle helped him to his feet. Palmer and Charlie rolled off each other, but in the crush they had difficulty getting up. Drawing breath, still on his knees, in full view of the news teams, Charlie tried again with Michelle Eastman.

'I only asked, how many trees will be lost?'

'I don't have specific figures,' she said coldly.

'Right, thank you. That didn't hurt now, did it?'

He heard a splat as he got to his feet. The air was suddenly rife with eggs, flour and tomatoes. The unfortunate Michelle looked like a rookie on a paintball adventure day, her white blouse splattered yellow and red. Several eco-warriors, on the other side of the gate, looked pleased with themselves as they lobbed their missiles into the throng. The news pack scattered. Palmer and Farrington ran for cover leaving poor Michelle to bear the brunt of the attack.

Jill greeted Charlie when he made it to the sanctuary of the glen. She looked every bit as happy as he did sad. Her cheeks were full of colour, her eyes bright and shiny.

'Stuff wants to see you,' she said, taking him by the arm.

'I'll bet he does.'

'You were on the news. It was great.'

They found Stuff, reading *The Times,* by the duck pond. He looked up as they approached and seemed delighted to see them. Pleased to see Jill anyway. Charlie had to wait while they greeted each other: first a smile, touching hands, a light kiss on both cheeks and then a long wet snog. Blooming heck, thought Charlie, how long since they last saw each other? Ten minutes? The great man himself was first to break the moment.

'Good morning, Charlie,' he said warmly. 'I'd like to thank you for taking the press conference.'

'Listen, Stuff mate, I'm sorry it went so badly. I didn't think anyone was interested in my personal problems.'

'It was fine. Now everyone knows about the party.'

'I don't think we've achieved very much. No one was interested in saving the trees. They only wanted to know if Palmer is sleeping with my wife.'

'This protest is all about raising public awareness. That's the reason for the party on Saturday. We bring the townspeople along to see the place, let them get a picture in their mind, let them savour the beauty around them and let them have some fun. When they realise their council intends destroying the entire forest we will have our support, and Palmer will have a fight on his hands.'

Chapter forty-eight

Charlie moped around all day. He refused Destiny's offer of a massage and the invitation to go swimming. The duck pond of all places. He sat by the water's edge for a while, watching them swim: eight girls, nubile and carefree. He didn't feel up to whatever he should be up to, while eight girls were frolicking in their underwear and begging him to join in the fun.

The field was alive all afternoon with the preparations for the party. A crew arrived to install a powerful sound system, huge stacks of speakers and a pair of giant video screens, on either side of the stage. Herbie's field resembled a site for a mighty rock festival like Glastonbury. Now all they needed was the entertainment and several thousand people, enough to make Palmer think again.

By late evening he could take no more of the activity. A great party it may turn out to be, but he couldn't see a victory in it. Feeling miserable, he wandered along the forest trails. He considered leaving altogether, heading home to a warm bath, a Chinese takeaway and a couple of Arnie DVDs. By the time he reached the gate, however, his chances of a pleasant evening at home seemed bleak. Three burly CAKE warriors stood guard, chatting to a policeman on the other side, sharing a smoke, and having a laugh. A couple of diligent reporters paced around outside the Portakabin. It was enough to stop him going any further. The last thing he wanted right now was to be hassled by the press. How the tables had turned. Besides, CAKE might not be terribly keen to see their PR man flee the scene of their intended triumph. He was trapped. Trapped, useless, tired and a bloody fool. This time, for sure, he would never touch strong drink again.

'Just look what it's done to my head. How did I ever get mixed up in all this protest shit? I report the news. I'm not supposed to be the idiot at the centre of it. All I wanted was for Barbara and me to live happy ever after.'

Retreating from the gates, wandering uphill through the woods, he came across a gap in the barbed-wire fence and stepped onto the deserted golf course. Staying close to the trees, avoiding open spaces, he traced the line of the fence until it met the road leading from the glen towards the Fir Tree Lodge. Hurrying along, round a bend, there sat his Polo now, with no other cars around, looking more abandoned than parked.

'Idiot!'

He searched again, but it was pointless. He kicked the door of the car; he wasn't getting in that way either. He hadn't needed his keys for days. Now, when all he could think of was a hot bath and a chicken chow mein, he didn't have them. He sat on the bonnet. He wanted to go home but, at the same time, he didn't want Palmer to win.

He'd already lost Barbara; there was nothing left to fight for. Should he stay or should he go? He weighed up the pros and cons.

'Would staying help Barbara?' He thought for a moment. 'No. I'm going home.'

'Do I care about saving the glen? Not really.' That was two for going home.

'Should I stay for Jill's sake? Yes.'

'To help Stuff? Go home.'

'Destiny? Stay.'

'Herbie? Stay.'

'Get Palmer? Stay. Get Farrington, Mr and Mrs? Stay.'

'Michelle Eastman? In-ter-est-ing.'

He was getting nowhere. He started walking, but the very thought of a three-mile hike to his flat tipped the balance.

'Stay,' he said.

An idea, and for a change a reasonably sane one, popped into his head. But he needed to get into the car. He pulled the door handle, tried the hatch, and kicked the door again. He found a large stone under a hedge and launched it at the window. He jumped; it made a bigger noise than he expected. There was no one around to witness this act of vandalism, although, on this car, it was more an act of mercy. He put his hand through the hole, flicked the lever, and the door opened. Climbing inside, over broken glass and into the back, he tugged at the seat, and it came away. He retrieved a brown envelope from the boot, climbed out and ran back into the forest, smiling.

His decision to stay was soon regretted. By the time he reached the inner sanctum of the protest site, he was soaked to the skin. Ballymenace Glen, during two weeks of sunshine, had taken on a romantic air; it had become a homely place. Everything was love and peace under glorious skies. But this was Ireland, the Emerald Isle. It took a load of the wet stuff from the heavens to keep it that way. Standing in the downpour, clutching the envelope, watching fields turn to mud, he wondered if things would ever be the same again. When at last he'd tracked down Stuff, sheltering under a tarpaulin, munching chocolate digestives and drinking coffee, he was a tad pissed off. OK, it was evening, and work was finished for the day, but it struck him that these people, the enigmatic Stuff in particular, were a bit complacent. He was about to tell them so. That was his trouble; he had a tendency to jump from the high board without checking if there was water in the pool.

'Taking things easy?' he said sharply.

Jill, seated on a log next to Stuff, looked up in surprise. Jemima, he noticed, didn't even have her clipboard, her mouth full of Jaffa Cakes.

'Had a tough day, Charlie?' Stuff asked in a friendly enough tone.

'You could say that. Although, by the look of you lot nothing much has happened. Tell me, Stuff, why are you really here?'

'To save the forest, Charlie. I thought you knew that.'

'I really don't understand how you're going to win.'

'What's the matter, Charlie?' said Jill. 'You seem annoyed.'

'I'm totally pissed off with the whole business. We're all camped here, nice and cosy. But what happens next? Do we let Palmer march in with the police and drag us off to jail? How are we going to stop him? Somebody tell me that?'

'There are plans,' said Stuff. 'We have our ways.'

Charlie wasn't impressed by the answer.

He tossed the envelope on Stuff's lap. 'In case you run out of your ways. Maybe that will buy us something.'

'Charlie, you apologise right now.' Jill was seething. 'Don't take it out on us.'

'We care about the trees as much as you do,' said Stuff.

Jill glared at Charlie, while Stuff had a peep in the envelope.

'The trees?' said Charlie. 'I don't care about the bloody trees. All I want is my wife and my house. I've had enough of this protest caper... Barbara! What are you doing here?'

Drenched, standing between two members of the Third Battalion of Moses Sandals, she looked every bit a lost orphan. Her jeans and T-shirt were spattered with mud, and rain dripped from her hair. Her eyes were fixed on Charlie.

'I need to speak with you, Charlie. Alone.'

A sickening dread took hold as he led her to the shelter of another tarpaulin, where there was no one else around. He sat her on a folding chair. She didn't seem capable of doing anything for herself. She looked older, her lips tight, her eyes staring at some point beyond him. All he could do was sit opposite and wait for her to speak.

'I need you to do something for me,' she said.

'What?'

'Please, Charlie, call this off. You've no idea what it's doing to us. Malcolm's behaving strangely; he's stressed, and he won't talk to me.'

Charlie wanted to say, 'Bloody marvellous. Serves him right, the pompous git.' But he knew it was pointless. Her mind was made up about Palmer. She trusted him and not her wayward husband. Otherwise she wouldn't be making this plea.

'It's gone too far,' he said. 'Palmer wants this glen, and we intend to stop him. It's out of my hands, Barbara.'

'Everyone knows our business. It's all over the papers and the television. I can't get to work, and I can't even drive to my mother's. It has ruined our lives.' She paused as if waiting for Charlie to reply, but he was spent. 'I suppose you'd be happy if Malcolm and I split up? That's what you've always wanted.'

'I never wanted you to get hurt, Barbara. But you wouldn't believe a word I said.'

'And so you've resorted to this?' She left the seat and stepped into the rain. 'I shouldn't have come. Malcolm would be livid if he knew I was here.' She hurried away.

'Barbara. Why won't you listen to me?'

She vanished into the trees, her two escorts trotting after her.

'Shit!'

'Is everything all right?' Jill asked.

'No it bloody isn't,' he said.

'Come and sit with us, have a drink?'

'I'm not in the mood.' He was still peering into the trees, undecided if he should go after her. Whatever happened, whether Palmer won or lost, she would get hurt, and for that he was truly sorry.

'I hope your friend Stuff has a good plan to save this place, or we're all going to look daft.'

'Why don't you trust someone for a change?' she said angrily. 'Sometimes, Charlie Geddis, you can be a right selfish bastard.'

She stormed off to join the others. Jill with venom, he hadn't experienced that flavour for a while.

Chapter forty-nine

He sloped off to bed in a huff. Destiny left the shelter and came after him, already dripping wet.

'For goodness sake, Destiny, my wife has just left. We shouldn't be doing this; go back to your friends.'

He watched as she walked back to the shelter knowing he'd hurt her feelings too. When he reached his tent, he pulled off his wet clothes, crawled inside and lay on top of the duvet. He craved sleep, but the patter of rain on the tent drummed up support for staying awake and thinking his problems through.

Suddenly he was overcome by a peculiar feeling. He sensed that he didn't belong there. Something around him was different. This was not the tent he shared with Destiny. He could see nothing familiar. Where were his meagre belongings? Where were Destiny's clothes? This was not his sleeping bag; it was a duvet. He sat up and gathered it into a ball. It was a Manchester United duvet. Under the blue nylon of the tent it didn't appear red, so he opened the flap to let in some light. He felt as though a big wrestler had just performed a flying leap, caught him on the side of the face, and knocked him to row six. Could it be his duvet? Don't be daft, he thought. Plenty of people own Manchester United duvets; they're world famous. But if it was the Shroud of Old Trafford then someone in CAKE had stolen it. That meant they had stolen the red-haired man from his flat. Someone in CAKE was a murderer. He was living among tree-hugging terrorists. All this time he'd blamed Palmer as a murdering land-grabber. Maybe he was an honest, hard-working businessman?

Everything fell into place. Herbie, for instance, hadn't believed him about the shooting at the duck pond. And then he invites CAKE onto his land. Herbie could be the killer; he was in the wood that night. All of them were in it together. They were prepared to kill people to stop Palmer from cutting down trees. He needed to tell Jill. They had to get out of the glen. He crawled back inside out of the rain.

The flap of the tent opened suddenly. It would have scared the pants off him, except he was naked.

'Mr Geddis?' His bum greeted Jemima. 'Really, Mr Geddis, if you're trying to shock me you won't succeed. I am a trained nurse. I have been witness to many greater and, I suppose, a few lesser things.'

'What do you want?' He sat up and found a blanket to cover his offending bits. Didn't seem right to use the duvet.

'You're in my tent,' she said.

He wasn't about to argue. He only prayed he hadn't aroused her suspicions. She mustn't find out what he'd discovered, or he was a dead man.

'Sorry, my mistake,' he said. Wrapping himself in the blanket, he scurried out of the tent and, glancing around, noted his mistake. He took cover in the next tent, the one he shared with Destiny.

He had three choices, he reckoned. Number one: get the hell out. Number two: confront them with the duvet and demand the truth. Number three: say nothing, hang around and find proof they had killed the red-haired man. Option number one had definite appeal, but if this were reality TV the phone poll would suggest number three.

'I wondered if you would like this returned?' she said. Jemima had followed him. She was holding the duvet, while it soaked up the rain.

'Where the hell did you get that?'

'Do you want it or not? I haven't got all night.'

She thrust the duvet into his tent. Just seeing it again sent a shiver up his spine. The thought of sleeping under it, even with a beauty like Destiny, forced him out of the tent and into the rain. Jemima ushered him back inside and crawled in after him.

'I suppose we should have told you earlier but we didn't know if we could trust you with the information,' she said, her voice resuming that low, esoteric quality she'd employed in the coffee shop.

'Why did you kill him?' he said.

'You think we killed him?'

'Well, you have my duvet. What happened to the body?'

'Our people took him from your flat. He is safe now.'

'Safe? He looked dead to me. Who was he?'

'His name was Steve Gerard. He was one of our operatives.'

Only Jemima could make it sound as though he worked for MI5 or MOSSAD.

'Steve Gerard? The Liverpool footballer?'

She rolled her eyes as if he should dare jump to such a ridiculous conclusion.

'His real name was Bradley Miller. He was a Liverpool supporter, and Gerard was his favourite player. He changed his name by deed poll.'

The poor sod, thought Charlie. Wrapped in a Man United duvet, the ultimate humiliation for a Liverpool fan. The shock could have killed him.

'And that's why he had red hair?'

She nodded. 'On the night he disappeared, Liverpool were at home to Chelsea. He was on his way to the pub to watch the match when they caught him.'

'He was murdered. I saw it happen.'

'We know.'

'Why did you leave him at my flat?'

'We didn't. We think Palmer organised it, or someone who works for him.'

'You know about Palmer's involvement?' said Charlie. The fulfilment of the entire Book of Revelation would've been less of a shock.

'Of course. By leaving poor Steve at your flat, Palmer was trying to implicate you in the murder. He probably got the idea after you printed the story in the paper, and he saw it as a means of getting you out of the way. We saw them put Steve at your place.'

'Why didn't you call the police? They would have caught them red-handed.'

'It wasn't the right time. We could never prove it had anything to do with Palmer, and it would have done nothing to further our plans to save the glen.'

Charlie shook his head in disbelief. Who was causing him the most pain, Malcolm Palmer or Jemima Pinkerton?

'What if I had called the police?' he said.

'We were very concerned about that. We couldn't be sure how much you knew of the situation. As it turned out, you were completely in the dark. It was a bit of a gamble, but it paid off.'

'And what have you done with Steve? Have you told his family? And why did Palmer have him killed?'

Charlie was bursting from the pressure of questions filling his head.

'Steve Gerard was one of our senior members. At the time he was killed, he was working undercover at Palmer Developments. As he got closer to Palmer, working his way into his confidence, he fed us information about the plans for Ballymenace and the glen. We think his cover was blown when he discovered Palmer's affair with Sheila Farrington and started asking too many questions. When his body was dumped at your flat we took him back, and he stays with us until we can prove that Palmer had him killed. Steve had no family that we know of, but he and Destiny were close friends. She has been very brave.'

Jemima rose to leave.

'Now, if you don't mind, I have other things to do.'

Charlie let her go.

With some questions answered, a whole new set popped into his throbbing head and merely added to the throbbing. Someone crawled in beside him. Assuming it was Jemima again, he jumped to his feet and his head almost went through the roof of the tent. Destiny giggled.

'You've been talking to yourself again,' she said. 'I could hear you from the river. You look so worried, Charlie. Let me rub your back; it'll help you relax. I don't want my precious Charlie to be so grumpy.'

She moved behind him and squeezed his shoulders just below his neck. Where had this princess been all his life? Her hands moved with loving dexterity, and all his troubles faded.

Despite the TLC, he didn't get much sleep. The rain passed, but the night became warm and muggy. Destiny always snuggled close to him: back to back, front to front, or spoons, but never apart. But tonight he was restless and gave her a bit of a kick. Eventually, she rolled away and he gasped for fresh air, but he couldn't open the tent, because the midges were holding a jamboree. Instead, he lay one way then the other, sat up, had a scratch, and fluffed his pillow. All was useless.

Chapter fifty

Heavy rain punished Ballymenace Glen throughout the following day and into the next, which was Saturday, the day of the grand party. The trickling stream through the forest became a torrent, and many of the tents had to be moved to higher ground. There was so much activity in Herbie's eleven-acre field with people, cars and vans, fetching and carrying, preparing for the party, the grass became mulch, and the mud became a hazard. The protesters, who previously looked clean and respectable, despite the Moses sandals, now resembled the eco-warriors most people would recognise: dirty, pathetic, and in need of a good home.

By late afternoon a few people, from around Ballymenace, gathered in the field. Many were bored teenagers looking for something to do on a miserable Saturday. Stuff had promised a 'grand time' but, since he was so far under-achieving in Charlie's eyes, a grand time might be a few CDs played through the sound system and a *Punch 'n' Judy* show.

At six o'clock loud music boomed over the fields, and the fledgling crowd rushed to the stage in hope of some live action. The video screens burst into life, and Kylie Minogue's lithe body gyrated to the music.

'What do you think?' said Jemima.

Charlie, open-mouthed, gaping at the screen, turned to see a different Jemima from the one he'd come to know. The penny glasses had gone. Her dull hair was clean, brushed and shiny. The blue eyes were heavy with a blue eyeshadow, which gave her a very blue countenance, although her cheeks were radiant and her lips cherry red. The chubby frame was squeezed into tight denims, blue, and her breasts were well-supported beneath a white T-shirt with 'DELUXE' printed, in blue, across the front.

'You look dressed to kill,' he said, without realising how inappropriate he sounded.

'I am allowed to enjoy myself, you know? If everything goes to plan it will be a fantastic evening.'

Charlie disagreed, but he didn't say so. Even at this stage, after two weeks of protest, no one had really explained *The Plan*. He understood they needed local support, but he reckoned he knew the people of Ballymenace rather better than Stuff. At best, they were impassive. Maybe tonight, if they bothered to turn up at all, they would support the protest and cheer for the cause. By tomorrow morning they would have done their bit, and still it would be up to CAKE to win the day. No one in the town had expressed concern that the building of Palmerstown would do them any harm. They had a council. It was the council's job to look after the people.

'Here's your speech for tonight,' said Jemima, handing him a folded piece of paper.

'My speech?'

'Stuff thinks it's wise for you to say a few words, since you're a local boy. It'll help the crowd identify with the core issues of the protest.'

'I take it Stuff has come over all shy again?'

Her face turned cold. Clearly an insult to Stuff was an insult to her and the entire CAKE organisation.

'We don't need your sarcasm, Mr Geddis. Stuff has his methods of handling these protest situations. He's had years of experience.'

'Not a lot of success though,' he muttered.

'If you want to help, just do as we ask.'

'Fine.'

Best not to upset these people. He accepted the paper and skimmed down the text. Nothing new, no inspiration. It wasn't exactly an 'I have a dream' sort of message.

'Ladies and gentlemen,' – a high-pitched voice rang out across the field – 'if I may have your attention for a moment.'

The music stopped, Kylie vanished from the giant screens and the audience gazed at Jemima on the stage.

'Welcome to our field of protest,' she said. 'Already you have lifted our spirits by your presence.' Several people cheered. About two. 'This evening we want to entertain you, but also alert you to the grave danger facing your town.'

Widespread mumbling broke out.

'Get on with it!'

'Where's the music?'

Jemima was not to be put off.

'During the course of the evening my comrades in CAKE, that's Citizens Against Killing the Environment, will explain why we are here, and why the people of Ballymenace must oppose unscrupulous and greedy property mongers...'

'Get off!'

'Give us some music.'

To her credit, Jemima remained steady and determined to deliver her message. Even Charlie was surprised by the apathy of the crowd so early in the proceedings. In one way, it was understandable. After all, Ulster was a land of protest, stand-offs, blockades, sit-ins, sit-outs and hunger strikes. A few people wearing sandals and swinging from the trees like monkeys was hardly a strike for freedom.

'We have some wonderful artists willing to perform tonight in support of our cause.'

There were more boos, more jeering, and one or two flying objects. Charlie was amazed how some people went to the bother of carrying tomatoes, flour and toilet rolls around with them for the sole purpose of chucking them at the first person they considered a legitimate target.

'Please give a big Herbie's Farm welcome,' said Jemima. 'To The Cider Drinkers!'

The Cider Drinkers, apparently, were a tribute band to the long-standing, best forgotten Wurzels, a comedy-folk combo hugely successful in the seventies. As the four men, who had to be keen, walked on stage and launched into *I've Got a Brand New Combine Harvester,* those in the crowd old enough to remember the originals were dumbfounded. It was like catching chickenpox twice. Those too young to know any better stood motionless, wondering if this was a crazy house or garage sampling outfit. Maybe the lead singer would step forth with a chain saw, rapping about death and cool things like rape and incest. Charlie hoped, prayed in fact, he was still trapped in a drink-induced nightmare.

The end of the number was greeted with lethargic applause but did little to discourage the band. Before anyone could protest they struck into *I am a Cider Drinker,* their signature tune as it were. Jemima came to fetch Charlie and led him backstage.

'One more act then you can do your speech,' she said above the din.

'Thanks, Jemima, you're all heart.'

When The Cider Drinkers left the stage, looking delighted with their fine performance, Jemima hurried to the microphone.

'Give a big hand once more for The Cider Drinkers!'

For a fleeting second the crowd were alarmed this atonal band would do an encore but, fortunately, they merely waved from the wings.

'Please give generously to sponsor our protests throughout the world,' said Jemima. 'Our team will pass among you with collecting buckets. We need your help to stop the destruction of our planet.'

The crowd cheered, a bit.

'Our next act tonight is known to you all.'

Reluctant cheers, suspicious looks.

'He's a local man, a singer with a big future. Please put your hands together for Jimmy Thorpe!'

If The Ciders Drinkers were something of a shock, the appearance of Ballymenace's own knocked the wind from every local in the field. Charlie gazed in disbelief. If this line up was intended to highlight the struggle for Ballymenace Glen, they would all be better off at home in bed.

The high point of Jimmy Thorpe's career was an audition for *The X-Factor*. It was, allegedly, the first time Simon Cowell had ever used the F-word in response to a contestant's performance. Jimmy did have a passing likeness to an older Elvis, in that his hair was dark and greasy and his face sufficiently puffy to resemble the overweight singer in his twilight years. Unfortunately, that's where the resemblance ended. Charlie, and everyone in the crowd, knew it. Poor Jimmy had a singing voice akin to Ozzy Osborne with laryngitis. After three songs – *Heartbreak Hotel, Are You Lonesome Tonight* and *Suspicious Minds* – he was coaxed off the stage by all in the audience cupping hands round their mouths and shouting, 'Bugger off!'

With Jimmy gone and dozens of people departing the field, Charlie was shoved on stage, a Christian to the lions.

'Give it up please for Jimmy Thorpe,' he said without conviction. He felt the breeze as a tomato whizzed by his head.

'I have here a note...' he began hesitantly.

'That's Charlie Geddis.'

'Get on with it, Geddis.'

'Who's he?'

'His wife's shaggin' Malcolm Palmer.'

'Who's he?'

'Get on with it, Geddis.'

He listened to their moans and their abuse. Much as he wanted to, he couldn't smack all of them in the face to make them listen. These people didn't care. They didn't give a damn about the glen. All they wanted was entertainment, free of charge, nothing in return.

For a few seconds he fell silent and gazed around the field, absorbing the beauty of the trees, the hedgerows, the green fields rising to the sky. He thought for a moment about CAKE and their coming to save a beautiful place from destruction. They had given their time and their effort, without question, to protect the world from money-grabbing hooligans like Palmer. And here they were, the people of his hometown, giving him dog's abuse. Suddenly he saw everything so clearly, an apple falling on his head on the road to Damascus. He crumpled the piece of paper in his hand.

'Right!' he shouted above their jeering. 'I can see you don't give a damn if this forest survives or not, but think about it. Next month, next year, it might be the trees beside your house. It might even be your home, if somebody decides it's in the way of a new road or a new town. One day you'll wake up and fancy a walk in the country, breathing the nice fresh air, taking in the lovely view. But you'll look around, and there'll be nothing but bricks and tarmac. You can't have it both ways. You have to draw a line. The trouble is none of you will care until it's too late and your piece of earth is marked for redevelopment. Wake up, Ballymenace; your time has come.'

The field was strangely silent, not so much a reaction to his speech, but because they were waiting for him to continue. Charlie, at last, had gained their attention. The problem was he didn't know what to say next. To his relief, Jemima waddled on stage.

'Ladies and gentlemen, please welcome the greatest band in the world...'

The lights died, and the crowd groaned. What next? Daniel O'Donnell? Please no.

Suddenly a wall of deafening sound, flashes of brilliant lights, fireworks, a huge curtain went up, and four figures walked on stage. It took a few seconds for the crowd to realise, and then came a mighty roar and thunderous applause. Charlie was gobsmacked, rooted to the spot.

'U2? In Ballymenace? It can't be happening,' he said.

Jemima pulled him out of the way as Bono reached for the microphone.

'How you doing, Ballymenace?' he called. The field erupted to the sounds of *Beautiful Day* and everyone freaked out.

'How can this be happening?' Charlie managed to say when he got off stage.

'Stuff has some very good friends,' Jemima replied, unfazed by the whole occasion as if this was her normal day job.

Charlie had to admit, he was very impressed.

'He wants to see us immediately,' she said.

'Don't we get to hear the band?'

'We have work to do.'

Chapter fifty-one

Stuff and Jill were seated beneath a tarpaulin in the middle of the forest, safely removed from the enormous crowds now descending on the field to see and hear U2. The leader of CAKE had a frown on his face, his eyes fixed on the screen of a portable TV.

'Brilliant,' said Charlie. 'How did you manage it? U2 in Ballymenace. Tell me it's really them?'

'It's them all right,' Stuff replied. 'Bono's a good lad. He was only too happy to help.'

'Jeez, Stuff, you're a cool customer. Sounds like you and Bono are the best of friends.'

His eyes widened in surprise, when Stuff didn't argue the point.

'Take a look at this, Charlie,' Stuff said, moving off the subject of super groups. He pointed at the television. It was difficult to hear because of the music, but it was clear that the concert in the glen was big news.

'This is great,' said Charlie. 'Just what we wanted.'

Stuff didn't look impressed. The body of the news programme was centred on the glen: live coverage of U2 in Herbie's big field. But the positive imagery was soon followed by pictures of Councillor Farrington. Stuff turned up the volume.

'These people must understand,' Farrington was saying from the steps of the council offices, 'this protest cannot be allowed to continue. For the past two weeks they have made their views known to all. However, Ballymenace Council and the owners of the land in the vicinity of the proposed development have given their support to this project. If the protesters do not leave the area soon we will take action to remove them. The Minister for the Environment has, this evening from his holiday in Barbados, rescinded the tree preservation order in respect of Ballymenace Glen. Following tonight's emergency meeting, the council has withdrawn the public right of way through the glen.'

There was a storm of camera flashes, shouted questions and jostling of the councillor as he battled to reach his car. Sheila Farrington, once again at the wheel of the Volvo, was ready to whisk him away. The news report continued to present details of the building project and gave a profile of Palmer Developments.

'That's my house,' said Charlie. 'That's my friggin' house.'

Crowds of reporters and photographers were laying siege to 47, Lothian Avenue.

'Apparently,' said one ITV commentator, 'Malcolm Palmer is sharing this house in Ballymenace with the estranged wife of Charlie Geddis, a leader of the protest at Ballymenace Glen. What is more intriguing is that number forty-seven, Lothian Avenue stands in the way of the Palmerstown development.'

'Shit,' was all Charlie managed to utter.

He watched in horror as the cameras picked out Barbara, arriving home, having to battle her way to the front door. She looked fraught as microphones were thrust in her face, and at times she disappeared in the throng. At last the front door of the house opened and there was Palmer to help her escape the baying photographers. Charlie seethed. Stuff switched channels, and the screen filled with the image of another familiar place.

'That's my flat.'

Outside the block of flats on the Yonhill Estate a dozen policemen held the press behind a metal barrier.

'What's going on?'

'They're looking for the body,' said Jemima. 'Someone has tipped them off.'

'At least they've got that wrong,' said Charlie, relieved that the body of Steve Gerard had been taken away by members of CAKE. Jill nudged him.

'Have a look at this,' she said, resting her hand on his shoulder. It proved a timely comfort. She set a newspaper in front of him.

The headline of the early edition of *The Sunday Life* read, 'TREE PROTESTER IN ROMP WITH PAPER GIRL'. On page four was a picture of Jill and Charlie, naked on her sofa. Charlie's recent life history followed, twisted beyond recognition even from the bizarre truth he knew. It was stated that while top businessman, Malcolm Palmer and Charlie's wife, Barbara were striving to make a success of their relationship Charlie indulged in bondage sex with a woman who had conned estate agent staff into believing she was nine months pregnant. There were allegations of Charlie's part in ritual killings, disappearing corpses, cult worship and impersonating a tabloid journalist. On page five, another photograph seemed to confirm the cult worship angle. Charlie stood naked beside a hooded figure in leather, with baseball bat and breasts, looking on as Jill removed her bra.

Sheila Farrington had been true to her word. She'd threatened to use the photographs if Charlie persisted with his 'get Palmer campaign'. Now he had lost everything. Barbara, his home, his job, even his grotty flat was out of bounds. Above all he'd lost his credibility. No one would take his view seriously when he had so much personal detritus.

'There's not much time left, Charlie,' Stuff said, switching off the television. 'Once the concert has ended, the authorities will move before we can rally support. With the tree preservation order lifted, Palmer will not waste any more time.'

Charlie wasn't listening. This was way too big for him. He was up shit creek in a leaky boat, and paddles were banned under a council by-law.

Chapter fifty-two

They put him in a tree, a huge sycamore overhanging the river, within earshot but sadly out of sight of the world's greatest rock band live on stage in his hometown. Several thousand people, braving the traffic and the police guarding their metal barriers, eventually found their way into Herbie's eleven-acre field to see what had been reported on radio and television. When the band played *In God's Country* it seemed that all had been won over to the cause. Now the members of CAKE had their crusade, and everyone could play their part.

By one o'clock in the morning all was quiet. U2 were long gone, a distant memory in the ears. The volunteers of CAKE manned their defences in the woods, confident that by morning the eyes of the world would still be upon them and Palmer would see justice. Charlie didn't share their optimism.

He dozed fitfully. His neck ached, and his ears nipped in the cold night air. Hard enough to sleep anyway, with all he had to worry about. On a wooden plank, twenty feet in the air, suspended between four branches, it was asking a lot. Everyone had a tree to look after, and Destiny had pleaded with Jemima to be given the one next to him. Very touching, but he needed more than comfort from a tree neighbour to get him through the night. His immediate future didn't seem too appealing. No job, no wife, a home crawling with cops, a dead body prone to disappearing to answer for and, most recently, a reputation for BDSM. If Palmer were to win the day, all Charlie would have left was a Volkswagen Polo with a smashed window and an uncanny knack of thinking only in clichés. His goose was cooked.

After four sleepless hours, he finally nodded off and timed it perfectly with falling out of the tree. A rope and harness saved him from disaster. The straps of the harness, however, were pulled tight around his crotch, and his balls were back where they started, pre-puberty.

Deep within this silent wood, damp and shiny from the summer rain, there was little to do except hang around and wait for something to happen. He would've settled for any of the following: rescue, his long overdue arrest, spiritual enlightenment, or simply for the rope to break launching him head first into the stream below. Swinging back and forth, he pondered his choice of landing place. Firstly, there was the long grass on the far bank. It might reduce the cracking of his skull to a dull thud when he landed. Secondly, the rocky stream where the cool flowing water would flush away the blood oozing from the massive fracture. Thirdly, and certainly the most dreaded of landing places, the barbed wire encircling the trunk of his cherished sycamore. He could picture his skin ripping as hundreds of tiny spikes broke his fall, the stinging pain, and then his head disintegrating on the rock at the foot of the tree. Definitely, given the choice, he would opt for the long grass every time.

Tossing and turning on the narrow plank had been his downfall. Now, dangling on a rope, trying to stay calm and quiet, he wondered if life could get any worse. But then he was the original case study for Sod's Law. He braced himself, realising he'd tempted fate once again.

Soon the police would swarm all over the place intent on clearing the woods now the concert had finished. U2, he still had trouble believing it. Stuff certainly kept all his major strategies to himself. It was a masterstroke; the crowd were jubilant. At the very least, they would have gone home with U2 in their ears and the thought that Bono and The Edge had played in Ballymenace to help save a bunch of old trees. Surely they would lobby the council, demanding the clearance must stop? He doubted it. Optimism was a mug's game.

At least in prison he could finish his novel. This and other strange thoughts fluttered in his weary head. If the police ever found the body of Steve Gerard, it seemed likely that he would be charged with the murder. After all, he'd written about it, they'd searched his flat, and he couldn't prove anyone else had done it. The pictures in the paper had suggested he was into some dubious practices. Why not the ritual killing of a Liverpool fan? As the owner of a Manchester United duvet, it could be said that he had motive. He was well and truly screwed but not in a nice sexual way. His life amounted to a failed escape from his hometown, a failed marriage and a failed career. Added to that was a severe lack of judgement, believing he could put everything right by destroying his wife's lover. Pretty damn stupid really but it's the thought that counts.

Piercing whistles emptied his head of further depressing notions. People shouting, air horns blaring, drums thumping, and everyone was suddenly awake. All he could do was swing. In days of old, he thought, this would be his hanging tree.

'They're coming!' A voice rose above the din.

'What direction?' asked Stuff, standing valiantly in a beech tree, a few yards downstream from Charlie.

'They're everywhere,' a girl cried in panic. Charlie watched her scrambling from one platform to another using the network of ropes and ladders.

'Stay high everyone,' said Stuff. 'Let's see what happens.'

'Isn't this exciting?' said Destiny from the next tree.

'Glad you think so. I suppose I may wait for a couple of lumberjacks to chop down the trees?'

'Charlie,' she laughed. 'What are you doing? It looks such fun.'

'Fun is definitely not the word I'm thinking of.'

He saw figures moving along the path. It wasn't quite dawn but bright enough to make out police in uniform, shining torches high in the trees where so many people were just hanging around. Flour, water and ketchup bombs exploded as they passed underneath. Then everything fell silent, and Charlie grew more anxious. If the climax of the protest was simply for them to be cut down and arrested then better now than later. He could be sipping on weak tea in his police cell in an hour if they got a move on. And, of course, helping Inspector Watkins with his inquiries.

'What do you reckon?' he called to Stuff.

'Shush! Keep your voice down,' said Jemima in a harsh whisper. Charlie couldn't see her, but he'd come to know that peeved tone.

'They've gone after the tunnel crew on the golf course,' said Stuff.

'The tunnel crew?' said Charlie.

'Will you be quiet, Mr Geddis?'

Mr Geddis? Was she narked, or what?

'It will take hours to get them out of there,' said Stuff.

Charlie was starving; he couldn't wait for hours; his tummy was talking, and it wasn't happy. His balls weren't too happy either. Added to that he needed to pee, assuming everything was still in working order.

'Am I going to dangle here all bloody day?'

'Shush!'

'Oh shut up, Jemima. You're doing my head in. What's happening, Stuff?'

'The chaps in the tunnel should keep them occupied for a while. It gives us time to get ready.'

'Ready for what?'

There was no further reply. Charlie had come to expect evasive answers from Stuff. Perhaps he had a few evasive tactics lined up. He watched as Stuff and Jemima negotiated the rope bridges, strung from one platform to another, finally dropping out of sight amongst the trees. Shouts and whistles could be heard from the golf course. Evidently the main body of protesters and the police had come face to face.

Jill looked abandoned on her wooden perch.

'How'd you sleep?' Charlie asked.

'I didn't. What about you?'

'Not much. Better off at home in front of the telly.'

'You don't mean that,' she said. 'Not after all you've been through.'

'There is a severe lack of communication around here.'

'I'm sure Stuff has his reasons.'

'I thought you might stick up for him. Getting very friendly, you two? Has he communicated his intentions?'

'None of your business, Charlie Geddis.'

'I think I'll climb down and stretch my legs.'

'No, Charlie,' said Destiny. 'You mustn't.'

'Only joking, love. I'm stuck on the end of this damn rope.'

Destiny climbed from her oak tree to his sycamore, unfurled a rope ladder, and lowered it to the ground. It hung quite close to Charlie, the dope on the rope, and he made a grab for it. Once his feet were firmly on the rungs he unhitched himself from the harness and climbed down. The bottom rung was three feet from the ground and, making a jump for it, he landed up to his thighs in the stream. Destiny followed him down.

'I'm not staying up here on my own,' Jill called from her horse chestnut.

'Then you'd better get a move on.'

'Stuff is going to be ever so cross with you, Charlie,' said Destiny.

'I'm not quaking in my boots over what Stuff might say. He hasn't put Malcolm Palmer off yet, has he?'

'No but...' The poor girl hesitated. She didn't seem capable of arguing.

'Come on,' said Charlie. 'Let's see what's going on around here.'

'Wait for me,' Jill called, scrambling down the ladder, swinging back and forth over the stream. She tried to make a jump for dry land, but her timing was all wrong and, like Charlie, she got a bit wet. Soaked actually.

Fortunately, after freeing himself from the harness Charlie could still manage to stand, although walking was uncomfortable. The best place to go, he thought, was Herbie's eleven-acre field. If there was to be any action he guessed that's where most people would gather. There might even be a burger stall open.

He was peeved this CAKE lot didn't seem capable of organising a decent fight. The first hint of trouble, and their glorious leader had disappeared. What kind of protest was this? They camp there for two weeks; have a big party – OK not just any party, it had U2, but he didn't even get to watch. Next thing he's swinging from the trees like Tarzan. This was no protest. And still he didn't know who these people were, or where they came from. The whole affair had reached a rather negative climax. Soon he would be arrested and charged with harbouring a dead body for a short time before losing it. He splashed on through the river, Jill and Destiny following.

When they emerged from the trees beside the pond, Charlie got a bit of a shock. It seemed the entire audience from the previous night had returned to the field. The front line of people held behind a safety barrier, forty yards away, was marshalled by several dozen police officers. Looking after safety barriers, Charlie thought, must be a major feature in police basic training nowadays.

They managed it so well. The crowd cheered loudly for no apparent reason. Jill, Destiny and Charlie looked around in case they'd missed something. But it seemed they were the object of the cheering. TV cameras were pointing at them, their images portrayed on the video screens still in place beside the stage. People were calling and waving.

'Charlie! Charlie! Charlie!'

He scanned their faces. Only a few did he recognise, but everyone seemed to know him. The last eighteen months of his life suddenly flashed before him.

Chapter fifty-three

There was a sudden blaring of horns as a convoy of vehicles cut a path through the crowd and came down the hill towards them. Some of the cars Charlie had seen before. There was the blue Aston Martin followed by a grey Volvo, a BMW, a Police Range Rover and, finally, a red Fiesta belonging to Barbara. They were allowed to pass through the police cordon and drew up in a line, close to the swollen duck pond, in front of Jill, Destiny and Charlie. Palmer and Farrington got out of the Aston Martin to a hail of boos, and stepped into the mud, this was greeted by raucous cheering.

'I trust you lot have come to your senses?' said Palmer.

'You should ask yourself that question,' Charlie replied.

'People are going to be seriously hurt if you don't call off this protest,' said Farrington, looking fraught.

'Is that a threat, Councillor?' asked Charlie.

'If the police are forced to climb the trees to get these hooligans out, they will do it. People will get hurt in the process. Are you going to end this now and save everyone a lot of trouble?'

'I'm not the one you should be asking.'

'You started all this, Geddis,' said Farrington, 'with your shoddy accusations in the paper.'

'I've had enough of these stalling tactics,' said Palmer. 'Get this sorted out, Jim. We have wasted too much time.' The two men exchanged hostile looks.

'Good morning, gentlemen,' said Stuff, appearing from the same spot in the woods as Charlie had done a few moments earlier. He was flanked by dozens of CAKE warriors, including a beaming Jemima. Her changing moods continued to be a mystery to Charlie.

'Mr Stuff,' said Farrington. 'I've just been telling Geddis that people will be injured if you continue with this action.'

Bodies began emerging from the other cars. Sheila Farrington, familiar in all black leather, stepped from her Volvo and tiptoed over the soggy grass. Michelle Eastman, resplendent in her business suit and white blouse, accompanied by Jeremy Bolton and his laptop, got out of the BMW and came to Palmer's side. Inspector Watkins left the Range Rover and chatted to a policeman standing proudly at his metal barrier. Barbara, looking forlorn, in jeans and a green sweatshirt, her hair in a ponytail, stepped through the mud and eased her way to Palmer's side, displacing the churlish Michelle Eastman.

Charlie glanced around him. It suddenly occurred to him that every woman with a current interest in his affairs, or indeed the subject of his affairs, was now in the field. Standing behind the police barrier was Lisa, his neighbour and friend, Joan, an old enemy, and Jill's mother, Mrs Barker, a woman who had good reason to believe she was privy to her daughter and Charlie's sexual proclivities. Other guests included, Trevor, his arm round Joan (wonders would never cease), Carol and Billy from the office, and a tall figure with ruby lips, smiling under a blonde wig and wearing a white halterneck dress. Tracy with her friend Zimmer, Charlie presumed.

'Councillor Farrington,' said Stuff. 'We have stated clearly our intentions. We will protect the trees in this glen at all costs. Your actions, and those of Mr Palmer, are highly improper and illegal. If the council wishes to discuss the matter we are willing to talk.'

'Talk,' said Palmer. 'I've had enough talking. Jim, you assured me this problem would be cleared up by this morning. I can't wait any longer. I suggest we pull out and leave the police to deal with these ruffians. I have work to do.'

He bounded to his car, ignoring the sneers from protesters. Farrington followed him, while Barbara, Michelle Eastman and others were left to wonder if they should do likewise. Palmer gunned his engine and tried to speed away, but the wheels of the Aston had a torrid dispute with the mud, and the crowd cheered again. Having got to know him quite well over the last few weeks, even Charlie was surprised at Palmer's cheek, when he lowered his window and calmly asked those people standing around having a protest if they would mind giving him a push. At least he got a laugh.

Stuff nodded to one of the warriors, who nudged another, and in seconds more than a dozen enveloped the car. A nod and a wink produced a chain and harness, which quickly was fastened under the body. A sharp whistle, the roar of a diesel engine and the Aston Martin, complete with Palmer and Farrington, was hoisted into the air. The crane, used by the bungee jumpers and in erecting the stage, evidently, had another purpose. The crowd cheered wildly as the prize swung over the duck pond. Sheila Farrington ran as best as she could through the mud to the water's edge. She was joined by Michelle

Eastman and Barbara. All three women looked to the sky as the rain drizzled on their faces.

'Be careful, Malcolm,' Sheila called.

Barbara glared at her in surprise.

'Let us down this instant,' shouted Palmer, raising his fist.

Rigid in his seat, Jim Farrington didn't seem at all happy. The CAKE volunteer, operating the crane, left the car swaying twenty feet above the centre of the pond. He had to lock himself inside the cab as four policemen abandoned their metal barriers and rushed to the vehicle.

'Get them down,' Sheila let rip at Stuff. 'You can't win by doing this.'

Stuff held a smug expression on his face. Charlie viewed him as well-educated and a well-mannered sort. But there he was having a laugh at the expense of an irate Sheila Farrington.

'Mr Palmer,' he called. 'Are you prepared to discuss the preservation of the trees in this glen?'

'No, sir, I am not. As far as I am concerned the Minister for the Environment has considered the matter. I am legally entitled to do as I please.'

'No matter what the cost to the environment?'

'The environment will not stand or fall because of a few rotting trees. Besides, we will give due consideration to landscaping the area. Now get me down.'

'And what of the cost to you, Mr Palmer?'

'Me?'

'You are willing to take full responsibility for your action?'

'My conscience is crystal clear.'

'In that case...'

Stuff, looking towards the stage, waved his arm in the air. Loud music boomed from the sound system. Tina Turner, *Simply the Best*. The crowd cheered, some began dancing and waving at the TV cameras. The giant video screens burst into life.

Suddenly everyone drew a sharp intake of breath. Shocked mothers turned the heads of their children away from the images on the screens. Charlie recognised his handiwork. It took Sheila Farrington a little longer.

'Oh my God,' she said, hands to her face.

Barbara and Michelle Eastman hadn't quite got there. Malcolm Palmer looked helplessly at Sheila in the brief second before her husband figured it out. Charlie stood in admiration. It seemed he had proved himself a true eco-warrior and, perhaps, a promising tabloid journalist. The faces on the screen were easily identified, and from there it wasn't difficult to attribute the correct body parts, although the most telling one was in the mouth of Sheila Farrington. Of that there was no doubt.

'Sheila?' Councillor Farrington called. 'Is that you?' He didn't wait for an answer before grabbing Palmer by the throat.

'Jim,' said Sheila. 'It's not what you think. Leave Malcolm alone.' Sheila looked at Charlie and Stuff in horror. 'You'd better get them down before they kill each other.'

No one seemed to mind that prospect as they watched Farrington throttling Palmer, who had now opened his door and was trying to jump.

'Jim,' said Palmer, gasping for breath. 'Calm down, I can explain everything.'

'I'll bet, you dirty wife-stealing bastard. I'll bloody kill you. All this time I thought we were doing business, but you were doing my wife. I let you talk me into this deal.'

'Jim, you don't know what you're saying.'

'I bought half the damn council for you.'

'Jim, they can hear you.'

'I don't give a damn. I want them to know what a lowlife you are, Palmer.'

'Let him go, Jim,' Sheila begged again.

Every punch was greeted with cheers, every comment reported live on television.

261

Charlie noticed Barbara, head bowed and stifling tears, slipping away to her car. Her wheels spun in the mud, but with the help of three CAKE volunteers she was soon motoring out of the field.

With all the commotion and a change of music to *You Ain't Seen Nothing Yet*, no one paid much attention to the sound of a helicopter approaching. It hovered above the field for a minute or so. Only when it attempted to land, did the police deem it necessary to herd several hundred people thirty yards to the right. Those standing by the pond hadn't taken much notice, their attention focused on the two men wrestling in the Aston. Charlie assumed the helicopter contained press, or a TV crew, getting an aerial view of the events. But when it set down on the grass three people stepped out and came striding towards them. Two burly athletic males in dark business suits walked either side of a woman in a white blouse, fawn riding breeches and brown boots. One of the suits held an umbrella above the woman's head. Charlie didn't recognise her, but she did not look happy.

Chapter fifty-four

'Malcolm?' said the woman, a tad shrill.

Malcolm was busy. The door of the Aston had closed again, but Malcolm's head was poking out of the window as he struggled to fend off the enraged Jim Farrington.

'Malcolm, what on earth are you doing?'

Her voice remained high-pitched but very upper-class. Charlie didn't know what to think. Another of Palmer's women? Very glamorous but too old for Malcolm, he would have thought. She looked trim and fit, her face well-tanned but taking on a leathery texture. Her bum was right up there with Jill's, though. Long ringlets of black hair fell over her lithe body; she looked a demon on two legs, dangerous yet appealing.

'Miranda?'

'Malcolm, come down at once. You have totally ruined my day with this nonsense.'

'Who the hell are you?' said Sheila.

The woman turned round, and peering down the end of her nose, inspected the stern-faced Sheila. Until that moment Charlie would have said Sheila Farrington was a confident woman, who wasn't afraid to speak her mind. But this stranger had a put-down look that could fell a tree in one go.

'To whom am I speaking?' she said, but in such a tone it seemed an answer was hardly desired.

Sheila's mouth opened, but nothing came out. The woman turned to another of the bystanders.

'James, darling. Wonderful to see you. I came as soon as I got your message. This bally... place was an absolute chore to find.'

'I'm terribly sorry, Miranda,' said Stuff. 'I'd hoped it would not come to this.'

Charlie felt dazed and confused, although lately this was his normal conscious state. He glanced at Jill who seemed ready to faint.

'I should apologise to you for my brother's behaviour,' Miranda said.

'Brother? Did you say brother?' Sheila had regained control of her mouth.

Charlie suddenly recalled the headed notepaper he'd found in Palmer's desk on the day he'd searched his office. Was that second M. Palmer, on the list of directors, Malcolm's sister, Miranda? He was about to find out.

'And why is that of interest to you?' Miranda replied curtly to Sheila.

'Malcolm and I are lovers.'

'How very quaint.' Miranda's attention returned to the Aston. 'Malcolm, come down at once. This is very tiresome. I've come to take you home.'

'Oh, Miranda, not now. Can't you see I'm busy?'

Jim Farrington pulled Palmer's hair forcing him back inside the car.

'James, if you could perhaps get him down, I shan't take up any more of your time. Besides, I really must dash. I'm playing a few rubbers with Prince Albert this evening.'

'Of course, Miranda.'

Stuff signalled to the CAKE warrior inside the crane. He opened the door of the cab and the police took over. They, however, were not so handy with the controls. A beleaguered constable pushed a lever, and the Aston suddenly nose-dived into the pond.

A standing account for dry cleaning would have proved useful to the unfortunate Michelle Eastman. The huge splash of water engulfed the poor girl. Sadly, everyone's attention was firmly on the car and its occupants, leaving Michelle to shiver alone.

The Aston quickly sank beneath the water, but seconds later two figures broke the surface, coughing and gasping for breath. Palmer was first to struggle ashore, squelching through mud and stones, arms drooping by his side. He came face to face with Charlie, who couldn't help looking smug. Panting for breath, Palmer didn't seem capable of words. He stared at Charlie, his nemesis. His arm swung, a brilliant right hook, and Charlie hit the mud. Palmer stood over him, rocking.

'I don't know how. I don't know when. But be sure of this, Charlie Geddis, I will pay you back.'

He turned in the direction he'd sloshed from and met Councillor Farrington emerging from the pond. The cold water had done little to cool his temper. Palmer landed in a heap beside Charlie. Farrington was also handy with the right hooks.

'Keep your dirty hands off my wife, Palmer.' He staggered over to Sheila. 'Take me home. You and I have some talking to do.'

'Oh piss off, you old fart,' said Sheila. 'I don't want you. I'm going to Spain with Malcolm.'

'What?'

'You heard. We were finished years ago. Malcolm and I love each other. Look up there.' She pointed at the video screen. 'See.'

'Oh, Malcolm,' said Miranda, also looking at the screen. 'I really don't have time for this. Daddy was right; I should never have let you loose. This really is the absolute limit, the third time in ten years. From now on you will stay closer to home.'

'Not now, Miranda,' he said wearily, struggling to his feet.

'Come along. I can't wait all day.'

Miranda Palmer embraced Stuff once more, a kiss to both cheeks.

'James darling, you must come to dinner the next time you are in Cap Ferrat?'

'I'll look forward to it, Miranda.'

'Please hurry, Malcolm,' she said. 'I'm really not in the mood for your tantrums. I feel a ghastly headache coming on. You know I hate flying before breakfast.'

'Yes, Miranda, I'm coming.'

'Wait,' said a female voice.

Michelle Eastman, soaking and bedraggled, caught Malcolm by the arm.

'What about the project, Malcolm? What's going to happen?'

Palmer had no answer. Looking despondent, in need of guidance, he turned to his sister. Miranda looked the pitiful Michelle up and down.

'And you are?'

'Michelle Eastman, PR and marketing.'

'I'll send one of my people to settle this matter next week.'

'Is that it?' said Michelle. 'The whole thing's off?'

She glared at Malcolm in disbelief. He turned away.

'You can't do this. What about the contractors? The investors? Malcolm?'

It was pointless. The man was deflated. He began a slow, dispirited walk towards the helicopter.

'What about us, Malcolm?' Sheila ran after him. 'When are we going to Spain?'

He trudged on regardless, no answers and no goodbyes. Sheila tugged at his dripping sleeve.

'You can't leave me here. I've given everything for you, Malcolm. You'll call me, won't you?'

Jill and Stuff walked part of the way to the helicopter with Miranda. Charlie nursed a bloody nose and so far hadn't made it to his feet. He had a bittersweet feeling because, despite Palmer's downfall, he was the one who got smacked in the face. He didn't get to thump anyone. But Jill soon lifted his spirits. With Sheila traipsing after Palmer, Jill came from behind, gave her a gentle push and sent her sprawling in the mud.

'Oops!'

She looked down at Sheila with a conceited smile. 'Funny who you bump into when you least expect it.'

The sound of another splash caught everyone's attention, except for Palmer. It took Inspector Watkins' hand upon his shoulder to stop him going any further.

'I believe that is your car in the pond, sir?'

'Yes,' said Palmer finally. 'I'll have my people remove it.'

Palmer was looking but not seeing. Whether he was in shock from crashing into the pond, or dazed by the fist of Councillor Farrington, he stared vacantly at the horrific sight. Something had bobbed to the surface of the pond from the boot of the Aston. The body of Steve Gerard, minus the Shroud of Old Trafford, had achieved something of a second coming.

'Would you care to explain that, sir?' said Watkins.

Only then did something begin to register with Palmer as he gazed at the plastic mummy drifting to shore. He turned to Sheila, on her hands and knees, dropping tears in the mud.

'You said you'd taken care of him, Sheila.'

Sheila glanced from Palmer to her husband. Perhaps in that fleeting moment she pictured her future. Whether it was years of bliss as Councillor Farrington's redeemed housewife, or twenty years in a prison cell, no one would ever know. Whatever passed through her scheming brain determined her reply.

'Malcolm, I haven't the slightest idea what you're talking about.'

'How about the pair of you coming for a nice cosy chat down at the station?' said Watkins.

Chapter fifty-five

This tree house thing was a good idea if you wanted to be alone. Nobody in the trees now, except a few blackbirds and the odd magpie. One for sorrow, he'd managed several times over. Two for joy was proving harder to come by. He pondered his future, now that Malcolm Palmer had taken his leave. He watched the crowd fritter away from the field and the crew dismantling the stage, where U2 had performed. That was a question on his list for the enigmatic Mr Stuff. Obviously successful in the matter of CAKE versus Palmer, he had still a lot of explaining to do. Charlie would insist on straight answers before this mysterious bunch fizzled into the ether.

'Charlie?' Destiny called.

He looked down from his tree. He didn't think it was a good idea to see her before she left. The past two weeks had been a bizarre holiday romance, but it was never meant to last. Her life seemed less complicated than his tangled mess, and she was more than he ever deserved. They'd enjoyed each other, and now it was time to part.

'Charlie? Where are you?'

But he didn't have the heart to ignore her calls.

'I'm up here.'

She looked up smiling, climbed the rope ladder and knelt beside him on the wooden platform. She kissed him firmly on the cheek, but he winced from the pain in his swollen nose, his memento from Palmer.

'What are you doing up here all alone?'

'Thinking.'

'You silly. What have you got to think about? Everything is fine now. We won; we saved the trees.' She threw her arms round him and squeezed.

'We did.'

Charlie wanted to be like her, free of troubled thoughts, free of malice, innocent and happy. Damned if he knew what she saw in him.

'Charlie? You're coming with us, aren't you?'

He wasn't the sort for long pauses. Usually he jumped right in with the wrong cliché, but today he was truly lost for the most considerate answer.

'Stuff says we're going to Canada next,' she said. 'It'll be fun. Please say you'll come?'

'It's a nice idea,' said Charlie. 'But I think I'll stay closer to home. Which reminds me, where is home for you?'

'Oh, you know.'

'I'm afraid I don't.'

She waved her hand in front of her face.

'You know, silly? England.'

Nice of her to be specific. He kissed her softly on the lips, and she blushed.

'You look after yourself,' he said. 'Send me a postcard from Canada.'

They climbed down from the tree, and holding hands, strolled along the path to the duck pond. The rain had stopped and the clouds were moving on. He stood on the bridge watching as she lolloped through the mud, up the hill to her friends, people of her own age and with the same outlook on life.

'I wondered where you'd got to,' said Jill, as if Destiny had just passed her the phrase.

'Hiya,' Charlie replied.

'You don't sound too happy. I thought you'd be over the moon now that Palmer has fallen from grace.'

'Bit of a hollow victory. I'm at a bit of a loss for what to do next.'

'Why don't you go after her?'

'Destiny?'

'You know who I mean.'

'What about you, Jill?' he asked, deflecting the subject. 'Did you and Stuff hit it off?'

'He's asked me to go with him,' she said.

'To Canada, I believe?'

'Not directly. There's a big protest planned in British Columbia, something about a big dam and flooding a whole valley, but that's not for a few weeks yet. He's invited me to his home.'

'That's nice; where exactly is home?'

'Scotland,' she said, unable to contain her delight and the rest of the story. 'Stuff is a real-life Scottish laird.' She was speeding up. 'His proper name is James Duncan MacGregor. He lives in a castle, a real castle. Dunarunnar, I think it's called. He wants me to spend the summer with him.' She was entering hyperventilation territory. 'Oh, Charlie, isn't it brilliant? Me, living in a castle? I can't believe it's happening.'

'Why's he hanging around with this lot if he's monarch of the glen?'

'He's interested in the environment, that's all. He has some special environmental projects running on his estate. His estate, doesn't that sound wonderful?'

Charlie pictured the Yonhill Estate, hopefully the wrong image.

The noble laird duly arrived clearly amused by his overexcited girlfriend. He was dressed in a more tidy fashion than previously, a tweed jacket over his jeans. He looked ready to leave.

'Charlie, thought I might catch you before I go.' The two men shook hands. 'I just wanted you to know how grateful I am for all your effort. We couldn't have done it without you.'

'Thanks very much, James, but to tell you the truth the whole thing is still a bit confusing. I'm not sure the matter *is* closed. Palmer could be back next week. Michelle Eastman could set the whole thing rolling again.'

'I don't think that's likely. You see, Miranda is an old friend. We go to the same parties, hunting, skiing, summers on the Riviera, you know how it is?'

'Yeah, sure.'

'Her father was Henry Palmer, you may have heard of him. Made his money in property development in the sixties, hotels mostly. She inherited all of his estate.'

'And what about Malcolm?'

'Miranda's brother. Runt of the litter, I suppose. Old Henry never saw much promise in him. Heaped all his praise on Malcolm's sisters, Miranda in particular, being the oldest of three girls. Every now and then Miranda has to clean up Malcolm's mess. There must be true love somewhere, I suppose. He doesn't have a penny without her, so he dare not wander too far. She feeds him little projects to keep him happy.'

'So Palmer Property was one of those little projects?'

Stuff nodded.

'Once he began to look foolish, with a battle against environmentalists raging, she simply ordered him home. He knows better than to disobey Miranda. She's had to pull him out of several deep holes over the years, although, I dare say, none quite as deep as murder. She wasn't too happy leaving here without him. But I think we did her a favour, in the long run, getting him off her back.'

'You think he did it then?' said Charlie. 'He's the one who killed Steve Gerard?'

'Didn't pull the trigger perhaps, but I'm sure he was aware of the killing. I would think Mrs Farrington knows a lot of the detail. She is a very determined woman. Had several hard men doing her dirty work. I believe you had first-hand experience of them?'

A shiver ran down Charlie's back, realising Sheila could have murdered Jill and him. Spending the night tied together was really no hardship at all.

They said their goodbyes, and Charlie watched as another woman strolled out of his life.

'Three in one day,' he said aloud. 'Barbara, Destiny and Jill. And it's only half past two. I suppose I'll have to settle for darling Jemima.'

'I beg your pardon?'

It had to be her. She'd been standing behind him, checking boxes off a list on her clipboard.

'Hello, Jemima. I thought you'd be gone by now. I hear the weather's nice in Canada at this time of year.'

'That's as may be,' she said smartly. 'But I have to stay here for a while. Things have to be cleared up and sent on, you know?'

She marched off to another stack of boxes.

'A wee birdie tells me you had a wild night at the party. One of the roadies?'

'None of your business.'

Chapter fifty-six

Alone again, staring at the pond, he could see the blue roof of the Aston just below the surface. Barbara must have looked stunning in the passenger seat, as she and Palmer roared along country roads. He had put an end to her relationship with Palmer, but he had also brought closure on his marriage. So much for his three-step plan. The solitary magpie wins again.

'Get the last of the burgers,' a young lad called to the dozen workers remaining in the field.

'Any chips?' Charlie asked.

'No chips, just onions.'

He found two quid in his pocket and paid for the dried-up meat and a few burnt onions. He smothered it with ketchup to hide the taste.

'Enjoy your meal,' said the lad with little sincerity.

Before he'd found a place to sit a shutter closed, an engine revved and the burger van chugged to the gate. A lone policeman, guarding his precious metal barrier to the last, waved it farewell.

He sat on a wooden pallet and took a bite of the stale roll, hoping to make it as far as the ketchup. At least it was something different to contemplate. He scarcely noticed a woman looking at him, until he glimpsed a pair of legs in jeans and boots.

'Baawbwa,' he said, his mouth stuffed with bread roll.

'I wondered if you'd still be here,' she said. She smiled, but looked nervous, her eyes swollen and tearful. He swallowed before speaking again, although he hadn't a clue what to say.

'What's wrong?'

'There's nothing wrong. I just thought I should come and see you.'

'Oh.'

'Jill called to see me.'

'Right.' He realised it was short and dry, but he was all out of small talk. He would have to practice on himself later.

'She told me everything.'

He blew in the air, bracing himself for an argument. After all, he was the man responsible for ruining her entire life, twice.

'Not just about today, I mean everything.'

'Everything?' That was a bit scary. Did everything include his night at Jill's and his sharing a tent with Destiny?

'I know Malcolm won't be coming back, and I won't be moving to a new house, but I wondered if you could ever forgive me for how I've treated you, for not trusting you?'

Those bloody clichés were back: water under the bridge, all's well that ends well, tomorrow is another day... He fought them off but not so eloquently.

'Yeah well, I mean, I tried to explain...'

'I know I don't deserve it, and you can tell me to clear off if you want. But you're welcome to come home.'

'Yeah, well I'll certainly think about it.'

Their eyes met briefly and then she backed away.

'I'd better go. I'm staying at my mother's until the press and police move away from the house.' She wiped her eyes with the back of her hand. He could feel her staring at him, but he hadn't the courage to look back. 'Bye, Charlie.'

'Barbara?'

'Yes?'

'One day at a time?' Such an original line, Charlie Geddis, ever considered Mills and Boon? Despite his corny phrasing, she nodded agreement with a smile and a tear. He got to his feet, burger in hand, and gave her a big squeeze, using a technique he'd learned earlier from Destiny. He took another bite of burger. Well, he'd hardly eaten all day.

'I love you, Baawbwa.' She held him tight.

'Hello there, young fella,' said Herbie, dressed in his old suit and flat cap, his collie standing by his side.

'Herbie! Where've you been? You missed all the fun.'

For a moment he realised Herbie was never about when something exciting happened. What's more, during the entire protest, he never once saw him in conversation with Stuff, and yet he had invited the noble laird to Ballymenace. Were Herbie and Stuff like Clark Kent and Superman, one and the same person? If so, Jill was in for a nasty shock when they got to Stuff's castle.

'I heard all about the happenings down here. Those young people sent that fancy Palmer on his way.'

'Herbie, there's someone I'd like you to meet. This is Barbara, my wife.'

'And a finer young woman I never did see,' he said, taking her hand and giving it a squeeze, as if he had some magical way of assessing a new acquaintance. 'And isn't your husband the finest man ever to walk these hills?' He shook her hand now as if to encourage a response.

'Yes, I suppose he is.'

'There's a lot of clearing up to do,' said Charlie, feeling the need to interrupt before he got embarrassed. 'Did you hear about Palmer's car dropping into the pond?'

'Is that so? Such a bright and shiny motor, too. Do you suppose he'll be wanting it back?'

'You never know, Herbie, it could belong to you now.'

The old boy studied the scene, the guys pulling down the stage, and the stall holders packing up. Charlie took Barbara's hand. It was the most wonderful feeling in the world. Herbie toddled over to the pond and peered at the car.

'Do you think I could take her for a spin?'

THE END

If you enjoyed this book, please let others know by leaving a quick review on Amazon. Also, if you spot anything untoward in the paperback, get in touch. We strive for the best quality and appreciate reader feedback.

editor@thebookfolks.com

MORE BOOKS
BY ROBERT McCRACKEN

THE DI TARA GROGAN SERIES

Merseyside Police detective Tara Grogan scarcely looks old enough to be a police officer never mind a detective inspector. Maybe because of this she is more determined than most to prove herself capable when investigating murder on the streets of Liverpool. But her tendency to become emotionally involved in cases frequently places her in great danger and undermines her efforts to get on in the force.

FREE with Kindle Unlimited and available in paperback.

BOUND TO RUN

A romantic getaway in a remote Lake District cottage turns into a desperate fight for survival for Alex Chase. If she can get away from her pursuer, and that's a big if, she'll be able to concentrate on the burning question in her mind: how to get revenge.

FREE with Kindle Unlimited and available in paperback.

OTHER TITLES OF INTEREST

BROWN BREAD by Pete Brassett

Most families have a problem with their freezer at some point or other. So too the Benardinos. Yet their problem is of a very unusual nature. Despite running out of places to store the bodies of previous unwelcome guests, gin-soaked Virginia mother has organised a party to celebrate her fifty-third birthday. Will anyone get out alive?

FREE with Kindle Unlimited and available in paperback.

HOPELESS by Diane Dickson

When a young man turns up Dick Whittington style in London, he soon finds himself in a pickle. With no money or place to stay, he'll be at the mercy of strangers. Can he find his feet or will he become another victim of the unforgiving capital?

FREE with Kindle Unlimited and available in paperback.

NEAR MISS by Traude Ailinger

After being nearly hit by a car, fashion journalist Amy Thornton decides to visit the driver, who ends up in hospital after evading her. Curious about this strange man she becomes convinced she's unveiled a murder plot. But it won't be so easy to persuade Scottish detective DI Russell McCord.

FREE with Kindle Unlimited and available in paperback.

www.thebookfolks.com

Printed in Great Britain
by Amazon